BLOOD RUNS COLD

HIDDEN NORFOLK - BOOK 14

J M DALGLIESH

HP

First published by Hamilton Press in 2023

ISBN (Trade Paperback) 978-1-80080-532-3
ISBN (Hardback) 978-1-80080-672-6
ISBN (Large Print) 978-1-80080-371-8

EXCLUSIVE OFFER

BLOOD RUNS COLD

PROLOGUE

The night air is humid; the only sound the whirring of the ceiling fan and the rattle of a loose part that'd been steadily worsening in the past few weeks. Lying on the two-inch-thick horsehair mattress, still smelling of urine, I'm alert, tense and more than a little excited. Glancing through the crack in the door between the iron panel and the wooden frame, and down along the corridor, I can see him, roughly sixty feet away. He's sleeping, as usual. It was now approaching midnight.

Daily, this place is a hive of activity and one of the noisiest places one can imagine. The raucous atmosphere is inescapable while the sun's up; the calling out to one another across the yards, the angry shouting, the jostling for position that takes place every day… and, of course, the screaming.

It's not so bad in this particular block, the one housing the foreigners. Once they'd been moved here things got a little easier. Easy in a place such as this is relative. But now, everywhere is quiet.

Looking across at his fellow conspirators, he points to the window. Torsten, his Danish friend, hops down from his bunk disturbing Sajan, who cocks his head at the interruption to his sleep. It is late January and the night-time temperatures are still hovering around thirty degrees with humidity in the high nineties. It never seems to change. In eight months, there has been very little change aside from when the monsoon rains hit between July and October. The cloud bursts were short in the early part of the season, perhaps lasting a few minutes to a couple of hours, whereas by October the rain became far more persistent.

"What are you doing?" Sajan asks, seeing Torsten move a small wooden stool against the far wall and stand upon it to peer out of the small window at the yard three floors below. The Dane ignores him, instead signalling a thumbs-up to the others. I slide down off my bunk. Kenji, their longest serving resident, a Japanese backpacker who'd got himself caught up in something he didn't fully understand, looks on warily but, unlike Sajan, doesn't seem interested in asking questions. That's his way; he stays silent as much as possible. I don't really trust Kenji. I don't trust anyone who is so unreadable. They're unpredictable. I'm good at reading Asian people. Americans… not so much.

"What are you doing?"

I signal to Torsten and he returns to his bunk, leaning down and grasping Sajan by the collar. He makes to protest but having the towering figure of a Viking bearing down on you, he must have thought better of it and shrinks back into the shadows of the lower bunk.

The others are gathering together the items of contraband we've been assembling for months. Bits and pieces sent in in innocuous parcels, a small bottle of oil, some duct tape and a pocketknife, purchased by gifting a substantial sum, by local standards anyway, to my personal guard, the trustee by the name of Aroon. My shadow during work parties or trips to the Christian church just beyond the outer wall, the last of seven standing between this room and freedom. The air smells sweeter on Sunday mornings, as sweet as it could in this god-forsaken place.

In the shower room, I take down the poster sent in by friends on the outside. The wooden runners, top and bottom, holding the poster straight are soon detached. The guards paid little attention to it when it came in. The vaguely religious phrase depicted on the canvas gave them pause to risk damaging it during inspection. They're a strangely superstitious people really; less focussed on good or bad, right or wrong, and far more interested in luck. If good things happen to you then it is luck, bestowed on you by the way you live your life, whereas the bad… is poor luck on your part; the vipãka, the maturing of your karma visited upon you. It is what you deserve.

Tomorrow will be one week from the day since my vipãka was handed to me, and it came far earlier than in the next of my seven lives spent upon the Buddhist Wheel of Life. Guilty. My contact at the US embassy has reliably confirmed exactly what I feared; they intend to make an example of someone. A westerner. In short… me.

The runners come away and inside are the two high tensile steel hacksaw blades. I pass them to Torsten along with the small bottle of oil and he runs back to the window while I move to the bookshelf. The plank of wood, not much longer or thicker than a scaffold board comes away easily enough from the wall. That had taken a bit of coaxing too; somewhere to keep our books. We have books, one or two. We would get more as time passed, but not for me. I have no time.

Crossing back to the door, I look down the corridor again. I can hear Carlos snoring in the next cell. The heat doesn't seem to bother him. It must be similar here to his hometown in southern Spain. The guard still sleeps as Torsten gets to work.

The first pass of the blade against the bar

sounds in the night like a squealing pig. I flick off the light switch, plunging the room into near darkness. The lights are never off in this stinking place. I bartered a switch two months ago. It cost a small fortune, but it was worth it. Not for the darkness, but for this moment. Torsten oils up the bar and gets back to work while I focus on the guard. Only twice does he stir and I have to hiss at my Danish friend to cease. He doesn't wake though.

The time. It's been an hour and Torsten finally manages to cut through that first bar. He looks over and I can read his pained expression in the reflective light from the corridor. I go to him. We should have been out of the cell by now. Sunrise is at a quarter to seven, in less than six hours' time, and they still have a long way to go.

"We should leave it," Torsten whispers to us. "We can go again tomorrow night."

I glance at the window. The bar doesn't look like it has been cut at the base. The guards probably won't notice, nor will Aroon when he comes to collect me for the work detail at the local factory. I see Sajan watching us in the corner of my eye. He's bricking it. It's written all over his face.

"No," I say. "It's tonight… or not at all."

"But… the bars," Torsten says with urgency. "They're too thick. They're stronger here."

He is right about that. The construction in this part of the prison is more solid than elsewhere.

They don't trust the foreigners. That's why we're on the third floor too. No amount of money will buy you a cell on the ground floor. We have no honour. No respect for the way they do things around here.

They're right about that.

Something in the way Sajan is looking at me… if we don't go tonight, then we will never go. Fixing Torsten with my steely gaze, I can read him. He never believed this would come to pass. We'd talked about it, planned it and smuggled everything in that we needed… and yet, he didn't believe we were actually ever going to do it. I look around the room at my two fellow conspirators and at those who are not involved. Everyone is looking to me to make the final decision.

"We… go… now," I say firmly.

The decision is made. The others nod and Torsten returns to his work on the bars. It is futile. I know it. It will take all night to cut through and remove all four of them. It shouldn't. Perhaps it's the weight of the masonry above the frame compressing the metal bars in their frame and therefore making it harder to cut than it should be? Or maybe they really don't trust the westerners, who are far too cocky for their own good, and they've actually spent some money on keeping us in?

I'm not staying. I can't.

Sajan looks ready to protest as Torsten forgets the oil and relies on his strength. His name is derived from the old Norse name of the god *Thor* and *sten,* the word for strength. Well, tonight it is fitting. The first bar is pulled aside with brute force, levering it to the side. Maybe, just maybe they can squeeze through. The other two have the same idea and they grasp the bookshelf, putting it on its side and sticking it out through the window. Another stool, hand made by a gifted craftsman serving ten years for murdering his wife, is used to wedge the plank in place so it will take their weight. Gathering Tosten's oil paintings together, a hobby he'd managed to bribe his way to exploring, I set about removing the canvas from each one. The frames are sturdy, over engineered for holding paintings, but not for use as footholds on a makeshift ladder. They'd tape these frames to two lengths of bamboo used in the yard below to hang out washed clothes for drying. Those seven walls will be a piece of cake.

Sajan clambers off his bunk. "You're going to get us all killed!" he hisses at me. It is a bold move. He's normally very reserved around me. I'm not sure why. Perhaps it's how I look at him, I don't know. I head him off and he back-pedals but not quickly enough. I'm in his face now, his eyes wide as I stare him down. I know now what he's thinking. He doesn't need to say. When that cell door opens tomorrow morning, Sajan will tell anyone who will listen what we have planned.

There will be no second attempt. It will be over. Especially for me.

"Sajan… I know what you're thinking… and you should know one thing," I tell him. "The only reason that you are still alive tonight is because I don't want to upset any of our friends by cutting your throat. They aren't murderers… none of them, but as for me… I don't care if you live to see the sun come up again or not. I'll kill you without a second's hesitation… and if you make one more sound tonight, that is exactly what I'll do."

Sajan swallows hard. I can see in his expression that I've cut through. Good. Because I meant every word. He returns to his bed and hunkers down.

"I reckon we can squeeze out," Torsten says.

"You sure?" Luigi asks. He's been silently getting on with his part of things up until now. Now he's concerned, standing below the window with tens of metres worth of webbing in hand. The mattresses on our bunks are supported by webbing, much like what you find lining military boots, and unfurled it makes a decent rope. Enough to lower us down to the yard below anyway.

"If Thor says so, then we go," I say and both men nod. The thought of getting clear of this cell is intoxicating. Grabbing our plastic bags, stuffed full of fresh clothing, we assemble beneath the window.

Torsten gives me the nod and I go first, squeezing through the tiniest of gaps between the bars, and I'm out onto the plank thirty feet above the yard. As expected, the guard who usually sleeps beneath our window is not there tonight. That's another reason to go now. He won't be missing again for another shift rotation. That's a week. I don't have a week.

Tying the first stretch of webbing to the plank, I tentatively look back into the cell. It's like an out-of-body experience. I'm no longer incarcerated. At least, not in that cell. We still have those seven walls to overcome. I lower myself to the ground. The silence around me as I touch down is incredible. Alien. Torsten and Luigi follow, both look like rabbits in the headlights as they touchdown and I grin at them.

The bamboo poles come free without a sound and we're away to the first of the inner walls. I've spent time casing the layout of the prison, but despite my best efforts there are still huge swathes of the compound I haven't seen. I think I know where we are, but at best, I'm guessing. Not that I'm telling Torsten or Luigi that. They'd bottle it. And it's too late for that now. Four Cambodians staged a breakout a couple of months ago. They didn't get past the second wall before daybreak. They turned themselves in before anyone knew they'd even escaped. Not that that helped them any. They were tortured to death; a slow and painful process over a matter of months… time in the depths of the prison, repeatedly beaten, whipped and starved until their bodies gave out on them.

No… there's no going back now. This is it.

The first and second walls are easy, less than eight feet high and without any barbed wire or other impediment. The guard towers are on the outer two walls and these walls have a trench between them as well as a moat encompassing the entire facility that spans at least twenty-five metres. The trench between walls is only two metres wide but it is lined with coils of barbed wire, and it also doubles as the sewage outflow for the entire prison. Even so, it is still more appealing than spending another day in that cell.

They're making good progress now, moving silently and efficiently. No one escapes this prison, they never have done, which must give the guards a modicum of confidence if not complacency. There were rumours that someone did escape once some years ago, a Swiss man or maybe he was Dutch, I can't remember. Most talk of it as myth or folklore. People leave here through the front door or in a body bag. It's that simple.

They can see the last wall now. It's bigger than I'd thought. It's ten metres tall, perhaps more and lined with barbed wire. The top of the wall is also electrified, so I'm told, but I'm assured it's only

240v… so if we grin and bear it… and don't fall off we should be okay. First though, we have the sewage trench to navigate. It's disgusting, truly horrifying. If we don't make it, perhaps, we'll die of typhus before they can arrange an execution or their preferred method of beating us to death with iron bars.

At the base of the wall now. I'm exhausted and I can see the same reflected in the faces of my friends. I don't think I have the energy to make the final climb. The ladder isn't long enough anyway and none of us are superheroes. They're thinking the same. I know it.

"I'll boost you," Torsten says, reading my mind and looking up. "If we can get to the top of the ladder, I can boost the two of you to the parapet and you can haul yourselves over." He smiles. "I'm too big for you guys to do it for me."

I want to argue. We can all make it, I think, but I know it isn't true. Luigi knows it too. So I nod.

"What will you do?"

Torsten looks back along the length of the wall. "I'll try and slip out the front gate. No one will be looking for us until first thing. They won't expect us to be this far out. And it's still dark."

Everything but the last is true. The sun is climbing on the horizon and within a few minutes they will lose the cover of darkness. It's a long shot for my Danish friend, but possible. I unhook my plastic bag from around my waist and take out the small umbrella I'd supposedly made at the factory in my day job. In reality I paid a local child to do the work for me. Money is king here, although it can't buy luxury or indeed freedom.

A few spots of rain are falling upon them and into the trench, causing ripples in and around the sewage. Not enough to drench them, but enough to warrant the use of an umbrella. He passes it to Torsten. At the very least he can hide his face under it although his sizable frame stands out like… a giant Viking in a country of midgets.

Without another word, Torsten facilitates them getting atop the wall. They've chosen their spot between two guard towers, one seventy feet in each direction. For a moment I could have sworn I could see someone looking at us from one tower, but it must be my imagination because the alarm isn't raised. Not yet.

Reaching down I grasp Luigi's arm in a warrior's grip and haul him to the top of the wall, feeling the wave of electricity pass through me, tingling, as if every muscle in my body is vibrating. He feels it too. I hold onto him, fearing he'll pitch backwards. Torsten drops to the ground, lifts the ladder up at full stretch so I can grab it and lever it up and over the other side of the wall. He looks up at me, sends me a brief wave and a resigned smile before setting off along the line of the wall, hugging it close so as to avoid being seen by the guard towers. That'll be the last I ever see of him.

Taking care, but feeling the need to move with purpose, Luigi and I climb over the barbed wire and lower ourselves down to the ladder in turn, carefully descending to the ground. Only the moat to go, but the sun is cresting the horizon. There's no time. It is deathly quiet, and swimming will make far too much noise. I meet Luigi's eye and he's thinking the same.

There's only one thing we can do. We're outside the walls. We need to get changed into our clean clothes and walk past the front gate. It's our only option.

"Let's do it," I say. Luigi nods. I'm impressed with him which I find surprising. If anyone wouldn't be able to cut it, I would expect it to be him. I wonder if I need to cut him loose, go it alone or risk capture. But it's my fault Luigi is here. Without me, he wouldn't be going through any of this.

It's my fault.

Dogs barking… shouting… we look at each other as we hastily get dressed into our civilian clothing. Trousers. We can't wear trousers in prison, it's not allowed. We're free, but for how long? We can't run, despite wanting to with every shred of my being, but we have to walk slowly towards the gate. No one is shooting at us. No dogs are snarling at us.

It's Torsten. It has to be Torsten. A gunshot. More shouting as we round the corner to see the front gate. More shouting and several gunshots. We can't look. We can't stop and so we bypass the meleé… walking to our freedom.

CHAPTER ONE

OLLY RESPONDED to the calls from his friends by pedalling furiously, his lungs bursting with the effort to catch up. He was nervous though. They'd only finished school an hour previously and he'd rushed home to get changed and then across the village to gather the bag he'd stashed in the old bomb shelter at the foot of his grandparent's garden the night before. Now he was cycling up the farm track in the dark, trying his best to keep up with his friends.

It was easy for them, they had newer bikes with lightweight frames whereas he was riding the most basic of mountain bikes, seemingly fashioned from concrete and weighing twice as much as those of his peers. It didn't help that Olly was almost a full school year shy of the others in development, and a late starter so his mum always tells him. That's another reason he wasn't particularly competitive when it came to matches; rugby, football… any of the contact sports if he was honest. Even those games he could play solo, tennis for example, he still struggled to match up to his opponents who were invariably taller and far stronger than him.

"Come on!" they shouted from the crest of the hill. He could sense their excitement. He shared it. They'd been planning this for a couple of weeks and the anticipation had been growing almost daily. It had taken him that time to figure out how to snaffle this stuff from his father's lock-up without being rumbled. He'd managed it, eventually. Not that he might not still get caught, but it would be after the event now. He'd take that in exchange for this moment, the moment when he got to be *that guy*. The one who puts the smiles on everyone else's faces.

The track was pitted and uneven, huge furrows gouged to both left and right of centre where the farm traffic had chewed up the terrain passing this way throughout the autumn, one of the wettest on record apparently. That was last month though. Now it was deep into November, frozen and crisp with clear skies and frozen earth beneath the wheels of Olly's bike. His approach was stalling now, despite the rousing cheers of his friends to spur him on. Even they appeared to be losing energy, their encouragement dissipating as he laboured up the track.

Finally, at least that's how it felt to Olly, he reached the crest of the slope and almost fell off his bike as he dropped it to lie on its side on the frosty ground. The sun didn't penetrate this side of the hill in the winter, sitting so low in the sky as it did now. Clouds of vapour exhaled from his mouth as he rested his hands on his knees, breathing hard; no doubt red-faced. His legs were numb and he felt dizzy, worrying for a second that he might pass out.

"Take your time, Olly," Andrew said, adopting his typically sarcastic tone, the one that always drew approving grins from the more sycophantic members of the group, of which there were many. He wasn't going to allow them to take this away from him. Not this time. "Did you bring it all?"

Arching his shoulders to unhook the straps of his backpack, Olly nodded, whipping it around to his front, clutching it like the prized asset that it was. He could see Andrew's mind whirring, wondering if he could take it off him and have all the glory himself. That wasn't happening. Olly had conceived the plan; run the risk and he was going to enjoy this moment. Maybe it would change things going forward, make him more of a central figure as opposed to one on the periphery, the figure of fun for some, abuse for others.

If not… then he'd just make the most of it.

"What's that sticking out?" Nobby asked, looking at the black length of poly pipe protruding from the backpack. "Is it drainpipe?"

He had a knack for stating the obvious did Nobby. Olly nodded.

"Launcher."

Several of them got it and started laughing, looking at one another in almost disbelief. Or was it nerves? Olly couldn't tell.

"Come on then," Andrew said, abandoning any plan to seize control of this event, arguably the highlight of this month's calendar. No doubt he'd try again once they got underway. He was always the one to do this, encourage others to act while he sits back watching and then steps in to claim the glory or deny responsibility, whichever way things went, good or bad. He was like the Charles Manson of their little entourage. "Let's go," he said, gesturing for someone else to unhook the gate. Nobby did so willingly.

The five-bar gate swung open with a shriek, the sound punctuating the darkness, and they funnelled through, pushing their bikes. Olly threw the backpack over one shoulder and followed. Nobby let go of the gate and it swung closed, slamming into several members of the group who cursed the little guy. Nobby, undeterred, cursed at them explaining it wasn't his job to hold the gate as he wasn't their slave. Fair point.

Mounting their bikes again they freewheeled down the gentle slope, picking up the old tarmac surface of the access road that looped around to meet the main Docking to Ringstead Road, long disused now, potholed and cracked with foot-high grass and weeds now growing through the surface, even at this time of the year.

If you weren't local, you'd never know about this place, particularly as the heavy traffic coming and going was a thing of the past now. They reached the main gate at the end of the access road. The gated entrance was seven foot high with multiple signs tied to the chain link fencing warning of the dangers of deep water, falling rocks and, above all else, that the site was not a play area.

Little did they know.

Abandoning their bikes, the small group began scaling the fence, the weight of their numbers causing the chain link panels to shake and pitch back and forth as they climbed. The top was a little tricky, particularly for those who were less adept at such things. Olly was one such child and bearing the weight and bulk of his backpack, he struggled to swing his leg over. His fingers were clasping the cold metal of the mesh at the top, but the distribution of his weight and the burden of the backpack were putting him off balance.

Fearing he may fall, he clung on, not wishing to lose face in front of his friends, he felt himself flushing as fear took over. Several of the others were already down by now, all of them were over the obstacle with only Olly to go.

"Give me the bag," a voice said, and he glanced up to see Andrew straddling the fence with one leg on each side, reaching down to him. He smiled at Olly, warm and supportive, but it was a mask, as usual. He'd seen the opportunity to assert control present itself and he was moving in for the kill.

"No, I've got it," Olly said without conviction. Andrew cocked his head, arching one eyebrow as if to say *really?* He didn't have it at all. Moments later, he handed the backpack over and Andrew flung his leg over to the other side and scrambled down to join the waiting group. Meanwhile Olly, was left to clamber over by himself.

By the time he'd managed to descend the other side, the group were already some distance away and he had to hurry to catch up. The contents of the backpack were laid out on the ground and the boys stood around in a circle perusing what Olly had managed to pilfer from his father's stash. It was impressive. There were a number of rockets, easily noted by the wooden stave they were attached to but the others were eliciting various excited responses.

"What's this one?" Stuart asked, holding aloft a

squat cylinder, shallow and fatter than others at almost four inches in diameter.

"That's a mine," Olly stated.

"I think you'll find it's mine now," Stuart said, grinning and making a couple of people chuckle.

"No, it's a mine," Olly said, exasperated at Stuart's idiocy. He wasn't the brightest of the group but he had the notion that he was something special. Heaven knows who gave him that idea. "It's a cannister, kind of like a shell, that is launched from a mortar. The charge is at the base with the effects packed into the top."

"Cool," Stuart said, rubbing the side of it as if a genie would appear.

"This one?" Nobby asked, reaching for a cluster of tubes all fixed together. Andrew leaned across to block his reach, gathering it to himself and sneering at the smaller boy.

"That's a cake," Olly said, enjoying his superior knowledge whilst shaking the blood back into his hands. He still had an imprint of the chain link in his palms and fingers.

"What's it do?" Andrew asked.

"Each tube is packed with different aerial effects, and they are combined on a fuse, so they go off in succession."

"What sort of effects?"

Olly shrugged. "Impossible to describe. Combined, these tubes can have hundreds if not thousands of different effects inside."

"Nice," Andrew said, his eyes gleaming.

Olly gathered up the length of poly pipe. It was only two inches in diameter and just over a foot long, but it would work to fashion a makeshift rocket launcher.

"Come on," Olly said, excitedly, carefully opening the rocket packaging. A murmur of excitement passed around the group as Olly 'loaded' the launcher, stepping away from the others who wisely intended on giving him a wide berth anyway. Rummaging in his pocket for the disposable lighter Olly had taken from his father's secret cigarette stash that he kept in a wall-mounted cupboard in his lock-up, the habit he mistakenly thought no one else knew about, he encouraged one of the others to step forward and light the fuse. He couldn't do that and keep the rocket from sliding out of the tube.

Andrew made to move and then hesitated, pushing Stuart forward as the sacrificial lamb. Reluctantly, the slightly rotund, blond boy with the floppy hair came alongside Olly.

"Are you sure about this?" he whispered so only he and Olly would hear him. The rocket was thin, but it was long and Olly had seen one of these go off recently. It was awesome.

"It'll be fine, Stuart. Just light the fuse and

gently push it back into the tube. Not too hard though or it'll fall out the back and then who knows where it'll end up."

Stuart, to his credit, looked unconvinced but as the discontent among the waiting group grew, he had to get on with it or face the taunts of his peers for bottling it. Taking a breath, he struck the wheel of the lighter and the spark flew from the flint several times until the gas ignited and he held the flame to the fuse. Olly heard the fuse start rather than saw it and Stuart pushed the rocket into the tube before running for cover. The boys started cheering and Olly turned the launcher towards the far wall of the flooded quarry, above the water, and waited. Seconds later, the rocket shot out of the tube with a whoosh, and he saw the smoke and caught a whiff of the gunpowder charge that propelled it away from him.

His friends cheered as the rocket shot across the quarry at frightening speed, striking the wall opposite before exploding in a shower of white, yellow and green. He had to admit it, it was awesome. They all gathered around him now, congratulating him, patting him on the back and confirming his newfound celebrity status. More rockets flew before Andrew set off the mine Stuart had coveted since it had come out of the bag.

"What would happen if we put a few of these together?"

Olly looked round. He hadn't seen who'd asked the question during their brief lull between launches. The novelty hadn't worn off as such, but the clamour to make bigger, bolder explosions was growing as they sought another high. It was like they were all chasing the dragon, which was ironic seeing as fireworks originated in China.

"A few of what?" Olly asked, seeing as they were all looking to him to answer the question. He looked at what they had assembled before them, a number of cylindrical tubes wrist to fingertip in length. "They're salutes."

"Huh?" Andrew asked.

"They usually go up for the finale. They're packed with flash powder and are designed to have a quick flash but primarily to produce a really loud report."

"A what?" Andrew asked, frowning. The guy really was a bit thick.

"A loud noise," Olly said, raising his eyebrows. "Mimicking an artillery shell going off. These ones have titanium added to give off some colour as well… but they're loud as hell."

Andrew grinned. "Stu… pass me that roll of gaffer tape."

"That's mental…" Olly said, watching Andrew assembling half a dozen of the tubes together before wrapping them with the tape. "You'll blow our eardrums with that. They're supposed to go off a hundred feet or more in the air."

Andrew looked at him, despondent. He wasn't keen to back down, not now that he had the group hanging on his every word. He shook his head, looking around. His eyes settled on the water, and he grinned.

"Depth charge!" he said. John, who had been quiet up until now, cheered.

"Yeah, man. Depth charge. Let's kill some fish!"

"There are no fish in there, you bell end," Stuart said, as if he knew.

"Will that work?" Andrew asked Olly. He didn't know if he was honest. He'd never tried to see if the fuses worked underwater. He shrugged. "I guess we'll find out," Andrew said, adding yet more tape around the tubes.

They transferred the makeshift bomb to the water's edge but before anyone called for the lighter, common sense prevailed… to a degree.

"If we horse it through the air into the water…" Olly said, "…what if it goes off before it hits the surface? Like, in our faces or something?"

Initially, Andrew's expression was dismissive, but the reality hit home as he looked at their improvised explosive device in his hands. He looked around. Olly's eyes drifted upward to the top of the wall at the steepest point of the incline to the rear of the man-made lake. The top was at least two metres or so above the water. He pointed to it.

"Let's drop it."

Andrew nodded and the two of them circumvented the lakeside and made their way to the high point. The others remained at the water's edge, looking on with curiosity. Once in position, Andrew smiled wickedly at Olly and indicated for him to light the fuse. Olly did so and then Andrew tossed the taped tubes over the edge and down into the water… where they broke the surface and sank with no effect.

The watching teenagers below moaned, their disappointment transmitting to both Olly and Andrew. The latter glared at Olly as if it was his fault.

"You idiot! We've wasted those because you don't know what you're doing."

He reached out to jab an accusatory finger into Olly's chest. Olly made to protest but was cut off by a loud boom and a trembling of the ground at their feet. A plume of water shot up from beneath them and the group cheered. Andrew burst out laughing, raising his hands in celebration, accepting the adulation from his wingmen. Olly, forgotten in all of this, stood back as the others high-fived one another, laughing and jeering one another.

That was the last of the fireworks. The last of what he'd taken from his father's stores. With a bit of luck, he might not notice until new year when the next wave of sales would come in. By then, he'd probably assume he'd miscounted on his late stock take… unless he looked in the next couple of days. With a bit more luck, Olly's new found kudos amongst his peers might last a while too. Although, seeing Andrew striding away to his waiting pack of hyenas without a backward glance, he doubted it.

His eyes drifted down to the water, watching the ripples fanning out across the still surface of the lake. *What's that?* Dropping to his haunches, he focussed on whatever it was. Could it be part of the firework casing or one of the tubes that'd failed to go off? No, it was far too big. The light clouds had settled in front of the moon, and it was tricky to see in the winter evening.

Hurrying back down, he lost sight of it as the darkness enveloped the object. By the time he reached the water's edge, gathering a fallen branch from one of the trees lining the eastern edge of the site, the moon had come out once more. Whatever it was, it was a similar size to his backpack. Several of the others saw he was up to something but only Nobby joined him at his side.

"What you got there, Olly?" he asked, squinting to see as Olly hooked what now looked like a package, wrapped in black plastic.

"I don't know… but I think the explosion brought it to the surface."

"Hey… maybe it's buried pirate treasure?" Nobby said, excitedly.

"Wrapped in black plastic… in a flooded quarry? I reckon the diggers might have found it, don't you?"

Undeterred, Nobby's logic didn't faze him at all. "You never know!"

Olly smiled, catching the package with his makeshift hook and drawing it to the shoreline. The others appeared at their shoulders now, keen not to miss out. Even Andrew, although he seemed poised to ridicule them as soon as the opportunity arose.

Using the tip of the branch to hook the slack of the wrapping, Olly levered the package onto dry land.

"What is it?" Stuart asked.

Olly glanced up at him, frowning. "Can't you see I haven't opened it yet, dumb ass?"

The others chuckled and Stuart's face flushed, visible even though his features were only lit by the moonlight. Intrigued now, everyone leaned in as Olly reached for the package. The plastic wasn't thick, likely a bin liner, but still of decent quality. His dad only ever bought the higher-grade liners and, having seen his dad's reaction when the cheaper ones split and sent the bin waste all over the kitchen floor, Ollie understood why. Gripping the slack of the bag, Olly pulled his hands apart, stretching and then tearing the plastic. A stench like no other greeted them and everyone recoiled but not only from the smell.

Before them, inside the bag atop other large chunks was one discernible feature that made it clear just what sort of treasure they'd uncovered; a discoloured, bloated human foot.

CHAPTER TWO

Backing into the door, Tom Janssen leaned on the bar, and it opened. Tom was immediately struck by a freezing blast of cold air. Usually, stepping out from the interior of the swimming pool area of the leisure centre in Hunstanton would be pleasant, a respite from the humidity of the viewing gallery. However, these days they heated the pool less than they would in normal times. These were far from normal times. Maintaining the usual temperature would likely bankrupt the centre within a month what with the current cost of energy. With a bit of luck that might change in the future; although when that future might arrive was an entirely different question.

Saffy complained bitterly now about attending her swimming lessons. She loved swimming, but being cold was something Tom's informally adopted daughter didn't care for. Oftentimes her friends would have a birthday party in the swimming pool, but on this occasion, it was a good old-fashioned roller disco, held in the rink just outside the pool enclosure.

The music was loud, blasting out from the pole-mounted speakers positioned at either end of the rink. Tom sidled up to Alice, handing her a cup of coffee he'd just bought from the cafeteria. She cupped it with both hands appreciating the warmth.

"Everything going okay?" he asked, watching the children doing laps. Most of them were seemingly competent skaters with only a couple using something resembling a Zimmer frame and one or two clinging to the sides of the rink and hauling themselves around. Saffy on the other hand was zipping in and out of others chasing a couple of her friends who were equally proficient on wheels.

"I'm only having a minor cardiac every time she changes direction on a whim," Alice said, removing the lid from her cup and gently blowing steam away from her face as she savoured the aroma. Tom turned his attention to Saffy, convinced she was about to suffer a collision only for her to adjust her feet, drop a shoulder and pass harmlessly between two friends. All three of them found it amusing as she passed through an impossibly narrow gap and continued on in her loop.

Tom shuddered. "It's like watching those nutters flying down the bobsleigh run on those… raft thingies."

"Raft thingies?" Alice asked, shooting an amused look towards him.

"Yeah, you know… the thin sled things…"

"The luge?" Alice asked.

"Exactly," he said, dismissing her amusement with a flick of his hand. "You know what I meant."

"I do," Alice said, grinning and then sipping at her coffee. "But don't say it too loud or she'll be hassling us to set her up with that."

"There are no runs anywhere near here," Tom said, frowning. "Is she still on about martial arts?"

"Of course. Purely as a form of self-defence, though."

"Naturally," Tom said.

"I've not heard her use the term *totally annihilate someone* to any of her friends for a couple of days now," Alice said coyly.

Tom shook his head. "She'll have to make do with the climbing wall at the moment. I don't think I could manage her doing anything else where she might break something." As if on cue, Saffy lost her footing and wiped out two of her friends drawing a collective gasp from a number of watching parents. Everyone involved got themselves, or each other, back on their feet and took off again without batting an eyelid.

"You know there's a family of four who come along to the climbing wall most weeks?" Alice asked. Tom nodded. "One of the children is an absolute nightmare. I thought Saffy was hyperactive but…"

"Do you want me to see if the parents have criminal records? Maybe I could have them all sent down or something," Tom said, sporting a wry smile.

Alice elbowed him in the ribs. "No, that won't be necessary… unless you could swing it?"

He looked at her, reading her expression. "I don't think that would go down well with the Det Chief Super."

"How is that going anyway? You never told me what his grand restructuring plan is."

"I've no idea yet myself. He's still playing it close to his chest. Not even Tamara is in the loop," Tom said, citing his boss, DCI Tamara Greave.

"She'll not like that."

"Understatement," Tom said. "I reckon it's just the new guy sabre-rattling."

"Rattling something," Alice said, "but I wouldn't go with a sabre."

Tom smiled. One of the parents caught his eye just as a lady came over to speak to Alice, distracting her from their conversation. Tom recognised her from the odd occasion where he did the school run, work schedule permitting, but he didn't know her name. Although, it was possible he'd forgotten it. Alice welcomed her warmly and they put their heads together. Tom excused himself, moving to meet the man who'd caught his eye.

"Tom, how the devil are you?" he asked, offering his hand. Tom knew Adrian reasonably well, but still only in passing. He was a local businessman, in the hospitality trade, owning a takeaway as well as a gastro pub or restaurant, Tom couldn't recall which.

"I'm well. How's business?"

Adrian's upper lip curled into a sneer, and he frowned. "Could always be better."

"It's a good time of the year for you now, surely," Tom said, looking up at the festive decorations already hanging despite it only being mid-November. "No one wants to be standing around outside at this time of year, it's sit-down meals and takeaways isn't it?" He appreciated the irony, since they were indeed standing outside at this time of the year.

"Tough times," Adrian said, "for everyone. I suppose in your line of work things are pretty constant, right?"

Tom shrugged. "Petty stuff seems to get worse when things are tight but, yes, the major cases roll on regardless of what's happening in the wider community."

"I guess that makes sense," Adrian said, his gaze drifting beyond the rink to the construction site at the rear of the leisure centre. A crane was in place, almost standing watch over the new buildings springing up from their foundations alongside the promenade. Tom sensed Adrian had something on his mind; he was brooding, his expression melancholy. It was a far cry from his default; a quick smile and an affable carefree demeanour. It was an assumption on Tom's part, but one born of honed instinct. He looked at him thoughtfully. Adrian noticed and shook off the look with an artificial smile.

"Everything all right?" Tom asked.

"Yes, yes of course," Adrian said, flexing his shoulders beneath his thick overcoat. "The weather's finally turned. Winter's arrived." It was cold, that was true, but it was no colder than it'd been these past few days, but Tom figured he wanted to change the subject. He saw no need to deter him. "It'll soon be Christmas."

"Gets earlier every year," Tom said, continuing the small talk and drinking his coffee. Alice and her friend had been joined by another mum and the three of them were laughing and joking. He liked to see her happy. These past few months had been something of a challenge what with her mum passing away shortly after being diagnosed with cancer. The impact of the loss had been substantial, but something good had come out of it, Alice reuniting with her estranged father. Their relationship still needed a great deal of work, from both of them, but it was positive that she still had a parent to go to.

"Isn't that the truth?" Adrian said, tutting. He glanced sideways at Tom. "Tell me… what do you do if you see financial irregularities going on?" Tom fixed him with a look, trying to ascertain if this was a fictitious scenario. Adrian appeared to read his mind. "I mean, hypothetically speaking obviously."

"Define irregularities for me," Tom said.

Adrian back-pedalled, waving the question away. "Oh… nothing, forget I said anything."

Tom smiled. "Look, if it's fraud or someone putting their hand in the till, then it's something I'd likely get into, but if you're talking about malpractice… then you'd take it to the ombudsman. Accountants, wealth advisors and the like are all regulated by the Financial Conduct Authority or whatever it's called this week."

"Ah… right, yes," Adrian said, nodding thoughtfully. "Yes, of course."

"Are you sure everything is okay?"

"Oh, fine," he said, dismissing Tom's concern. "It's nothing… just a couple of things. Nothing for the police to be concerned about."

"Always available for a chat, if needed," Tom said, smiling. "In private or just in confidence."

"Much appreciated, thank you... but there's no need, as I say."

Tom was startled by a large bang alongside him as Saffy crashed into the hoardings like a crazed ice hockey forward, grinning up at him maniacally as she hoisted herself up.

"Can we do this more often?" she asked him. "I love skating! Can we go ice skating?"

"Erm... yes, I suppose so," Tom said, trying to recall where the nearest ice rink to them was. He had no idea.

"And I want to go to the dojo in town," Saffy declared.

"Yes, your mother mentioned that to me."

"When can I go?"

"We'll see."

"Can I go this week? The class is on Friday. Jenny and Olivia go already... and Jack does too."

"Who's Jack?" Tom asked, glancing to his right at the retreating form of Adrian who'd left without saying anything. "Do I know Jack?"

"Yes, he's the horrible one. Remember, I told you how he pulled Olivia's hair and told her he was going to kill—"

"Yes," Tom said, holding his hand up to stop her in mid-flow, conscious of the other parents nearby and not wanting to feed the gossip machine.

"I remember. And you want to hang out with him?"

"No, I want to hammer him into the ground like a tent peg."

Her stance was so matter of fact that it brought a smile to his lips.

"There's an image. But violence isn't—"

"The answer!" she said, dropping back onto her wheels and pushing away from the barrier. "I know!" she called over her shoulder as she skated away, building up speed.

"Poor Jack," Tom said aloud.

"Poor who?" Alice asked, coming to stand alongside him and slipping her arm around his waist.

"Some poor soul who has found himself in Saffy's cross hairs."

"Oh dear. I feel for him… and the boy he once was."

"Are you sure training her to be a lethal killing machine is the best course of action?"

Alice shrugged. "It's a dog-eat-dog world, Tom, I don't want my daughter to wind up in a tin of Pedigree Chum."

"Fair point," Tom said, just as his mobile phone rang. Fishing it out of his pocket, he saw it was Cassie. Winking at Alice, he answered. "Hey, Cass. What's up?"

"Dead fella," she said flatly. "I think."

"Anything more than that…" he said, glancing down at Alice and she removed her arm from his waist so that he could move out of earshot of anyone else, "or do I have to guess?"

"Some kids found it whilst exploring pyrotechnics out at the old quarry on the Docking Road."

"I expect that's a story in and of itself."

"Too right."

"You said *it*, male or female?"

"Um… that's tricky to answer right now," Cassie said. Tom could hear some movement in the background along with the wind noise whistling over the mouthpiece. "Looking at the size of the foot we have… and yes, it isn't connected to a leg, I'm guessing it's a guy but some women have big feet too, so maybe not."

Tom frowned. "Please tell me you have more than a foot?"

"Yes, of course… well, it's hard to tell what we do have to be fair." Cassie sniffed. "But we definitely have at least one foot."

Tom sighed. "The old quarry you said?"

"Aye," Cassie said. "And I hope you haven't just had your tea because it's a bit ripe, if you know what I mean?"

"I'm on my way."

He hung up and returned to Alice's side, meeting her expectant look with an apologetic smile.

"You have to go?"

He nodded. "Cassie has something I need to take a look at." He leaned in and kissed her cheek. She smiled. "Are you going to be all right getting home?"

"Sure," Alice said. "One of the others will drop us back." He nodded and turned to leave. "Don't forget my dad is arriving tomorrow… with his lady friend."

Tom held a finger up to her. "Now, you promised to play nicely."

She raised her hands in submission. "I know… and I will." She cocked her head. "Mostly. Although, she was the reason my dad left us high and dry, so…" she shrugged, "you do what you have to."

"He did have a say in it too, remember."

Alice scrunched her nose and rocked her head from side to side. Tom shook his head, stroked her cheek affectionately and walked away. Saffy came alongside him, slowing to match his pace.

"Are you off to work?"

"I am," he said. "But I'll be home for bedtime, I promise."

"Are you going to see a dead body?"

He checked his walk, turning to face her and Saffy pulled up, leaning on the barrier.

"What makes you ask?"

"You've already been to work… so if you're

going in again then it means someone's died. Right?"

He nodded. "Not necessarily. It's not always because of that."

"It is this time though. You get that haunted look when it's something gruesome."

He frowned. "Do I?"

"Yes. So, is it? Gruesome, I mean?"

"Sometimes you're too smart for your own good, young lady."

"You can never be too smart," she said, grinning and wheeling away to catch up with her friends skating by. "Stay safe!" she called, and he waved to her before resuming his walk to the exit.

"Not even into double figures and she's parenting me already," he told himself quietly.

CHAPTER THREE

THE ENTRANCE to the old quarry wasn't easy to spot. Tom was a Sheringham boy and although he was familiar with seeing the aggregate lorries transporting sand or gravel all over the local area, he'd never actually visited the site. There was another working quarry just outside Snettisham but that one was right on the main road, useful for access with the heavy vehicles. This site however was positioned over the crest of a hill and separated from the passing Docking Road by an agricultural field. If you didn't know it was there, you'd never see it.

Thankfully, a liveried police car was stationed at the end of the access road, closed to through traffic by a simple metal gate. Tom pulled up and the constable ducked to see inside the car, recognising him and quickly opening the gate for him to pass through. He stopped and the officer came around to the driver's side.

"Good evening, sir," he said, glancing up the track which wound around to the rear of a copse before disappearing over the crest of the hill. "Forensics are already here… along with the parents."

Tom started. "The parents? Whose parents?"

"Local kids, sir. They found the body… or what there is of it."

Tom nodded. "How are they taking it?"

"The kids or the parents?" He asked with a wry smile.

"I was thinking of the children."

"Well, I reckon they're coping better than their mums and dads."

Tom could understand that. The last thing any parent wants, besides them coming to harm, is for their child to bring the police to their door. To do so because they were not only trespassing on dangerous ground, blowing things up and disturbing a mutilated corpse at the same time would be a lot to take in.

The constable stepped aside, and Tom continued on up the road. Once this route would have been well maintained, necessary due to the volume of traffic as well as the sheer weight of the vehicles coming and going fully laden. However, it was clear now that the upkeep was minimal, if not non-existent. In places the road surface had slipped with the land beneath shifting, likely due to water erosion, heating and cooling. Both a Norfolk summer and winter could swing between extremes, facilitating the formation of great cracks in the asphalt.

Large potholes were appearing elsewhere and seeds, carried on the breeze, were allowing wild grasses and no doubt overspill from the neighbouring farmlands to take root. It wouldn't be long before Mother Nature reclaimed what had once been hers.

The quarry was a hive of activity, nestled at the foot of a gentle slope. Tom was aware of the local planning decision to designate the former quarry as a nature reserve, allowing it to be flooded and then re-wilded to form a wetland habitat. Popular with local people as well as wildlife enthusiasts, the site had received some negative press of late due to the lack of funds seemingly allocated to complete the project. The local water company had been approached to see if the site could be repurposed into a domestic serving reservoir or as a storage sink hole for local farmers. However, due to costs and a lack of enthusiasm from many parties, the decision was taken to create a natural drain for the surrounding farmland and to allow nature to take its course.

Pulling up at the massive chain link gates and eyeing the fencing encompassing the entire site, Tom had to wonder if the criticism was indeed justified. The place looked a far cry from a nature reserve and much more like an abandoned industrial site that'd been given the bare minimum of care prior to locking the gates.

He parked next to Cassie's car and got out acknowledging the greetings of several uniformed officers who were ensuring no unauthorised eyes got too close. Three scenes of crime officers along with a police photographer were deep in conversation beside their van, all dressed in their blue paper coveralls. A tent had been erected at the nearby waterline and he could see Cassie standing at the entrance coordinating events. She smiled as he approached.

"Sorry to call you back out," she said.

"No problem. You saved me from children's party hell."

"Oh… I've not missed her birthday, have I?"

Tom shook his head. "No, don't worry. It's a school friend of Saffy's. They could only book the roller skating for this evening, something about weekend maintenance. Either way, it was pizza and cake after the event and, trust me, the music was loud enough outside before a load of pumped-up kids get stuck into fast food and additives."

"I'm surprised you didn't insist on carrot sticks and broccoli as appetisers, Tom."

"Who's to say I didn't?"

Cassie smiled, indicating beyond Tom to where a gaggle of adults and children stood along with two uniformed officers.

"Some of the natives are a bit restless," she said.

Tom followed her gaze. Three of the parents were standing together, their children in close proximity but there were others who were keeping themselves separate and clearly insisting their children did likewise. Not that any of the children seemed particularly vocal, bearing in mind what they'd been up to.

"I'll speak with them in a bit. Any of them I need to be aware of?"

"The big chap is a little bit precious, I must say."

Tom knew who she was talking about. He was one of the ones standing away from the others, his son, presumably, was within a step of him but evidently not keen to be any closer, his head bowed. As for the father, his expression was one of thunder.

"Feeling aggrieved, is he?"

"Aye. His son must have been led astray by the others. You know, the usual."

"I've met them, yes."

"Well, this one is full of demands… knows his rights and all that. Although, what rights he's talking about must stretch back to Magna Carta because I've never heard of them."

"Terrific," Tom said, frowning. "Come on then, what have you got for me?"

"Come join me in my magic tent and I'll reveal all," Cassie said, putting on her best Mystic Meg impression. He followed her inside; a portable lamp was clipped to the frame above them illuminating the space.

Dr Fiona Williams, their on-call forensic medical examiner, looked up from her position kneeling beside what Tom figured was a black bin liner, torn open, revealing some of its grisly contents. She had a clipboard resting on her thigh and was making notes.

"Hello, Fiona, having fun?" Tom asked.

She arched her eyebrows, looking glum. "Well, it's more interesting than my midweek bridge club which is where I should be right now."

"Sorry," Tom said, looking at the contents of the bag. "It doesn't look like we'll be keeping you out long, not based on what I can see there."

She nodded. "Yes, I'm afraid your man has lost a fair bit of his bodyweight since he passed away."

Tom appreciated the dryness of her sense of humour. The contents of a small to medium-sized kitchen waste bin would likely hold more material than he could see at his feet.

Cassie looked at Tom. "I've already contacted

the dive team, but they won't be here until the morning. There's no chance they'll see anything in that water in this light, but they'll go under first thing."

Tom nodded, turning his gaze back to the bag. Fiona continued.

"I think I can be confident in saying that your victim, and I'm presuming it is a victim, is male judging by the size of the foot and by the muscle definition of the lower leg, which is separated from the foot within the bag. Despite your glamorous assistant here proclaiming to have an aunt with size fourteen feet, whether that's commonplace in Newcastle, I couldn't say, but in my experience, not so much here in Norfolk."

"The land of the Hobbit people," Cassie said, nodding approvingly.

"As I was saying, a male, I'd estimate five foot ten to six feet tall, based again on both the foot size and the calf muscle. I know it's not an exact science, but shorter people tend to have smaller proportions in almost every department."

"Again…" Cassie said, "if you'd dated the same people as I have over the years you wouldn't be so confident in that assertion."

Tom glanced at her and sighed. Cassie smiled but made it clear she wouldn't interrupt again.

"And please… I've already been asked by some of your team," Fiona glanced at Cassie, "if I can ascertain a cause of death. Clearly, that's not possible with what we have here."

"With a bit of luck, the rest of him is still in the water," Tom said.

"I do hope so, Tom, because otherwise you will be struggling for an identification let alone a potential cause of death."

"Toxicology?" Tom asked.

Fiona took a steep inhalation, screwing up her nose. "If there's anything suspicious in his bloodstream… maybe it will show up. However, with this length of time in the water I would expect any trace of the majority of drugs, recreational or poisonous, could be long gone."

"How long has it been in the water do you think?"

She shrugged. "Hard to say." Turning her attention back to the body parts, her brow furrowed. "The quarry is deep, and the water is very cold at this time of year, so it will have acted as a refrigerator of sorts. It seems microbial activity is limited, likely for the same reasons… so… a week to ten days. The skin, as you can see," she said, indicating the foot, "is discoloured with a blue green tinge to it. The flesh is bloated, so that would indicate time of death of a few days ago if it were summer, but in these conditions, this air and water temperature… gives you the week to ten days."

Tom nodded solemnly. "So, the body… parts… were in the water?"

Cassie nodded. "Yes, North Norfolk's answer to the Peaky Blinders gang were up here detonating explosives—"

"Explosives?" Tom asked.

"Fireworks," Cassie said. "Enough firepower to launch a coup in a small Central African Republic by the sounds of it, and some bright spark – no pun intended – thought to drop one under the surface to see what happens." She pointed to the bag. "That popped up as a result."

"Weighted down?" Tom asked.

"Could be in a larger container," Cassie said, "which was disturbed by the shock wave, perhaps?"

Fiona looked thoughtful. "Possibly. Any explosive force is magnified by the confines of the water around it, so it is certainly possible that the disturbance freed it from whatever was keeping it at the bottom. The children tore the bag open, and I'm not sure what they were expecting but it wasn't what they got. Looking at the tightness of the knot, along with the grade of the plastic, I'm not seeing any holes in the exterior, it is quite possible that the gas build-up of the decomposition helped bring it to the surface as well."

"Really?" Cassie asked.

Fiona nodded. "I used to walk around here

with my dog, prior to her passing, and I remember this quarry. If you are on the bridleway that runs along the field boundary to the east you have a great view down over the site. I know this quarry wasn't as large as some of those monster ones you see in Africa or North America, but it was deep. The sides were stepped, I think that's what you say, and so when they flooded it, it is only at its deepest in the centre. If this bag, or bags, were deposited fairly close to the edge then it may not have been more than a couple of metres deep. Therefore, the build-up of the gases could aid in it rising to the surface if it's not properly weighted down."

Tom thought about it. "How close to the water's edge did it surface?"

"Close enough the boys could snag it with a branch."

"Thrown in from a standing position on the bank rather than taken out by boat."

Cassie agreed. "And if they were horsing it in from around here, then they wouldn't have thrown it far."

"Probably not expecting anyone to come looking," Tom said. "Who's going to drain a freshly made lake two years after creating it."

"No one is ever likely to drain this," Cassie said. "They couldn't have known it was still shallow so close to the edge."

"Great place to dispose of someone without anyone seeing," Tom said. "It'd have to be a local."

"Or a contractor familiar with the site," Cassie countered. "Truck drivers coming and going, local builders, landscape gardeners… all of whom would have had reason to come here to load up. The list might be longer than you think."

Tom exhaled, turning back to the doctor. "Fiona, is there anything else you can tell us?"

"Whoever chopped him up did so very crudely. I think you can chalk off anyone with surgical training. I would expect more skill from a butcher than I can see on display here."

"An amateur?" Tom asked.

Fiona frowned. "Someone not familiar with the process of dismemberment… or someone who doesn't care particularly for accuracy which, to be fair, if one isn't used to butchery then they might wish to be quick about it. Although…"

"Although?" Tom asked.

"The number of times they've slashed at this ankle to detach the foot… it would have taken a while. Much longer than it needed to."

"Someone who definitely doesn't know what they're doing then?" Cassie asked.

"Or someone in a rush," Tom suggested. "More haste and less speed, so the saying goes."

"Maybe they had a dinner reservation?" Cassie said dryly.

"How much of the body do you think we have here?" Tom asked.

Fiona checked her notes. "One foot, the lower leg, separated at the knee - presumably for the same foot, the right foot and leg anyway – plus the thigh and another calf. I have an upper arm, separated at the shoulder and above the elbow. I'm hoping that all these bits are all from the same person, but we won't know that until you've reassembled every part you can retrieve from the depths and, I dare say, run some DNA comparisons."

"You think it could be more than one victim?" Tom asked.

"No, I wouldn't say that, only that I can't be certain with so little to work with."

Cassie sighed. "We could always have a rather macabre pick and mix going on here."

"I hope not," Tom said. "One victim is more than enough to be getting on with. Is there anything else you need, Fiona?"

"Well, a head and hands… and perhaps a torso might prove beneficial when it comes to establishing what happened to the poor soul."

"Not much to ask then."

Fiona smiled. "Oh… I nearly forgot. We do have this," she said, opening a fold in the bag to reveal more detail. Tom dropped to her side, and he could see what she had revealed, a tattoo.

"Is this the arm… segment?"

She nodded. "Upper left arm. I'm afraid with my limited knowledge of ink that I can't shed much light on it for you, and it does seem to be a generic design, so that may not help you either, but it's something."

Tom looked at the tattoo. It was a series of interlocking Celtic patterns that seemed to wrap around the entire section. Dr Williams was correct; it did look like many other tattoos and not very distinctive.

"You're right, it's not much," Tom said, "but it is something. Have you had everything out of the bag yet?"

Fiona shook her head. "No, the photographer has taken his shots, but we were waiting on you."

"Right, Cassie, have SOCO come in and start cataloguing what's here. You never know, there might be something else in there. While they're doing that, we'll go and speak to the children."

"I hope you've had your vaccinations," Cassie said. "I reckon this lot are borderline feral."

Tom grinned, thanked Fiona and headed out of the tent. Cassie went to speak to the forensic officers while he walked towards the waiting parents and their children.

CHAPTER FOUR

TOM NOTICED several of the parents reacting to his approach. They must have assumed he was quite senior, two of the dads appeared to stiffen as he came to stand before them. PC Marshall greeted Tom and made the introductions. A couple of people offered their first names while others merely nodded. There was an air of apprehension around the group and Tom saw that one man, who Cassie had pointed to, was standing slightly apart from the others, although he too had come over to him.

"Thank you, everyone, for your patience this evening," Tom said. "I'm sure you can appreciate this is a challenging situation we have here."

"Are you going to keep us here much longer?" the big man said. Tom looked at him sternly.

"May I have your name?" he asked, the man hadn't spoken when Tom arrived.

"Aitkin. Nicholas Aitkin."

"Mr Aitkin," Tom said, meeting his eye directly. "I'm sure you can appreciate the gravity of the situation we all find ourselves in tonight." He looked around the group seeing solemn faces. "And it is important we get things straight before anyone leaves. Obviously, we can follow up with official statements tomorrow but, in the meantime, I would like to know what was happening here tonight."

"You can't think any of our children have anything to do with this?" Aitkin said, unfazed by Tom's monologue. "Don't you think these boys have been through enough?"

"Nevertheless," Tom said, "here we are and *here* we will all stay until we get to have this conversation. Feel free to leave, Mr Aitkin, if you please, but your son…" he looked at him, the young Aitkin was looking at his feet.

"Andrew," his father said.

"Andrew will remain here. I can always contact social services, if you prefer. They can provide a suitable adult to stand with Andrew—"

"That won't be necessary," Aitkin grumbled.

"Good. The right choice," Tom said. "Now, what were you all doing here this evening?"

Tom asked the question directly towards Andrew. The boy's father seemed to be the most domineering character and in Tom's experience that would often translate into similar patterns of behaviour by the offspring, perhaps attempting to mimic the parent, even if it was entirely a front.

"Why are you asking my boy?" Aitkin said, turning and pointing at another lad two over from where they stood. "He's the one with access to the explosives and so I'll bet it was all his idea."

Tom looked and one man flushed through embarrassment. He swallowed hard, his eyes flickering between Aitkin and Tom. His son was standing in front of him, and he had his hands placed gently on his shoulders.

"I must admit," he said, "I will need to up my security after all of this." Tom shot him a quizzical look. "I have a business selling and distributing fireworks." He looked apologetic. "We supply retail outlets all over East Anglia… and this is the busiest time of the year."

"Where do you store your stock?" Tom asked.

"In secure containers…" he looked at his son, "but I guess I never suspected Judas here." He gave his son a playful shake. It was mockery spurred on by humiliation.

"We'll get to the fireworks and general safety another time," Tom said. The boy looked up at Tom, tears welling in his eyes.

"We were just messing around," he said. "Honestly. We didn't mean any harm… that's why we came out here."

"What's your name?" Tom asked.

"Olly."

Tom fixed him with his gaze. "Did you see anyone out here tonight, Olly?"

He shook his head.

"How about any other night when you've been here?"

"I'm sure they—"

Tom raised a hand to stop Nicholas Aitkin's newest protest.

"I'm sure the boys have planned this little escapade in great detail," Tom said. "Isn't that right, Olly?"

The boy nodded. "We wanted to make sure it was safe. Rather than let them off at the beach." With the last comment he involuntarily appeared to look across at Andrew who flinched. Aitkin looked to complain again but catching Tom's eye and reading his expression made him think twice. It would appear Andrew was the driving force in this little group but seemed quite adept at deflecting blame onto others. Yet another skill he'd adopted from his father figure, no doubt.

"Have you seen anyone else out this way?" Tom asked.

Olly shook his head, but another lad objected.

"What about that car we saw?" he said. All eyes

fell on him. He was a short lad, stocky with close cut hair but he seemed genuine.

"Shut it, Nobby?" Andrew said, only to receive a cuff across the back of his head by his father. Tom ignored him.

"What car, Nobby?" he asked.

"It was a white hatchback, wasn't it guys?" Nobby asked, looking around.

One of the others nodded and Olly agreed after thinking about it for a moment.

"Any idea of the make?" Tom asked.

"A German one, I think," Nobby said. Olly bobbed his head. "Four doors… a hatchback."

"Was it new or old?"

Nobby shook his head. "Don't know. We was too far away to see it."

Tom exhaled. "Okay, where did you see it?"

Nobby pointed back up the access road to the crest of the hill alongside the copse. "Just there, heading away."

"And when was this?"

"Last week… maybe Tuesday night?" Nobby said, looking at his friends for support. They all agreed, aside from Andrew who had his arms folded defiantly across his chest. He wasn't going to speak if he could help it.

"Had they been here, to the quarry?" Tom asked. All of the boys shrugged. They didn't know. "And the driver… the occupants, can you tell me anything about them? Male, female, old or young?"

Again, they all shook their heads.

"How about the time?"

"Around seven," Olly said, thinking hard. "We were home by eight, so it would have been around then."

"Okay, boys, you've been very helpful, thank you. Now, tonight, aside from bringing the bag out of the water, is there anything else you've found or seen here that might be of interest to us."

The boys exchanged nervous glances and Tom wasn't expecting anything from them. They were hardly likely to be concealing more body parts elsewhere. However, after a moment or two, all eyes drifted over to settle on Andrew. He must have felt the weight of their eyes upon and buckled under the scrutiny, lifting his head and glaring at them.

Tom looked at him. "Andrew?"

He stared at Tom, his eyes burning with indignation. His father, having first stood in silence pretending there was nothing going on, eventually relented and gave his son a nudge in the back, putting him off balance.

"Whatever it is, boy, you'd better spit it out."

Andrew looked down the line at his friends, then glanced at his father, appearing to wilt as he read his father's expression. His shoulders sagged.

"It wasn't tonight."

"What wasn't?" Tom asked.

"I didn't find it tonight," he said, barely audible.

"Find what?" his father asked, shaking him gently, barely controlling his frustration. The man must be a nightmare to live with and Tom hoped his controlling tendency only came out in words and not violence. He decided there and then to ensure uniform stopped by their house the next day just to make sure he was behaving himself. "Come on, lad, get it out."

Andrew relented, speaking to his feet. "I found it over there," he said, lifting his hand and pointing to the gate. "It was on the floor… I was going to hand it in."

Nobby scoffed and Andrew shot him a dark look.

"I was!"

"Yeah, right," Nobby said, grinning. There wasn't any love lost between these two, clearly.

"What did you find?" Tom asked.

Reluctantly, Andrew met Tom's eye.

"A wallet."

"And do you still have this wallet?"

He nodded. "I kept it here… seeing as I knew we were coming back. I figured if the owner came back to get it, then he'd find it."

"And where is it?" Tom asked. Andrew pointed to the undergrowth to the right of the gate. "And the owner was going to find it in there was he?"

The boy shrugged and his father snarled from behind him. "Just wait until you get home, boy!"

"There's no harm done, Mr Aitkin." Tom said. "Certainly, no reason to overreact at this point."

Aitkin bristled but didn't reply, averting his eyes from Tom's gaze.

"Is it still over there?" Tom asked. The boy nodded and Tom sent him over to the bush with PC Marshall to retrieve it. They soon returned with a black leather wallet now safely inside a transparent evidence bag. PC Marshall handed it to Tom who inspected it. Aside from some signs that it had been outside in the elements, a bit of mud and a few scuffs to the leather, it was in good condition if a little worn by time.

"Did you take anything out of this?" Tom asked, holding the wallet aloft.

"No, not yet," Andrew said, immediately regretting it. "I meant… no, I wouldn't… haven't."

"Thank you,' Tom said. He looked around the waiting group. "I think we can leave it there for now. You can all go home, as long as PC Marshall here has all your details. We'll be in touch in the next couple of days to take formal statements from your children."

The group began to break up, those who were still to give their contact information lingered whereas others made to leave. Tom gently gripped Nicholas Aitkin's forearm and the man stopped.

Tom leaned into him, close enough that no one else would overhear them.

"I'll be sending officers around to your home tomorrow, Mr Aitkin, and I do expect to see your son safe and well." Aitkin met Tom's eye, looking down at the grip he still had on his arm. Something unspoken passed between them and Aitkin nodded.

"My son will be fine, Detective Inspector."

"I'll look forward to having that confirmed in due course."

They stared at one another for a moment longer and then Tom released his grip, Aitkin walking off to meet his waiting son. Tom had met enough of his type over the years to recognise what he might do under certain circumstances. He hoped he was wrong but, somehow, he didn't think so.

Cassie came to meet him, spying the bag in his hand.

"Something interesting?"

"Possibly," he said. "Anything else in the bag?"

She shook her head. He donned a set of forensic gloves and removed the wallet from the bag, beckoning the police photographer over to take some pictures of the wallet before he examined the contents. That took a few moments then Tom set about emptying it. There wasn't much inside, no credit cards or identification and only twenty-five pounds in cash. Tucked behind the notes was a small business card. It was faded and a little dog-eared. Tom took it out and held it aloft. Cassie shone the light of the torch function on her mobile onto it so they could read it in the darkness.

"A148 Services," Cassie said aloud. "What's that about?"

"No clue," Tom said. "An agency of some sort, I think. Let's find out." He took out his own mobile and dialled the telephone number on the front of the card. The call cut to voicemail, but there was an automated message that Tom listened to. He hung up after a moment and Cassie shot him an enquiring look.

"Well?"

"A labour agency," he said, puzzled.

"Well… maybe they offer contracts to clean up dead bodies… or other people's problems?"

Tom saw the glint of mischief in her eyes.

"I doubt it," he said, "but this seems a strange place for someone, anyone, to be hanging about all the way out here." He glanced towards the children and their parents being escorted from the scene. "Unless you're planning to blow things up, obviously."

Tom flipped the card over. On the back was a handwritten message and a mobile number. It read, *Louis, any problems, call me.*

"I wonder who Louis is?" Tom asked, arching his eyebrows and revealing the message to Cassie.

"And if he's missing his wallet?" she added.

Tom looked around the scene. There wasn't much more they could do at this time of the night short of securing the scene and having the specialist dive team hit the water at first light. With a bit of luck, the remains of their victim might flash up on the DNA database, but that wasn't anything to rely upon. For now, all they had was a tenuous link to a labour agency which could be purely coincidental.

"Lock everything down for the night once Fiona and SOCO are done," Tom said to Cassie. "We'll keep a uniform presence here overnight and start up again at dawn."

"I know the agency will be closed at this time, but should we chase up this mobile number tonight?"

Tom shook his head. "No, we'll be there tomorrow when the doors open. In the meantime, get onto the mobile phone operators and trace who owns this number. We can always pay them a visit tomorrow as well."

CHAPTER FIVE

TOM TRIED THE DOOR, but it was still locked. The opaque glass set into the frame was such that he couldn't make out anything of the interior. Stepping back, Tom looked along the line of shops in this little precinct set apart from the high street opposite. There was an architect's office, a warehouse shop selling a vast array of goods, a takeaway, a laundry as well as a restaurant.

The agency, however, was a solitary door off the street with no apparent frontage. They couldn't expect, or possibly didn't need, to have any trade from passing footfall. He tried the door again, rattling it in the frame, glancing at the sign displayed on the door along with the opening hours. A shadow appeared on the other side, and he heard the lock turn,

"I'm so sorry," a young woman said, opening the door and smiling at him. "I'm not used to callers so early in the day."

Tom smiled warmly, showing her his warrant card. "DI Tom Janssen. Is this your business?"

She shook her head. "No, Mr Hakimi owns the agency… but I run all of the administration side of things. I'm Claire Markham, the office manager."

She seemed very young to be the office manager, but Tom found himself thinking that quite frequently these days. The sight of the newest recruits into uniform frightened him.

"May I come inside and ask you a few questions?"

She was surprised, moving a wisp of hair away from her eyes and nodding. "Please, come in."

He entered and she led him down a narrow corridor to the rear of the building. It seemed as if the agency was renting space within a unit shared with another business, the space partitioned by a simple stud work wall as he could hear voices coming through the wall from the laundry next door. At the end of the corridor, they passed through a door and the space opened up into a small office with three desks. Only one computer screen was active, Claire was alone in the office. She offered Tom a seat and he took it.

"What can I do for the police?"

"We're looking for someone," Tom said, reluctant to share too many details at this point. "Do you have staff under contract, or do you merely facilitate people moving between jobs?"

"We are just an agency. We introduce staff to our clients, and they process all the paperwork with us taking a cut should anyone go on to work for them."

Tom nodded. "Business is good?"

She smiled. "It's always been good, although times are challenging right now."

"In what way? The labour shortage?"

"It is a problem, yes. Vacancies with our clients are higher, so the demand is there but the bodies available to do the work are more limited."

"Good for wages, so I hear?"

She laughed. "You would think so... but it doesn't really matter what we pay – what our clients pay – if the people aren't here, they're just not here. We're working on encouraging the economically inactive to come back into the workplace, but with the roles we have on offer it's not particularly appealing."

"You mean retired people or those choosing not to work, right?"

"Correct."

"And you are admin based, is that what you said?" Again, she nodded. "So, you're familiar with workers... clients, people who come and go?"

"Yes, that's me," she said smiling broadly. "Without me, this place would fall down around us. Not that the boss would like to admit it."

"I'm looking for someone specific," Tom said. "Do you know Louis?"

"Louis? Louis Taylor?" she asked.

"Possibly… but could you tell me a little more about him?"

"Yes… Louis was one of our successes while he was with us."

"In what way?"

"Well," she said, cutting a wry smile, "he stood out from the others… most of them anyway." Tom's quizzical look saw her explain. "You see, the nature of the work our clients have to offer isn't… exactly fulfilling for many. The pay is generally lousy, and the hours are peculiar, split shifts, early starts and late nights. Granted the holiday parks – who are always short staffed these days despite their best efforts – have regular hours due to changeover times, but the shops and professional businesses, such as the local banks, estate agents and so on, don't want contract cleaners coming and going, shampooing carpets and running vacuum cleaners during office hours."

"So, the cleaners are in before opening and again after closing?"

"Yes… and that means unsociable hours, early

starts and late finishes, a lot of running to and fro between sites. It's a certain type of person who has the… determination to succeed in that environment."

"That sounds to me like you struggle to find these people. Is that fair to say?"

"We always used to," she said, biting her bottom lip before shrugging. "These days, it's getting harder and harder to find quality staff. You see, with the labour market the way it is, people have options now. And, as I said, the work our clients have just isn't very appealing." She sat back in her chair. "I mean, the hours suit some people, just not enough."

"Which type of people does it suit?"

"Those who perhaps have childcare issues during the day. Young children who are pre-school age but whose parents can only stretch to limited nursery places, the state-funded ones for example. Perhaps their partner can be home early and in the evening which gives them time to go out to work. Others are people who maybe cannot manage a full-time job and juggle several smaller roles throughout the week."

"The gig economy?" Tom asked.

"That's right, yes. Then there are the migrant workers. Many of them are qualified to work in other fields but either their qualifications aren't recognised here, or their language skills are a barrier to making it into the workplace. Some people are content to work by themselves in a job with little stress and these roles suit them. There are all manner of reasons why people work with our clients."

"And Louis... Taylor, you said?" She nodded. "Where on your scale does he fit in?"

She smiled. "Louis was a godsend to someone like me; intelligent, diligent... a great guy to have around. We only ever had good feedback about him for eighteen months. He never wanted a permanent contract... liked to flit around between jobs, never allowing the grass to grow under his feet. He was in and out of here regularly."

"You've mentioned him in the past tense several times now. Is there a reason for that?"

The smile left her face, replaced by a frown. "I'm afraid he hasn't worked with us for some time now."

"He sounded like a model employee the way you just described him."

"He was..." she said, glumly.

"Until?" Tom asked, sensing reticence on her part. Claire looked around as if concerned someone would hear but they were most certainly alone.

"We... had a number of complaints," she shook her head, fiddling with a couple of items sitting on her desk. "It was nothing too major, but one came from one of our major clients. None of it went down well, really."

"What was the nature of the complaint?"

"I probably shouldn't say," Claire said. "Not without speaking to the boss."

"It's important," Tom said. "I wouldn't ask otherwise." He couldn't compel her to answer, but he kept his tone amiable.

"Well, I guess there's no harm," she said, smiling nervously. "Louis was offering to work cash-in-hand for one of our clients, offering to keep things off the books. Mr Hakimi wasn't very happy about that. You see, we receive payments for a set period once we've introduced a worker to a client who goes on to employ them. Louis would be doing us out of money."

"Why would he do that, if he wasn't worried about staying in one place?"

She shrugged. "I've no idea… but that wasn't the worst of it. Another client accused him of stealing from their offices."

"Stealing what, money?"

"No, no… nothing like that. Any shops or hospitality businesses have secure processes around money. The contractors are never exposed to that level of temptation."

"Then what did he steal?"

"Nothing was ever proven… and no one called the police or anything." She leaned forward, a conspiratorial look on her face. "You know, I never quite believed it."

"That he might have stolen from them?"

"Exactly. I think there was something else going on."

"Such as what?"

She shrugged. "No idea, but I'm not buying it. Louis wasn't a thief. If you knew him… you'd understand. He was kind, well mannered… not the type, not at all," she said, shaking her head. "Believe you me, we get people through here all the time who have been arrested, prosecuted and convicted of all manner of things. Trust me, they are hard people to find work for. Usually they end up on the building sites, labouring… doing the donkey work because no one will give them a break."

"I hear that a lot."

"It's a shame," Claire said. "They are often the hardest workers of the lot but just can't get their feet through the door."

"These complaints against Louis, what was their effect?"

"Mr Hakimi had him blacklisted from our books," she said. "He said it was a matter of reputation and we couldn't be seen to be offering our clients suspect characters."

"And how did you feel about that?"

"Gutted," she said. "Absolutely gutted. I knew that whenever I sent Louis on a job, first that he'd get it done and we'd get the money in the pipeline and secondly, that he would be a great advertisement for the agency. How he was doing what he was doing or why, I will never know."

Tom cocked his head at that comment. "Why do you say that?"

She was thoughtful. "It's difficult… you see, we have a number of people who pass through here, often, and they have only half the work ethic of Louis and far less ability. You'll not be surprised to learn that many of those on our books are below average when it comes to their education but Louis… he was different. The way he spoke, carried himself… he was articulate… I don't know how to explain it really…"

"Educated?"

"Yes, that's good. He seemed educated."

"Do you have his CV to hand?"

"I can certainly bring it up for you, if you like, but it's not particularly enlightening if you want to learn about him. There's so little on it. Just more agency work prior to moving to the area."

"Where was he from originally?"

Claire arched her eyebrows. "Somewhere in London, I think. What's your interest in Louis anyway? What's he been up to?"

Tom smiled. "Just routine."

Claire's gaze narrowed and she seemed unconvinced, but she turned to her keyboard in search of the file holding Louis' details. "Here we are," she said, glancing sideways at him. "Do you want a copy to take with you?"

"Please," Tom said as she tapped a couple of keys and the office printer fired up on the other side of the room. "Do you have a photograph of him?"

"Louis?" she asked, then shook her head as Tom confirmed with a nod. "We don't keep photos."

"Aren't you required to check identities when registering potential workers these days?"

She chuckled. "We do have to check a person's right to work these days. Although it's just logging into a database and running the code the worker provides us."

"Is that for anyone who comes onto your books?"

"It's all got a bit more complicated since 2021, but we don't deal with workers who come here for roles in a professional capacity. I'd wager every worker on our books was in the country prior to that and so the legislation doesn't cover them."

"And as long as they have a National Insurance Number and a PAYE code, then…"

"It doesn't matter," she said, smiling. "Although, as time passes, we are finding we have fewer people registered with us. I know Mr Hakimi is exploring setting up abroad to act as a go-between to bring workers here, but it's all red tape and bureaucracy these days."

"I thought it was supposed to be easier now?"

She laughed. "Yeah… that's what they say. It's an employee's market now for sure."

"One more thing," Tom said as she handed him the copy of Louis Taylor's CV, "which business was it that made the allegation about stealing?"

Claire checked they were alone, which of course they were. "You didn't hear it from me…"

"Off the record," Tom said.

"Thomas James."

"The accountant?"

"The very same," Claire said, nodding vigorously. "The senior partner, James Newell, called Mr Hakimi and I could hear him shouting down the phone from my desk. It was unpleasant. Mr Hakimi was not pleased."

"Why would it be his fault?" Tom asked.

Claire shrugged. "Do you know James Newell?"

Tom shook his head. "Only the name of the business."

"Well, a word of advice, don't get on the wrong side of him. The man is such a stress-head that he looks likely to either implode or explode at any moment. Highly strung if you know what I mean?"

"We all know the type," Tom said. Claire

agreed, nodding sagely. "Tell me, Louis, does he have any distinguishing features?"

She frowned. "Distinguishing?"

"Anything that stands out… features, tattoos, anything at all you can think of."

"Not really."

"Can you describe him to me?"

"Yes… slim, athletic. Black hair… he has lovely hair. I don't know what product he uses, but the shine is quite lovely."

Tom frowned.

"Sorry, I digress. He's a little shy of six feet tall… clearly works out."

"Does he attend a gym?"

"I think so. He is quite the fitness guy… nutrition and all that type of thing."

"Aren't all agency cleaners?"

She smiled at that. "Most of them, I would say… not, no. Oh, he spoke other languages as well. I don't know if that's relevant."

"What does he speak, do you know?"

"I remember he was chatting away with one of our ladies… now where was she from? Italy, I think. Or Spain."

Tom found that frustrating because the languages were quite different in many ways. He didn't expect a contract cleaner to be bilingual, but on the other hand he had come across all sorts in his line of work, so he shouldn't have been surprised.

"And you've described him professionally and intellectually, but what was he like as a person?"

Claire considered the question for a moment. "I can't say I knew him all that well beyond speaking in passing when he came through here looking for work, but I always had the impression he was a decent guy. He was quick with a smile, but he was also serious, not flippant or offhand like so many people I have to deal with."

"Did he have friends that you know of?"

She shook her head. "I couldn't speak to that, I'm afraid. I barely knew him… which I think was his way."

Tom pondered that for a moment, then cast an eye over the CV in his hand. It was all written on one page; not as a stylistic choice but through necessity. The employment history listed A148 as the most recent company he'd worked through and there were two others, one in Birmingham and another in Manchester.

"You said Louis was from London?"

"I think so. That's his accent anyway. Why?"

Tom angled the sheet of paper towards her. "There's no history documented in or around the capital."

She shrugged. "What can I say? Maybe he moved around a lot."

"His education has no details at all, just the name of his schools."

"You don't need qualifications to vacuum a carpet or wipe down a toilet, do you?"

"I suppose not. How long ago did you last see Louis?"

"It's been a few months. I've seen him out and about in passing. He still smiles at me, so there's no hard feelings. Not towards me at any rate."

"How about towards your boss or James Newell?"

Claire arched her eyebrows. "No love lost there, with either. Louis went mad when it all kicked off. I've never seen him angry like that before. He was always such a calm, assured man. It was very unlike him, I have to say. But, I suppose that was all in the moment. He denied doing anything wrong but calmed down when Mr Hakimi said they weren't calling the police or anything."

"He was pleased to hear that?"

"Oh yes. I saw real fear in his eyes when the theft was mentioned. It was anger borne of panic, I'd say. Strange. Louis was such a clean-cut guy. I can't believe he'd stoop to such a low level to ever steal something. Like I said, he's not the type. I'd put good money on it."

Tom nodded, looking down at the schools Louis attended. Both were in the north of England, primary in Liverpool and the secondary across the river on the Wirral. The information was scant though. Something seemed odd here, very odd indeed but Tom couldn't put his finger on what.

Turning to Claire, he set the CV down on her desk. "Do you think you could write Louis's name on here along with your contact number? A mobile if you have one?"

"Sure," Claire said. If she found the request odd, she didn't say anything, scribbling down Louis's name and her own mobile number before handing the paper back to him.

"Do you have Louis's address to hand as well?"

"Yes, I can get that. Presuming he hasn't moved of course."

Moments later, she passed him a slip of paper with the address written on it. It was here in Hunstanton. Thanking her for her help, Tom left the agency. The sun was shining and for once the breeze coming in off The Wash was light allowing him to feel a little warmth on his skin. He took out his mobile and called Cassie.

"How are you getting on, Cass?"

"The divers are in the water, but so far they haven't found anything," she said. "We're working on the theory that whatever was keeping that bag from bobbing to the surface was weighted down but in shallow water. They've surveyed the area close to the water's edge, but no joy so far. It's possible that our local yobs with their improvised explosive devices have sent what remains to the deep. It's slow going. Apparently, they can't see their hands in front of their faces down there."

"Is there a back-up plan if nothing comes up?"

"They have a sonar rig coming today, so that'll show up larger objects. How did you get on with this Louis guy?"

"He used to find work through the agency but hasn't done so for months. Seemingly there were a few complaints levelled at him and they ceased working with him."

"Complaints? Anyone angry enough to chop him up and dump him in a man-made lake?"

"We can only hope," Tom said. "Although maybe he was angry enough to chop *them* up and dump them in a lake."

An old lady passing Tom stopped and stared up at him, searching his face having heard what he'd just said. He smiled and she shook her head before shuffling away.

"Are you still there?" Cassie asked.

"Yes, sorry. I was just terrifying a pensioner."

"I do that a lot," Cassie said. "I checked missing persons data last night after I contacted the mobile phone companies."

"How did you get on?"

"Mobile providers are useless. Call centre staff… polite but haven't got a clue or clearance to authorise release of data or anything… apparently management will call me back today."

"And the missing persons' register?"

"Nothing," she said. "To be fair, we haven't got a lot to go on. No fingerprints – no fingers – a generic Celtic tattoo… a white guy. That's it. I'm surprised the computer didn't burst out laughing when I put the data in."

"When you get back into the office, can you run the name Louis Taylor and see what pops up? Originally, he's from London but I don't know where—"

"Oh… small place. That won't be hard."

"And spent time in Manchester and Birmingham, schooling in Liverpool."

"Excellent… narrows it down loads. Thanks."

Tom appreciated Cassie's dry sense of humour, even if it did get her into trouble with alarming frequency. "See what comes out, and keep me posted on what, if anything, they find in the water too. I'm going to stop by this guy's address on my way back to the station. He might not be related to this at all."

"Okay; Danny is coming over to relieve me in a bit, so I'll see you back at the station."

He hung up and slipped his mobile into his pocket, looking at the copy of the CV Claire had printed for him. Taking out a folded plastic evidence bag from his pocket, he unfurled it. Inside was the business card they'd found in the wallet found at the quarry and he reversed it, placing it alongside Claire's handwritten name and number, comparing her writing style with that on the card. They were clearly written by another hand. It had been a long shot. He put both away in his coat pockets, zipping himself up as he felt the nip in the air despite the sun.

CHAPTER SIX

The address Claire Markham gave Tom for where Louis Taylor lived was the annexe to an old Victorian end-of-terrace property on Church Street, a narrow, leafy residential street in Hunstanton. The entrance to the annexe was found at the rear, accessed by Austin Street that ran adjacent. A small, gravelled parking area was set out before the property marked into two sections with a line of concrete paving slabs down the middle delineating the bays, a small hatchback was parked to the right. Tom approached the door and rang the bell. There was no pane in the door and he chanced a quick look through the one window off to his left offering a view into a kitchenette.

There was no sign of movement from within and taking a bit more time to peer into the interior,

Tom saw the kitchen surfaces were clean and tidy with everything neatly put away.

"Can I help you?"

He turned to see an elderly man standing in the rear garden of the adjoining property behind a waist-high gate. Tom smiled and stepped away from the window, the man watching him warily. Brandishing his warrant card, Tom identified himself and the man visibly relaxed.

"Police, DI Janssen," Tom said, putting his warrant card away. He inclined his head towards the annexe. "I'm here to see Louis Taylor, do you know him by any chance?"

"Yes, of course. I'm Gary Bowers, his landlord."

The man was in his eighties, wearing cream slacks, a thick knitted woollen pullover and Tom could make out a set of clasps for braces clipped to his waist band. His near white hair was thin revealing dark patches across his scalp.

"Mr Bowers, do you know where I can find Louis?"

"Oh… you'll have a wait I'm afraid. He's not here."

"Do you know when he'll be back?"

"Not for another week, I think. He's gone away," Gary said. "On a holiday."

"I see. Where did he go, do you know?"

He shook his head. "He was a bit cagey about it… I joked he must be going to Thailand, to take care of himself, seeing as he lives like a monk. Not that he cared for it, but I was only joking."

Tom found that interesting. "How do you mean, *lives like a monk?"*

"Well, I never see him with any lady friends… or male friends either, although the wife tells me that's just as likely these days. Not that Louis seems the sort."

"Keeps to himself, does he?"

"I'll say he does, yes," Gary said, nodding. "A man of few words, although Marjorie does have a word or two with him from time to time."

Tom glanced towards the annexe. "When did you last see him?"

"When he paid his rent," Gary said, thinking hard. "It would have been around ten days ago. Thereabouts anyway, the beginning of the month. He's regular is Louis, never late with his rent. Perfect tenant. Not like that last piece of filth we had in here before." Gary shuddered. "Waste of space that boy, we should never have rented it to him in the first place. I told her, Marjorie, that but she wouldn't listen. Thankfully, he moved on otherwise I'd have had to… well, give him what for, if you know what I mean?"

Tom smiled, picturing the diminutive figure before him squaring up to an individual half his age.

"And Louis was making to leave you say?"

"Yes, nine or ten days ago. He had a bag packed in the hall and everything."

"But he didn't say where he was going?"

He shook his head. "No, I can't say he did, but as I said, he's a quiet lad. Not one for sharing."

Tom thought about it. "Do you happen to have a key to the property?"

Gary's eyes narrowed. "I do, yes. Why do you ask?"

"It's a welfare call above everything else, Mr Bowers. Nothing to be concerned about. You may accompany me if you're not sure."

He frowned and then nodded. "We respect Louis's privacy, you understand. He's a polite young man and a darn good tenant. We wouldn't wish to lose him."

"I understand," Tom said. "We'll be in and out in a matter of minutes."

"Okay. Hang on there for a second and I'll get the spare key from inside the house."

Gary Bowers returned a couple of minutes later looking flustered. "All right, love… I said I'd go with him."

Approaching Tom, he looked contrite shaking his head as he unhooked the garden gate and came out to stand alongside Tom at the entrance to the annexe.

"Are you married, Detective?"

"I am."

"Then you'll know not to make an independent decision without running it past the organ grinder."

Tom smiled, stepping aside to allow the landlord room to unlock the front door. He pushed the door open and moved aside so that Tom could enter. The entrance hall was tight. The kitchen was to his left and there were three doors off the hall. One was open and Tom could see a living room at the rear and the other two would be a bathroom and the bedroom. It was compact, but an annexe often was.

"I'll just hang back out here, if you don't mind?" Gary asked.

"Sure," Tom said, pleased for the opportunity to look around. He'd seen the kitchen was clean and tidy, the surfaces uncluttered. Opening the fridge Tom found it was reasonably well stocked, but he could see the open bottle of milk had turned, a thick white residue forming around surface level. Pulling out a salad drawer he found a bag of mixed leaves which had blackened and turned to mush along with some broccoli, the florets yellowing.

Closing the fridge, he went back into the hall and walked towards the living room. The landlord was peering past the door and watching him. He eased open the bathroom door. It was an internal bathroom with no exterior window. He pulled the cord, and the light came on with a clunk. The basin was clean, as was the bathtub. A small, mirrored cabinet was fixed to the wall above the basin and Tom opened it, making sure not to use the handles, thereby not disturbing any potential fingerprints. As far as he knew, this wasn't a crime scene, but he was diligent, nonetheless.

The cabinet had the usual toiletries present, shaving foam, a razor, deodorant along with some basic medicines, paracetamol, aspirin and dental floss. Everything was remarkably clean considering it was a bachelor pad. The bedroom was in a similar state, the bed made without any clothing strewn across the floor or thrown over the bed. On the bedside table he found books on economics and accounting, which made for interesting bedtime reading. Perhaps it was to put him to sleep. A free-standing wardrobe stood in the far corner and Tom crossed to it, opening the door. Several ironed shirts hung on hangers and trousers, polo shirts and underwear were neatly folded and arranged on shelving beneath the rail. Below this another shelf had several pairs of shoes set out side by side. One pair of dress black brogues were beside trainers, one pair gleaming with a well-polished sheen to them and the trainers didn't have a speck of dirt on them.

"Feel free to come around and tidy our house anytime you like, Mr Taylor."

"What's that you said?"

"Talking to myself, don't worry," Tom called back. The man may be infirm but there was nothing wrong with his hearing. Making his way through to the living room, he found it matched everywhere else, neat and tidy with everything in its place. There was a small television on a stand in the corner of the room, a little occasional dining table tucked in the opposite corner. A two-seater sofa was the only other furniture in the room. Tom saw a bag on the floor, leaning against the sofa and he dropped to his haunches to inspect it.

He donned a pair of gloves he had in his pocket before unzipping the holdall. It was a similar size to a sports bag, albeit a large one. It was full and not wishing to pull out the contents without just cause, Tom scanned the interior as best he could. There were clothes, all folded neatly, along with toiletries inside a clear plastic bag including a battery-powered toothbrush. It struck Tom as an overnight bag, but why would Louis leave it here if he was planning to go away?

Taking out his mobile, he rang Eric who answered almost immediately.

"Morning, boss," he said.

"Good morning, Eric. I want you to get onto the Border Force and have them run the name Louis Taylor through their system."

"Will do. What are we looking for?"

"It's possible he was planning to leave the

country a week or so ago, destination unknown. I'm not sure he was headed abroad but," Tom paused, looking around the room, "I don't know if he made it."

"Is this our guy from the quarry?"

"Let's not get ahead of ourselves," Tom said. "I've already asked Cassie to run his name through the database when she gets back to the station, but if you get through with the border team before she does then see what else you can find through regular channels."

"On it."

"Is the DCI in yet?"

"Yes, she's in her office. Do you want me to transfer you—"

"No, don't worry. I'll be in myself in a bit."

"Dr Paxton has left a message for you though. Nothing urgent, and he's left it on your desk."

"Right, thanks Eric."

Tom hung up, casting another look around the room. On top of the dining table, Tom spied a wicker basket. Crossing to it, he saw it sat atop a couple of leaflets advertising books on finance, history and architecture. They were the sort of fillers that came with mail-order products rather than letterbox stuffers. In the basket itself, he found a key ring with two simple metal keys and a bar-coded plastic tile. Tom recognised this. He had a similar one for the local leisure centre that he would swipe to gain access. This one was different to his though. Flipping it over, he saw a logo printed on the reverse for a place called *DG Fitness*.

Having seen enough, Tom made his way back outside to the waiting landlord. His expression was borne of concern and Tom reassured him with a warm smile.

"Everything all right?"

Tom nodded. "Yes, there doesn't seem to be anything of concern inside." He glanced at the car parked behind him. "Is that your car?"

"Yes, it is."

"Does your tenant own a car?"

Gary Bowers shook his head. "No, he has a push bike. He cycles everywhere. He can't stand petrol cars, polluting the air and causing cancer. He said if he was in charge, he'd have banned the internal combustion engine years ago." Gary frowned. "I'm not sure how that would've worked, but he's a passionate one is young Louis."

"He would speak to you about his interests then?"

"No, not really. Only if they came up in general conversation, you know? I said we were thinking of getting one of those new electrical cars that people are always going on about. I read they were bad for the environment, but Louis put me right."

"Bad for the environment?" Tom asked, curious.

"Yes, all those batteries being thrown away…

leaking toxic metals into the sea. Nasty stuff, or so I thought. It's not true though."

"Good to know. Tell me, where does Louis store his bike?" Tom asked, looking around and seeing no garage. He suspected the annexe was once the property's garage.

"Oh, we let him keep it at the back of our garden, in my old potting shed out of the rain."

"Is it there now?"

Gary pursed his lips, frowning deeply. "You know what, I've no idea. I tend not to go out there at this time of the year. It's far too cold."

"May we take a look?"

Gary shrugged, leading the way into the garden and around to the shed. It was unlocked and he pulled the door open, the hinges shrieking as he did so.

"Hmm… no, it's not here," Gary said, puzzled. Then he laughed. "I can't see him taking it on a plane." He turned to Tom, aghast. "I never lock the shed. Do you think someone's broken in and stolen it? What will I tell Louis?"

Tom glanced to either side of the door. It didn't appear that the shed had been ransacked and it was tucked away behind the annexe at the foot of the garden, away from prying eyes.

"I'm sure that's not the case. Perhaps Louis took it with him, travelling away by train rather than going abroad as you first thought."

"Oh… yes, I suppose that's possible." Gary looked troubled, but accepted Tom's logic.

"You said Louis was a polite man, timely with paying his rent?"

"Oh yes, the model tenant. We couldn't have hoped for more when he called us after seeing our advert in the local paper."

"You rent the annexe directly? You don't use a lettings agent?"

Gary shook his head. "No need. We live here, so are around if there's a problem. Agents scythe off a huge chunk of your money and what do they do for it? Nothing, as far as I can see anyway."

"So, Louis just called up… came around to view it and you took him on?"

"Yes, it was as simple as that. He had a month's rent in bond, another two months up front in cash," Gary said, smiling. "We never would have asked for that much, but it was great. Then he pays us at the beginning of the month, sometimes after a couple of days if his pay is late coming through, but never more than that. He's reliable, quiet… tidy. What more could we ask for?"

"And what work does he do? Do you know?"

Gary's brow furrowed. "No… I did ask once but he said he was freelance."

"A freelance what?"

The furrows deepened. "I don't know."

"Fair enough," Tom said. "Don't worry, I was only curious."

"Is Louis in some kind of trouble? You said this was a welfare call."

"Yes, it is," Tom said. "Nothing for you to worry about, so please don't be concerned. Does Louis have any regular friends that you know of?"

He shrugged. "Can't say I do. I mean, we're not nosy people. Let others live their lives. I've seen a car parked in the driveway from time to time. A dark blue BMW, I think. I thought it was a tourist once or twice being cheeky to avoid parking charges, but then I realised she was in visiting Louis, so I let it be."

"I thought you said he lived like a monk?"

Gary smiled. "Well, even monks have to partake of refreshment once in a while, don't they?"

Tom returned the smile. "Do you know who she was by any chance?"

He shook his head. "No, I never actually saw her except for that one time when I was struggling to get the back door closed in a storm… it'd swollen in the frame. Shocking weather that week, I can tell you."

"And the visitor?"

"I saw her flash by on the other side of the gate and jump into her car. A tall sort, for a woman anyway."

"Can you describe her at all, aside from her height?"

"No... not really, it was dark, and I was getting soaked. She had a big coat on, collar turned up," he said, screwing up his nose. "Her shoes were click-clacking on the paving slabs down the middle of the drive though. I heard that above the sound of the wind and rain. A fancy sort, I reckon."

"Heels?" Tom asked.

"I dare say so, yes. She had that pitched forward walking gait as well, the type women have when they're tottering along, so they must have been tall ones." He shrugged. "Anyway, I got back to it, and she leapt into her car and drove off."

"How often does she visit?"

"I suppose it's... once or twice a fortnight. Maybe more, but as I say..."

"You're not nosy."

"That's right, I'm not." He sighed. "It'd be nice for Louis to settle down with a woman, someone decent. It's such a shame to see such a decent young man go to waste."

"Maybe he likes it that way," Tom said. "Being by himself."

"Nonsense! Who wants to live by themselves the whole time? Not unless you're a weirdo..." Gary chuckled, "...or you've got something to hide." He tapped the end of his nose with the tip of his finger. Tom didn't comment.

"Do you happen to have a contact number for Louis? I wouldn't want to interrupt his holiday, but it would be great to make sure he's okay."

"Yes, I think that'd be a good idea, but sadly I can't help you. Louis doesn't have a mobile phone."

"He doesn't?"

"No," Gary said, firmly shaking his head. "Doesn't believe in them. Something about radiation…"

Apart from the television, Tom hadn't seen any tech inside the property either. Nothing about this man seemed consistent aside from the fact he was well liked by his landlord and by Claire Markham, both describing him as a man of integrity. However, Tom was seeing him more as a square peg being placed into a round hole; Louis, working as a contract cleaner but reading economics and finance in his spare time. People could have all manner of interests that were very separate from their work lives but, in this case, he found it to be quite a stretch.

The fact Louis had also fallen foul of James Newell at a local accountants could be worth exploring further. His mobile rang. He excused himself, seeing it was Cassie, and moved out of earshot.

"Hey, Cassie. Have you found something?"

"The dive team have found a bag… a suitcase.

It's one of these hard plastic ones. It looks like the kids' improvised depth charge blew it open."

"We have the rest of the..." Tom checked he couldn't be overheard, "...rest of the body?"

"I would say... most of it... but we're missing a few bits. The case is likely carry-on luggage, rather than hold storage, if you know what I mean?"

"Right. What do you have?"

"Easier to say what we're missing, *look, boss, no hands,*" she said jovially, before reading the room and turning serious. "And no head either."

Tom sucked air through his teeth, grimacing. "Are the divers still looking?"

"They are, yes," Cassie said, "but it's painfully slow going. It's possible we'll find what we're missing down deeper, but the sand and clay of the ground here is making the lake floor so murky it's making things tricky."

"All right. Keep at it and I'll see you back at the station later."

CHAPTER SEVEN

Tom found DC Eric Collet and the DCI, Tamara Greave, deep in conversation in the ops room when he arrived back at the station. Tamara touched Eric's forearm and left his side to greet Tom.

"Cassie called through from the old quarry," Tamara said. "Danny's gone over to relieve her, but she's not back yet."

"I spoke to her a short while ago. Have the dive team found any more remains?"

"Head or hands?" Tamara asked, shaking her head. "No, not yet. Cassie says you were asking her to run a check on Louis Taylor?"

"That's right. It looks like it was his wallet the kids found out at the quarry the other night. I've been around to where he used to work as well as to his home. No sign of him. His landlord says he was going away on holiday, so I'd like to know if he did."

"Do you think he might be our victim?"

Tom shrugged. "Stands to reason that it might be. The FME believes the body has been in the water for a week or so, maybe more. The landlord told me he was supposed to leave ten days or so ago. If it's him, then it might explain why he hasn't been missed yet. We'll see."

"Eric has been running his name through the system this morning." Tamara beckoned Eric over and he bounded across the room to them, notebook in hand, greeting Tom with a broad smile.

"Morning," Eric said, without looking up and reading through his notes. "I've been having fun researching this guy."

"Cassie was pleased when I gave her what I had," Tom said dryly.

"I'll start with the positives," Eric said. "He's been paying his council tax here in Hunstanton for the past two years. I'm assuming, without any evidence to the contrary, that this was when he moved into the address you visited this morning," Eric said, glancing up. "However, he isn't entered onto the Electoral Register. Perhaps this is an oversight…"

"Or he chose not to fill out the separate form," Tom said.

"That's right," Eric agreed. "You need to fill out

two applications. Now, it's possible he forgot or thought they were one and the same thing but… the council send out reminders every six months or so. I get them all the time and I am on the register. So…" Eric rocked his head from side to side, "that's a bit weird. Anyway, HMRC has him paying tax up until six months ago—"

"That will likely be when he was fired from the agency he was working through," Tom said.

"Likely, yes. However, he's not been working since or if he has then he's been doing it off the books. I had a quick look on social media… do you know there are over fifty people by the name of Louis Taylor originating from or presently living in London? I was surprised, but there it is. So, with very little to narrow down the search—"

"Like a fingerprint," Cassie said, entering ops behind them and hanging up her coat."

"Yes, that would help," Eric agreed.

"Or the traditional means of identification like a head to put the face to the name, so to speak," Cassie added, joining them and perching herself on the edge of the nearest desk.

"Right," Eric said. "So, I ran his National Insurance Number through the system, the one attached to his tax code I got from HMRC, and that helped a lot."

"What did you find, Eric? Does he have a criminal record?" Tom asked.

"Or a well-documented and often lamented history of dismembering people?" Cassie asked, smiling.

"Hardly," Eric said, frowning. "In fact, he has never so much as been issued a parking ticket. He's clean as a whistle," he said, glumly.

"Where was he before he moved up here?" Tamara asked.

"Ah... now that is a little more interesting," Eric said. "I couldn't find any information on him at all."

"And that's... interesting to you?" Cassie asked, mock grimacing.

"Yes, it's fascinating," Eric said. "Now, I say I couldn't find anything, but that's not strictly true. He had numerous jobs, part-time judging by the size of the payments passing through HMRC, the businesses he was working in, catering, hospitality, security contracting jobs through an agency, all over a three-year period. He's thirty-five and based on when this employment took place, fourteen to sixteen years ago, it's fair to say he was—"

"Working his way through university," Tamara said.

"That's what I reckon," Eric agreed.

"And after he graduated, let's assume he graduated, where did he go?" Tom asked.

"That's the interesting part," Eric said, looking at Cassie and arching his eyebrows. "Nothing for the next twelve years straight." Eric slapped the page of his notebook with the palm of his hand. "The guy vanishes… like a ghost."

Cassie sighed, shaking her head. "No, not possible."

"He does, I swear," Eric said. "I've checked and double checked. The employment stops… no tax records, no NI payments… nothing."

"It's not the 1800s, Eric," Cassie said. "You can't just vanish in the twenty-first century. Everything's digital these days. My old mum has a hell of a job just booking a hotel room when she comes down to visit. If you're not online these days, you can't get anything done. And my mum is a classic technophobe. I forced her to get a mobile phone last year just so I could get a hold of her if I need to."

"I don't disagree," Eric said, "but… the system has no record of him right up until he pops up here in Hunstanton two years ago. And it's not just the tax. There's no driving licence, no pension contributions… mobile phone contracts, no entry on the electoral roll anywhere after his time in education."

"Oh, bloody hell, we've got 007 living in Hunstanton," Cassie said.

"I mean, it could be that I'm just missing something," Eric said. "I'm going to check if he's changed his name through deed poll. People have been known to do such things to try and skip out on debt collectors and the like or maybe he got married and took his partner's name." Eric shrugged. "It is possible."

"Could he have been in prison?" Tom asked.

"Or abroad?" Tamara said.

"I will look into it," Eric said. "I've not even been on it for an hour yet."

"You must have missed something," Cassie said, shaking her head. "It's not possible."

Eric bristled but didn't say anything, glancing between Tom and Tamara.

"Keep at it, Eric," Tamara said. "Good work."

"If he's a degree graduate," Tom said, "why is he working out of an agency on the Norfolk coast doing what is quite menial work. Honest work, but not what you aspire to with a university education."

Tamara arched her eyebrows. "Eric, have you found any relatives?"

"No one local that came up, no," Eric said over his shoulder, now back at his desk. "I'll see if I can look them up. Do you want me to get in touch if I do?"

"No, no," Tamara said. "Don't do that. We don't know what we're dealing with yet. We don't even know if he's caught up in all of this. Just find out if there are and with a bit of luck the divers will come good for us."

"I wouldn't bet on that," Cassie said. They all turned to her. "They were cracking open the big guns as I left. The sonar. They can't see their hand in front of their face down in the depths, so they were trying to locate anything else with sonar. Now, it's useful for an entire body, but when it comes to things the size and shape of hands… or even a human skull, it's tricky."

Tamara nodded. "Tom, you've been to this guy's home. Was there anything that could be used to run a DNA comparison? A hairbrush with hair still in it… I know, I'm reaching, but we need to identify our victim."

"The place was immaculate. Everything neat and tidy. I had the impression he had a bit of amateur OCD; it was so clean. You'd be having palpitations," Tom said under his breath.

Tamara smiled. "I know, long shot. What about this car? The one the children saw driving away from the quarry?"

Tom pursed his lips before speaking. "We don't have the make, let alone the model. All the way out there, there's no chance of pulling up any CCTV that might help. Our best bet is still to identify the body and go from there."

"Okay, anything in the house that could help with that?"

"The landlord says he largely kept to himself. Paid his rent on time, in cash, curious bearing in mind he hasn't been working these past few months. He did have an occasional visitor, a woman driving a BMW. The landlord says she was classy, or at least she wore high heels."

"Does that pass for classy these days?" Cassie asked.

"You'd fail," Eric said bitterly.

"No argument from me," she replied.

"No name for this woman?"

"No," Tom said. "Sadly. However, in better news, he has a bar-coded pass card for what looks like a private gym, so we can go there. Maybe someone there will recognise him or perhaps be friends with him."

"Sounds good. Anything else?"

"The reason he was fired from the agency," Tom said. "One of their clients accused Louis of stealing. There was a bit of a flare up around it and ultimately Louis lost his work through the agency. Something he wasn't particularly happy about by all accounts."

"Motive?" Tamara asked.

Tom shrugged. "In the absence of a stronger one, we should check it out."

"Which client?"

"Thomas James," Tom said, "here in town."

"The accountants?" Cassie asked, her head snapping up.

"Yes. Are you familiar with them?" Tom asked. "Because I'm not."

Cassie wrinkled her nose. "No, not really. I

mean, what do I need with an accountant on the pittance of a salary you pay me for risking life and limb."

"Yes, cutting edge threat here in sleepy north Norfolk," Tamara said with a wry smile.

Cassie returned the smile. "I just know someone who works there, that's all."

"Good, then you can come with me to speak to them," Tom said. "We'll find out what all the fuss was about."

"Oh… no," Cassie said. "I mean… me?" She shook her head. "Probably best if I—"

"Get your coat, Cass," Tom said. "If you're well behaved, I'll even treat you to a cup of coffee seeing as your poor, measly wage won't stretch to cover the basics."

"Any chance of a muffin to go with it?" she asked hopefully.

"Only if we get a result from your contact."

Cassie frowned. "Ah… well I'm not hungry anyway."

CHAPTER EIGHT

THE OFFICES of Thomas James were located in a large end-of-terrace Victorian property on Greevegate, sandwiched between two traditional guesthouses. A narrow driveway led to the rear where the once large garden was now repurposed into a car park for a half dozen vehicles, but Tom chose to park on the street at the front. The sun was shining as they got out of the car and made their way up to the front door and the main reception.

"Your contact here, what do they do?" he asked.

"Um… contact might be a bit optimistic a description if I'm honest. She's just someone I sort of know… a little."

"Well, any familiarity might be advantageous."

"Yes, that's… possible."

Tom sensed her reticence, curious as to the nature of the relationship, but he had no time to ask further as he pushed open the large wooden door which opened into a reception hallway. A woman was seated behind a raised counter that wrapped around her position in a horseshoe shape. She looked up as they entered, offering them a warm, if artificial, smile in greeting. When she clocked Cassie coming in behind him, Tom saw the corners of her mouth change slightly but she maintained the welcome.

"Good morning," she said. "Welcome to Thomas James."

"Good morning," Tom said, approaching the counter and taking out his warrant card. There were no others in the waiting area, but Tom looked around just to make sure. Having the police in a business could cause some consternation among clients and Tom was well aware of this. "Detective Inspector Tom Janssen and DS Knight," Tom he said, indicating Cassie.

"Hi, Melanie," Cassie said cheerily.

"Cassie," Melanie said with a curt nod. The smile was long gone. Cassie pursed her lips, acknowledging a sideways glance from Tom.

"We're here to speak to James Newell, if that's possible?" Tom asked.

"Is Mr Newell expecting you?"

"No, he isn't," Tom said, "but this is official business."

"I see," Melanie said, not reacting to his comment as she scanned a diary planner on the desk in front of her. "Mr Newell doesn't have an appointment until half-past ten, so I'll just give him a call. If you'd care to take a seat in the waiting area," she said, gesturing to a row of cushioned chairs in front of the bay window overlooking the street. Tom thanked her and the two of them wandered over to the area but neither of them sat down. Melanie picked up the phone on her desk but cast a watchful eye over them as she dialled.

"I take it that's your contact?" Tom asked, lowering his voice to all but a whisper.

"Yes. That's her. Melanie Strutt," Cassie said, peering out at the passing traffic, hands deep in her coat pockets. "Strutt by name, strut by nature."

Tom glanced at her, deep in conversation on the telephone, lowering her gaze to her desk. She was a similar age to Cassie; her hair and make-up were styled as one might expect for a person whose job was front-of-house operations. Tom's eye drifted to a sign on the wall listing businesses. Presumably these were all firms represented by the accountant and their businesses were likely registered at this address. He recognised some of the names but not all.

"Do I detect a touch of animosity between the two of you?"

"You're good at this," Cassie replied, smiling. "You might have a shout at a career as a detective."

Tom grinned. "You never know—"

His reply was cut off by Melanie replacing the receiver. She looked up at them. "Mr Newell will be right down to see you."

"Thank you," Tom said. Melanie's eyes fell on Cassie and her expression darkened. Tom turned his back on the counter, arching his eyebrows. Cassie smiled as if she didn't care, but the atmosphere was thick between them.

They didn't have to wait long before footsteps could be heard descending a creaking staircase and a man entered reception, looking around as he did so. Melanie pointed them out, even though they were the only ones present. He walked purposefully towards them, and Tom took his measure.

His shirt and trousers were tailored rather than off the rail and he wore his hair swept back and off to one side, using a fair amount of product, Tom guessed. His expression sported a broad smile, one which was as well-groomed as his appearance.

"Detectives," he said, shaking Tom's hand, "James Newell. What can I do for two of Norfolk's finest?"

"We'd like to speak to you about Louis Taylor, if we may?" Tom asked.

Newell was taken aback and the smile faded. "Louis? That's a name I haven't heard in a while."

He frowned, breaking eye contact with Tom, he looked over his shoulder and indicated towards a closed door to the right of Melanie's desk. "Please, come through to the consultancy room."

He led them across the reception and pushed open the door, walking through first and then holding it open for them. Originally this would have been the front sitting room and many of the period features, the deep skirting boards, cornicing and the decorative tiled fireplace were still in place, although the room now had a hard-wearing blue carpet and was now adorned with little more than a desk and several plastic chairs to sit upon. Tom figured this was as Newell had described it, a room used to consult with clients which otherwise remained empty throughout the day.

He offered them a seat before taking one himself on the other side of the desk.

"So, Louis? What's this all about?" Newell asked.

"He used to work for you, didn't he?"

"Indirectly, yes," Newell said, sitting back in his chair and pitching a tent with his fingers before him. "He worked through a local agency, cleaning the offices, for a time."

"How long?"

Newell blew out his cheeks, thinking hard. "A few months… maybe six at the top end. Why do you ask?"

"What did you make of him?" Tom asked, ignoring the question. If Newell was perturbed by that, he didn't show it, but continued on.

"Nice enough guy, I suppose. Not that I had a great deal to do with him. The cleaning staff come in towards the end of the day once our clients and most of our staff have left. It's a bit hard to work with the vacuum cleaner going in the background," he said, smiling. "And it looks unprofessional."

"You had him fired, didn't you?" Tom asked, fixing him with a stare.

"Fired," Newell repeated, raising his eyebrows and smiling awkwardly. "That's a strong word."

"Then what word would you use?" Tom asked.

He sighed, angling his head to one side and staring out of the window at some point in the distance. "It's true, I did have to speak to his line manager and… we requested that he no longer attended our site."

"So, you had him fired," Cassie said, "but by someone else?"

Newell laughed nervously. "Yes, I suppose you could say that. What's this about?"

"We'd like to know why?" Tom asked. "If you don't mind telling us."

"Not at all," Newell said. "I'm just surprised, that's all." He sat forward, resting his hands on the desk before him. "Louis was a good worker… conscientious… but when we caught him…" he hesitated, pursing his lips.

"Go on," Tom said, seeing his reluctance.

"It's just that I don't wish to be accused of slander."

"Trust us," Cassie said, "I think that'll be the least of Louis's problems."

Newell cocked his head but didn't press further. "Okay, we caught him stealing."

"Stealing?" Tom asked. "Stealing what?"

Newell shook his head. "We don't really know what he was doing… but he was seen at one of our terminals." He shrugged. "The man was a cleaner. He had no business doing so. I had no choice when it was reported to me."

"By terminals, you mean?"

"Oh, sorry. I mean one of our desktop computers."

"What was he doing?" Tom asked.

"I've absolutely no idea!" Newell said, shaking his head dismissively. "Was he trying to access confidential information, banking details… altering files for a dare… or just being nosy? I really do not know. What's more, I don't care." You'll understand that I can't be seen to allow that sort of thing. We have a code of conduct that we have to follow, an agreement of trust between parties, and that is paramount to our ongoing success. If we don't respect that, then our clients would lose faith in us.

Business is a fragile theatre to work in, Inspector Janssen. Confidence is everything, be it the property market, banking or indeed accounting. Without it, we are all sunk. He had to go," he said, splaying his hands wide. "Had to."

"And did you investigate what he was doing?"

"Of course. Industrial espionage is always a possibility—"

"In Hunstanton?" Cassie asked, barely suppressing a snort.

"Yes, even here in sleepy Norfolk," Newell said. He wagged a casual but pointed finger in her direction. "You know we manage the accounts of over sixty clients in the wider north Norfolk region, more when you factor in our offices in Norwich and Great Yarmouth. Our portfolio of businesses is worth annually in excess of a hundred million pounds, and so… yes… we manage some significant clients."

"Sleepy Norfolk has joined the twenty-first century," Cassie said sternly.

"In many ways, yes," Newell said, then grinned. "But not all."

"And did you find that Louis was accessing any accounts?"

"Heavens no!" Newell said, grinning and shaking his head. "I've no idea what he was up to, but all our files are password protected and the data encrypted as a routine matter of course. I think he'd just sat down at a desk and was playing, seeing how a keyboard works, that type of thing." He chuckled. "I think the man was barely literate. I mean, he's only a cleaner for crying out loud."

Tom nodded. "You're sure he didn't access any files?"

"Absolutely. There's no way he got into anything. We checked."

"But you still saw fit to have him sacked for… playing with a keyboard?" Tom asked. Newell's laughter ceased and his expression darkened.

"Now look," he said, fixing Tom with a stern gaze. "If there is any semblance of doubt… at all… then he had to go. Zero tolerance."

"We understand that there was a bit of a fuss made," Tom said. "That you contacted the owner of the agency who supplied Louis Taylor to you and that things got a little heated?"

Newell took a deep breath, and he offered Tom a curt nod. "I did raise my voice, I admit. Perhaps I overreacted a bit, but under the circumstances I believe it was justified… if a little unprofessional. I've since spoken with Aboud about it all and he's forgiven me." Newell grinned. "Totally."

"Aboud?"

"Hakimi," Newell said. "He owns the agency although he rarely works there. He leaves the day-to-day running to… oh, I can't recall her name."

"That's okay, don't worry," Tom said. "What about Louis? How did he take it?"

Newell sucked air through his teeth. "Not well, but what can he expect when caught abusing the trust shown in him? I mean, he had a set of keys to come and go as he pleased. But he's there to wipe down the desks, vacuum up and empty the bins. If he'd done what he was supposed to be doing, then there wouldn't have been a problem."

"Which account was he trying to access?" Tom asked.

"Like I said, he didn't get access to anything," Newell said, frowning. "Our client accounts were never breached. Not for a second." He glanced at his watch and then fixed Tom with a look. "Now, I think you'll agree that I've been cooperative, but now I must ask you what this is all about? What's Louis been up to?"

Tom smiled. "We're just making enquiries at this time, Mr Newell. But you're right, you have been very helpful."

"Is that it?" Newell asked as Tom stood up.

"Yes, for now," Tom said. Newell seemed surprised. "Although did you ever see Louis outside work, away from the office?"

"No," Newell said, also standing. "I can't say I ever did. He's been up to no good elsewhere, hasn't he?"

Tom found the comment curious. "What makes you think so?"

"He always had quite an opinion of himself, did Louis," Newell said. The comment was laced with a hint of venom. "And he didn't mind sharing them."

"Opinions on what?" Cassie asked.

"You name it, he could talk about it. He was one of these typical Joe-nobodies; the security guard on the door who knew how to run the company better than the CEO. That type. Irritating."

"I see," Tom said. "Well, thank you for your time."

Newell escorted them out to reception but didn't stick around to see them off. He shook Tom's hand, smiled at Cassie and made his way quickly back upstairs.

"Well, he didn't have a high opinion of Louis, did he?" Cassie said, watching him go.

"Louis?"

Both of them turned to Melanie, who appeared to have surprised herself by speaking. They crossed to her.

"Do you know Louis Taylor?" Cassie asked. Melanie's eyes flickered between them and then across reception towards the stairs. She raised a hand, gesturing for Cassie to keep her voice down. She did as requested. "Do you know him?"

"Yes, of course," Melanie said, glancing nervously around to make sure no one else would hear. "I like him. He's a nice guy. Why are you asking about him?"

Cassie ignored the question. "How well do you know him?"

"Well enough," she said, shrugging. The wariness and animosity she'd greeted them with, at least Cassie, were returning and her guard was going up.

"It's important," Cassie said, setting aside any grind there was between them. "I wouldn't ask if it wasn't."

Melanie seemed pensive but relented after one more nervous look towards the stairs. "He's a nice guy. Everyone here liked him. Well, almost everyone."

"Your boss doesn't."

"Yes, well… he doesn't seem to like anyone. Especially someone like Louis, well mannered, fun, intelligent… gentle too in some ways." Cassie glanced sideways at Tom but didn't comment. "Men like James, those who like to see themselves as some kind of alpha male, always struggle with guys like Louis and so they try to undermine them. It works too."

"It does?" Cassie asked.

Melanie shrugged. "With other shallow, wannabe tough guys, I guess."

Cassie laughed. "So, James didn't get on with him. Was the feeling mutual?"

Melanie leaned forward, speaking in a conspiratorial tone. "Well, I'll tell you, James really didn't like Louis speaking to his wife. I think he thought Louis ought to be seen and not heard, like he was a servant… staff who lived under the stairs, you know?"

"I take it she didn't agree?"

Melanie made to speak and seemed to think better of it, dismissing the question with a flick of her hand. "I doubt I'm the only one who would rather hang out with Louis. He's a handsome chap, after all. Not my type though."

The door opened and a man entered. He was in his seventies, well dressed and sporting a trilby. Melanie smiled at him politely.

"I'll be with you in just a moment, Mr Reynolds."

"Thank you, my dear," he said, tipping his hat towards her. She turned back to Cassie and then Tom. "Mr Newell's appointment is a little early. I should get on."

"One more thing, if you don't mind?" Tom asked. She shook her head. "Do you know if he had any friends that he saw regularly?"

"Louis?" Melanie asked in a whisper. It didn't seem like the client was listening in, but she clearly didn't wish to be overheard. "I don't know of anyone specific but he worked out, attended a gym somewhere local… not one of these chains but it was a fitness studio. That's probably your best bet. I'm sorry, I don't remember the name."

"That's okay. Thank you," Tom said warmly. "You've been very helpful."

"Is… is Louis in some kind of trouble?"

"Not as far as we know," Cassie said brightly. The phone on her desk rang and Melanie picked it up, listening intently.

"Yes, Mr Newell, your half-past ten has arrived… Yes, I'll bring him up now." Melanie hung up, glancing up at the corner of the room and then smiling apologetically. Cassie followed her gaze to the CCTV camera mounted on the ceiling. "I'm sorry, I need to get on," Melanie said, rising from her chair. "Mr Reynolds, if you'd care to join me, I'll take you up to Mr Newell's office in the lift?"

"Thanks, Mel," Cassie said as the receptionist came around from behind the counter.

"Say hello to Lauren for me," Melanie said over her shoulder as she guided her client towards the stairs.

Tom and Cassie stepped out into the street, the cool breeze stiffening as they walked down the path, funnelled up Greevegate from the water at the foot of the hill.

"How do you know one another?" Tom asked.

Cassie shrugged as they reached the car. "Mel and Lauren go way back."

"Way back? As in before you and Lauren got together?"

"Lauren and Mel used to be together," Cassie said, opening her door as soon as Tom unlocked the car.

"A-ha," Tom said.

"And it's possible that there… may have been a bit of an overlap when Lauren and I met."

"May have been?" Tom asked.

Cassie coughed and got into the car. Tom smiled and followed suit.

"Interesting, wasn't it?" Tom asked, looking back at the building as he reached across his chest and drew his seatbelt around him.

"Which part?"

"James Newell described Louis in rather unflattering terms, his lack of intelligence which is not the perception of others I've spoken to."

Cassie shrugged. "I don't know Melanie all that well, but from what I know she is a pretty shrewd judge of character. After all, she got my number when I started hanging out with…" she grimaced. "Never mind."

"Do you think Louis was hamming it up, playing the idiot in front of James?"

"Why would he do that?" Cassie asked.

"Why indeed?"

"Maybe James just had it in for him and saw what he wanted to see."

"Perhaps," Tom said, arching his eyebrows and pushing the start button. The engine fired into life. "Have you got a decent signal on your mobile?"

"Yeah, pretty good. Why?"

"I want to swing by this private gym that Louis is a member of. Can you look it up on your phone and get the address?"

CHAPTER NINE

THE GYM WAS LOCATED in one of the industrial units on a small park on the outskirts of the town. There were only a half dozen units there and several of those were occupied by the coastguard with a window company and a martial arts studio making up the numbers. Tom parked the car and they got out just as it started to rain. Crossing the small car park, they found the door unlocked and they entered to the sound of loud music and shouting coming from within.

There was a small reception area with a counter, but this was unmanned. To their right was a door through into the main body of the building. Peering around the corner they could see a class was underway. About a dozen people were taking part in an exercise class, all following the lead of the instructor; a muscular man who stood before everyone else, taking the lead.

Tom and Cassie entered the main area but stayed close to the door, Cassie leaning against the wall. They watched as the group were put through their paces.

"He certainly works them hard," Tom said quietly, not that they'd be heard above the music and the encouraging shouts between instructions.

"My idea of hell on earth," Cassie said.

"I had you down as something of a gym bunny."

She scoffed, knowing he was making fun of her. Tom looked around. Equipment lined the walls, but it wasn't the same as you'd likely find in one of the national chain gyms or even what you found in upmarket hotels. This place seemed to be more of a cross between a gym and hiring a personal trainer. They didn't have to wait too long before the class broke for a rest period, several people almost collapsing to the floor and gasping for breath.

"And this is fun for some people," Cassie said under her breath as the instructor approached.

"Good morning!" he said in an upbeat manner. "How can I help you today?"

It seemed like a scripted welcome, one he would give to potential clients walking in off the street.

"Good morning," Tom replied, subtly showing

him his warrant card. "Is this your business?" The man nodded, glancing at Tom's identification.

"I'm George Melior and this is my place," he said, slowly waving an arm in an arc to his side. "What brings you here?"

"I'd like to ask you about someone who I believe trained here with you. Louis Taylor?"

George smiled, nodding. "Yes, I know Louis. Good guy. What's he done?"

The question was asked so amicably that Tom guessed he was having fun at Louis's expense.

"Are you friends?"

George shrugged. "As friendly as you can be when someone is paying you for your time."

"Some people get very friendly when they're paid to be," Cassie said, dryly.

George looked at her, turning the corners of his mouth down. "Different line of business, I reckon." He winked at her, and Cassie rolled her eyes. "Well, Louis is a good guy. He trains with us two, maybe three sessions a week."

"What sort of training do you do?" Tom asked.

"General fitness… along with some strength conditioning," he said. "We run classes here throughout the day. Someone is here for a 6 am class to catch people before they head off to work and then we have a morning class, lunchtime and evening sessions."

"Seven days a week?"

George nodded, noting Cassie's uncomfortable expression. "Yes, every day, but obviously people don't attend every day. We operate a monthly subscription model and that gives access to as many classes as you wish to attend. Book online, come and go as you please."

"Sounds like… heaven," Cassie said.

"It is once you get into the routine."

"And Louis, two to three times a week you say?" Tom asked.

"That's right. Regular as clockwork is Louis, same sessions each week." He frowned. "Although, I've not seen him for a week or two."

"Is that unusual?"

George thought on it. "Yes, I would say so. Unless he was ill, he'd be here."

"He didn't say anything about going away?"

George shook his head. "Not to me, no."

One of the others in the group called everyone together and they began a fresh round of circuit training. George waved to the lead runner, and they set off without him.

"I'm sorry to delay you," Tom said. George waved the apology away. "Do many of your clients have a similar routine in coming to the same sessions."

"Yes, many do."

"And is Louis close with any of his fellow regulars?"

"Close? No, I wouldn't say close as such."

"Then what would you say?"

George frowned. "He is a quiet guy, Louis. He doesn't say a lot but when he does speak, he comes across well. He was popular… but he doesn't attend any birthday drinks or anything like that. People here do spend time together away from the gym, but Louis always seemed to prefer to keep his distance. If you know what I mean?"

"I do," Tom said. "Did he have anyone he spoke to more than others?"

"Oh, he got on with everyone, to be fair." George's brow furrowed. "Although… he also spent time with Stacy and Marcus."

"And they are?"

"The Bell brothers. They work over at Burnham Overy Staithe, maintaining and looking after boats moored out that way. They get a lot of trade from the yacht club types. You know, the weekend sailors who don't care too much for the day-to-day maintenance of their vessels. Stacy and Marcus have carved themselves out something of a niche."

"Bit like yourself here then?" Cassie asked.

He laughed. "Yeah, you could say that. Gyms are really busy the first couple of months of the year as we all try to get that holiday gain off, but their footfall is sparse after a while. We try to offer a service that encourages people to keep at it all year round."

"Anyone else?" Tom asked. "Apart from the Bells?"

George thought on it. "I know he was doing a bit of extra training with Nicholas… helping the guy out with some spotting. Lifting the weights, you know?"

"Nicholas?"

"Craft. Nick Craft. He's a semi-retired guy, obviously a bit older than the rest of the group but he holds his ground."

"Where does he live, do you know?"

"Blakeney, I think." George's face lit up. "And Annabelle, of course. I can't believe I forgot about her. She and Louis get on well too." Tom gave him an enquiring look. "Annabelle Cook."

"And what does she do?" Tom asked. "Do you know?"

"Very bright woman, Annabelle. She's a marine biologist. The last time I spoke to her about work, which isn't often because she may as well be talking witchcraft, she was doing some consultancy work for one of the energy companies building an offshore wind farm down Lowestoft way." He pursed his lips. "I think it was Lowestoft."

"Thanks very much," Tom said. "Do you know if he fell out with anyone at all, recently or in the past?"

George shook his head. "No, not Louis. He's a decent guy, like I said. He gets on with everyone. I can't see how he'd fall out with someone. They'd have to be going hard at it for that to happen, I reckon."

Tom and Cassie exchanged a brief glance. Aside from James Newell, no one appeared to have a bad word to say about Louis.

"How do you find him?"

"Me?" George asked, pointing at his chest. "He's all right. I quite like him. Why, what's he done?"

"You said he hasn't been here for a week or two. How was he when you last saw him? Was he happy, committed, motivated…"

"I'd say he was in good spirits. He has a remarkable drive to push himself beyond what you might think are his limits. It's impressive. I wish all my clients were the same."

"How much do you charge?" Cassie asked. George looked at her, casting an eye up and down.

"Are you looking to get into shape?"

"Say I am," Cassie said, "how much will it cost me to join?"

"We don't do contracts here. It's a monthly subscription and we are not your standard gym. Think of us more as slotting between a gym and employing a personal trainer. There are several membership bands, but I reckon if you attended three sessions a week then you'd see a significant improvement in a short space of time."

"And three sessions a week would set me back how much?"

"One hundred and fifty pounds a month would cover it," George said. "That's for joining the communal classes, but if you wanted something more tailored to your specific needs then we can negotiate."

Cassie smiled. "I'll bear that in mind, thanks."

George returned to his group, issuing encouragement as he reached them. By the strained looks on several faces, his words wouldn't do much to pick them up.

"I hope they have a defibrillator around somewhere because some of these lot look ready to expire," Cassie said. She turned to Tom as they made to leave. "One hundred and fifty a month? Louis lived an expensive lifestyle for a man who was out of work, didn't he?"

"I have the distinct impression there is more to Louis Taylor than we are aware of."

"He's certainly caught my attention," Cassie said. "And he has an interesting peer group to associate with too."

Tom's mobile rang. It was Eric.

"I've heard back from the Border Force," Eric said, the sound of his fingers passing over his keyboard in the background. "British Airways had a Louis Taylor booked on a flight to South America via Madrid for a brief stop to transfer planes before flying on to Tocumen Airport in Panama."

"Interesting holiday destination," Tom said. "When did he leave?"

"More interesting than you realise," Eric said. "The flight departed eleven days ago, but our man wasn't on it."

"He didn't show at the airport?"

"No. He checked in online three days prior to departure but was a no show on the day of the flight."

Tom sighed. "That is interesting." Cassie looked over at him and Tom inclined his head, conveying he'd just been told something significant. "Right, I want you to speak to the DCI and fill her in. We're at the point where we need access to Louis's bank records, credit cards and the like. It's starting to look like he's our guy and we need to build a timeline on his movements as well as his associations. We'll need a magistrate to sign off on a warrant for that."

"I'll speak to her now," Eric said.

"Quick as you can Eric."

Tom hung up, touching the top of his mobile to his lips as he thought through the significance.

"Penny for them?" Cassie asked.

"Louis Taylor was due to fly out of the country eleven days ago, to Panama," Tom said, "but he never made the flight."

"Maybe he went for some extreme weight loss classes and a deep swim instead?"

Tom nodded. "It's looking that way." He was thoughtful for a moment, absently rubbing the side of his head. "Right, we've barely scratched the surface on who this chap really is. All we have to work with are these people who have flimsy connections with him—"

"As far as we know," Cassie said. Tom nodded. "It's really weird though, don't you think?"

"Yes, very. I think we look into these people, the ones in and around him, and find out who he was really hanging around with. He'll be close to someone; we just haven't spoken to them yet. But you're right, something here isn't adding up."

CHAPTER TEN

Blakeney Quay was quiet when Tom parked his car in the small parking area overlooking the River Glaven which wound its way through the nature reserve and past the small town. In the tourist season the little town of Blakeney was a hot spot for visitors looking to hire boats, take short seal-watching trips or simply to make their way along the raised paths through the marshes towards Cley. At this time of the year much of the town was in hibernation until these people returned in the spring.

A line of boats was moored along the quayside and Tom crossed the road to the buildings opposite the quay. Originally warehouses for the trade and commerce that passed through the old harbour, the changes in tidal patterns along with the movement of the sands made Blakeney's historic harbour a place for servicing private vessels and the tourist trade rather than the continental commerce of its heyday. The old warehouses were now broken up into different businesses selling crafts or housing art galleries, tea rooms or estate agents selling holiday homes. The largest building on the waterfront was the Blakeney Hotel which did a roaring trade.

Tom paused at the end of the line of old buildings noting the plaques mounted on the brick wall denoting flood levels reached in particular years. In 2015 a storm surge raised the tidal level to Tom's chest, thereby flooding the lower end of the town. Looking back across the nature reserve, such a beautiful and peaceful spot, it was hard to imagine the force of nature that must have struck at that time. It'd happened before and it would undoubtedly happen again.

Resuming his walk, the brisk breeze saw him button up his coat as he looked for the business Nicholas Craft operated from the quay. He found the door locked, a typed sign stuck to the glass in the front window, along with a mobile number, for all enquiries out of season. There was little passing footfall, and Tom rang the number on the off-chance Mr Craft would be nearby. His registered home address and phone number was also in Blakeney, but there'd been no answer there either.

"Mr Craft?" Tom asked when the call answered.

"I'm down at the quayside, standing outside your shop. I was hoping to have a word."

"Sure, I'm only on my boat in the harbour."

"Then I'll come to you," Tom said, keen to set foot on a boat again. He seldom had the time these days to take his own out on the water. Nowhere near as much as he'd like at any rate.

"Great. It's the Raven Black, a thirty-three-footer. I'm up on deck, so I'll keep an eye out for you."

Tom hung up and returned to the water's edge, crossing the road and walking towards the moored boats. There was a real mix of vessels at anchor in the inlet as well as tied to the quay, from small single-occupant boats to the yachts such as the Raven Black which stood out as one of the larger ones. Nicholas Craft saw him coming. There was no one else about and he signalled for Tom to come aboard.

Gripping the guardrail, Tom adeptly swung a leg over and climbed aboard.

"Managed like a true professional," Craft said as Tom offered him his hand.

"It's been a while," Tom said, taking his hand and looking around the deck. "DI Tom Janssen from Norfolk Police."

"Police?" Craft said, surprised. "And here was me thinking you were after some sailing lessons."

Tom smiled. "I'm afraid not. I have that covered."

"You sail?"

Tom nodded. "But as I say, it's been a while."

Craft pursed his lips. "You couldn't keep me off the water. I'd go mad if I had to stay on dry land. It doesn't suit me."

"Do you go out a lot?"

"As much as I can. This time of year, I can do as I please. Once spring comes around then I'm pretty much servicing the tourists much like everyone else in these parts. Those who aren't retired anyway."

"You mentioned lessons. Do you teach then?"

"I do, yes. Mostly that comes through the local sailing clubs, local schools… that sort of thing." He inclined his head. "There's not a lot of that to be honest. Much of my business is in kayaking and paddle board hire."

"Perfect location for it," Tom said, resting a hand on the boom as he looked out towards the spit and the access to the North Sea. Blakeney was sheltered from the ravages of the sea by the headland that culminated in Blakeney Point. At low tide the water receded to such an extent that smooth golden sand was revealed for several miles along the coast and sometimes as far out as a half mile. When the conditions were right though, the picturesque area could turn lethal. Lives had been lost in previous storm surges along this coast.

"So, what brings you out here, DI Janssen? You can't be that desperate to be out on the water?"

Tom smiled. "No, I wanted to ask you about Louis Taylor."

"Louis?" Craft asked, raising his eyebrows. "Interesting young man, that one."

"You know him well?"

"Fairly well, I would say." Craft put down the lubricant he was using to grease the winch he was working on. "He approached me a while back about taking some classes… oh, it must have been six months or so ago, I guess. I took him out on the water a few times, but it sort of fizzled out when I got busy with the regular trade."

"Was he not up for it then?"

"I wouldn't say that necessarily, but he seemed far more interested in me than learning to sail."

"In you?"

"Don't be too surprised, Detective Inspector," Craft said with a sideways grin, "I'm quite an interesting person. At least, I've been married three times, so I must have something going for me." Tom arched his eyebrows at that, a reaction that broadened the grin further. "Widowed once, divorced twice," he said, sighing.

"I'm sorry to hear that," Tom said.

"Which one, the widowing or the divorces?"

"All three?"

Craft laughed. "Thanks, but there's no need. My

first, and greatest love passed away after thirty years of wedded bliss… and the next two were but shadows in her honour. Expensive ones as they turned out to be too." He frowned. "Although, I do get a Christmas card from my solicitor every year, so the end result isn't all bad."

"In any event, my condolences."

"So, what's your interest in Louis?"

"Just routine."

Craft chuckled. "Does anyone ever buy that line when you say it?"

Tom smiled. "Some do, others… not so much."

"He's in trouble then?"

Tom shrugged. "I don't know, and that's the truth."

Craft seemed to study Tom, his eyes narrowing. It was a genuine answer and Craft accepted it.

"I met him at the gym," he said, moving the tin of lubricant aside from where he'd put it at the stern and leaning back against the push pit, resting both hands behind him on the tubular rail. "Did you know he went to the gym?"

"Yes. Forgive me for saying so, but it seems a strange—"

"Friendship to have, between myself and a man almost half my age?"

Tom nodded. "The thought occurred to me, yes."

Craft nodded. "True, but I still feel like I'm in

my thirties… at least mentally. My knees are shot, along with much of the rest of me, but I can still keep up with the youngsters, albeit at a distance. Besides, Louis isn't your average thirty-something."

"I think I can agree with you there. So, if he wasn't interested in learning to sail, what do you think he was out here for?"

Craft thought on it, his brow furrowing. "I'm not really sure, to be honest. I thought he might be unhappy in his work and looking for a new opportunity. If he liked the idea of sailing then perhaps he might be trying to fulfil some ambition, but I quickly quashed that thought. He barely knew the stern from the bow. I don't think he'd ever been out on the water before." He chuckled. "Perhaps on a ferry or such like."

"You said he was interested in you?"

"More my business, I should say. I know what I said, but I'm not that interesting. He has quite a business mind that Louis."

"He does?"

Craft cocked his head. "Well, he graduated from the London School of Economics."

Tom was surprised to hear that but didn't let on.

"What interest did he show?"

Craft thought about it, his forehead creasing. "He was keen to hear about passenger numbers, the number of trips I would make… that sort of thing. After a while I figured he was hatching some sort of business plan."

"To present to you or to set up a rival offering?"

Craft grinned. "Now that would be a sight; Louis out on the water teaching people to sail." He shook his head. "I doubt it was that. More likely, I thought, that he was looking to join me in a consulting capacity or something like that. I mean, I'm good at what I do, but the admin side of things is anathema to me. Left to my own devices I would likely be bankrupt within a few years." He sighed, straightening his back. "And besides, I fancy retiring soon, so I need help to keep me focussed."

"Do you think Louis was planning to help or offer advice?"

Craft shook his head. "Like I said, that was a thought I had but… he didn't ask anything about where I earn most of my income, so I figured I was overthinking it a little."

"The kayak hire side of things?"

He nodded. "Exactly, and I've been very open with people that that's where I earn the bulk of my corn."

"And he didn't show any interest in that?"

"No, not a single question as far as I can recall. So, I dismissed the notion and then the sailing lessons dried up and Louis was a little vague when

I asked. After a while," he said, shrugging, "I dropped it and he never brought it up either."

"I see," Tom said, puzzled. "Tell me, when did you last see him?"

Craft blew out his cheeks. "The week before last, I think. I didn't make any training sessions this past week or so… this damned hip of mine," he said, theatrically rubbing at his right side. "It happens when you get old, your mind thinks you can do more than your body can handle. I've had to take a bit of a break, rest and revitalise, George calls it."

"The fitness instructor?"

"Part-time fitness and nutrition consultant and full-time torturer of lazy people," Craft said with a wink. "He works us damn hard does George. I feel better for it." He rubbed absently at his hip again. "Most of the time."

Tom smiled. "You said you know Louis fairly well?" Craft nodded. "Did he mention any troubles he was having recently, with work, friends or anything else?"

Craft exhaled heavily, thinking hard. "I don't think he had troubles, as far as I know. I would say that recently, he's been… preoccupied."

"With what?"

"Now that," Craft said, raising a pointed finger, "I can't say, but he's definitely had something on his mind. As a lifelong insomniac, I can tell you I know a troubled night's sleep when I see one and Louis hasn't been getting the rest he needs, that's for sure."

"But he has never said anything to you about it?"

Craft shook his head. "No, sorry. I'm really starting to think he's in some kind of trouble, Detective Inspector. Should I give him a call?"

"Do you have a number for him?" Tom asked.

Craft rolled his tongue around the inside of his cheek, frowning. "Come to think of it, no. Louis always arranged things in person. I don't recall ever speaking to him on the phone." He laughed. "Isn't that odd? I've never noticed that before."

"Have you ever been to his home?"

"No, I can't say I have. I always had the impression he was a bit embarrassed about where he lives, you know? I've had him out to mine a few times and I know the others in the class – from the gym – have socialised with him on occasion too. I'm not sure if they've ever been to his place or not."

"Was he particularly close with anyone from your group?"

"Besides me? I know he got on well with Annabelle, but then she gets on with everyone. She's really quite lovely. I think they have a shared interest in ecology, the environment and all of that green stuff."

"You don't share it?"

He laughed. "I'm a bit long in the tooth to change what I do these days, Mr Janssen. I'm so set in the way I do things that even changing which toilet roll brand I use comes with a fresh wave of anxiety." He shook his head. "No, I think the saving of the planet will be the mission for the young… and more energetic… although, I would say one thing… having spent decades out on the water, if you treat nature with disrespect, then she will turn on you without a lot of notice. And none of us will like those consequences."

"Spoken like a true environmentalist," Tom said, eliciting a smile from Craft.

"I'll be gluing myself to aeroplanes any day now," he said, his smile broadening.

Tom took out one of his contact cards and passed it to him. Craft took it, glanced at the front and then the reverse.

"If you do hear from Louis, please could you give me a call?"

Craft cocked his head. "I'll say yes, and I'm a law-abiding citizen, but without knowing what he's done, betraying a friend will not come easily to me."

"I appreciate your candour, Mr Craft, but I meant what I said. I don't know what Louis is caught up in, if anything, but it will be better for all concerned if he were to speak to me directly."

Craft's gaze lingered on Tom and then he nodded, almost imperceptibly. He held the card aloft.

"If he gets in touch, I'll encourage him to call you… and I will let you know."

"That's all I ask, Mr Craft. Thank you for your time."

CHAPTER ELEVEN

TOM WALKED into the ops room and made a beeline for Eric who glanced up at him as he approached.

"Where are you with the warrant for Louis Taylor's personal information?"

"The warrant has been approved and I'm just waiting on feedback from his bank for access. The mobile phone companies are being a little slower in their response though."

Tom bit his lower lip, wondering whether Nicholas Craft was right in that Louis didn't possess a mobile phone. "Have you tracked him down?"

"Yes, well, sort of," Eric said, smiling and then frowning as he turned back to his screen. "It's really unhelpful that he doesn't have any photos of himself in his home, you know? It would help with the search. However, as you know we have the National Insurance Number that they used through the agency payroll and so I've gathered a fair bit of stuff about him."

"Okay, good," Tom said, sitting on the end of the adjacent desk and folding his arms across his chest. "Give me the headlines."

"Right," Eric said, his brow furrowing as he switched pages in his browser, "Louis Taylor. As you already knew, he was from Essex, grew up in that area… local schools… no known contact with our counterparts in the Met… he graduated from college with four A-Levels, two in languages – Spanish and Italian – plus two others in maths and economics."

"Bright guy," Tom said quietly.

"I'd say so," Eric agreed. "He applied for and was offered a place at the London School of Economics… graduating with a first class degree in 2007. The student loans provider has Louis on their records, and they've been very helpful, by the way. He hasn't made any contribution to his debt at all. Seemingly, you don't start repaying the loan until you hit a certain threshold of earnings and he's never met that, so his payments are deferred."

"You won't if you're cleaning offices on minimum wage," Tom said.

"Quite right, although he does have to provide information to them, address and the like… which he has done. Now, I cross-referenced all of that information with the short list of social media names I'd already come up with and… I don't think it'll be much use."

"Oh? Why not? Can't you find him?"

"I'm pretty sure I found him," Eric said, changing windows in his browser again and pulling up a social media account from the web. He clicked on a picture and it enlarged. It was a party shot of a group of twenty-somethings, Tom guessed, taken at a bar or a club. Some of the group were dancing whereas others were clutching drinks. Everyone appeared to be having a good time. "Louis is tagged in this photo. Tagged is when—"

"Yes, I know what tagged is, Eric, but thank you for making me feel old."

Eric smiled. "Well, Louis is tagged in this picture, although it doesn't help me work out which is him. These days, if you're tagged then your name appears over your image in the photo, but this was taken back in the day when the technology was much newer and less… accurate."

"So, we don't know which is him?"

"That's right, I don't," Eric said. "And before you ask, yes, I've looked at other pictures and I have the same issue. Most of the content was taken from university parties, along with other social gatherings and so there are a lot of people – the same people – all together. What I can say though, is that after graduating, Louis had been offered a place on the graduate programme of an investment bank in the City."

"Way to go, Louis," Tom said, arching his eyebrows.

"But he was taking a gap year beforehand," Eric said, exhaling. "He went on the backpacking trail, planning to head off to South America and then on to East Asia and down to Australia before coming home to take up his new post. He never took up that post as far as I can tell. I called the bank, but I'm waiting on their HR getting back to me. They've confirmed he never joined their company though."

"So, where did he go?"

Eric shrugged. "He flew out of London, landing in the USA where he spent a few weeks, likely hitting some of the big sights, before continuing down in Central America."

"By car or flying?"

"Flew out of LA and landed in Panama," Eric said. "His passport pops up on multiple border posts across Latin America before he flies into Thailand, Bangkok, in late 2007."

"And then?"

Cassie joined them and Eric spun his chair to face Tom, spreading his hands wide. "Then… he disappears."

"What do you mean?"

"Exactly that," Eric said, puzzled. "He doesn't reappear until he shows up on the payroll at the agency here in Hunstanton."

"That's not possible, Eric," Cassie said. "No one just disappears."

Eric looked apologetically between them both. "I can only tell you what I see… and Louis Taylor vanished off the face of the earth. Although…"

"Although?" Tamara asked, coming to stand beside Eric having heard the tail end of the conversation.

Eric's eyes flicked up at her and away. "Although, his passport does have a couple of random hits on it in the meantime."

"Where?" Tom asked.

"One in North Macedonia, as it is now, in 2012 and another later that year…" Eric checked his notes, "when crossing into Romania." He shook his head. "Nothing else though. I've asked the Border Force to check their records again because that's way too random. I'm thinking it might be an anomalous record. These countries are not, or certainly were not, as advanced in their systems as we are. There were no biometric systems in operation at the time. Weird."

"That is odd," Tom said. "It would be good to have some confirmation. Do we know anything about Louis's family?"

"I have a list, primarily those who were registered at his home address but that was prior to leaving for university. I need to update it. Are we still following the policy of not contacting them?" Eric asked, looking at the DCI.

"For now," Tamara said. "I agree with Tom. We don't know that our victim is Louis yet and we're not going to cause a panic unnecessarily. Besides, we've still not gone public and once we do all hell is going to break loose. The moment we contact the relatives we lose all control of that situation and we're not ready."

"Hey," Cassie said with a grin on her face, "maybe Louis is a spook?" Her suggestion was met with a roll of the eyes from Tamara. "No, seriously. I'm only half joking. He graduates with a first-class degree from a decent university and then disappears. The security services recruit the best and brightest straight out of university, don't they? It might not be as daft an idea as you think."

Eric frowned, suppressing a smile. "And MI6 are very prolific in and around the north Norfolk coastal region. A lot of FSB agents floating around these parts…"

Cassie reached over to slap the back of Eric's head but he avoided it easily.

"I'm just saying…" Cassie replied to Eric's amusement, "that it might not be as weird as we think. That's all."

"Okay, Mrs Bond," Eric said in his best Connery inspired voice, winking at her. Cassie snarled at him which only made Eric laugh.

"Although I don't share Cassie's enthusiasm for the presence of spies in Hunstanton," Tom said, "it is all very strange. Nicholas Craft was of the opinion that Louis might be trying to learn about his business, perhaps to join him in a consultancy role. It all came to nothing, but then we have James Newell complaining about him interfering with the computers at the accountancy offices. Eric is right, it's weird. I say we keep an open mind."

"Agreed," Tamara said. "We should keep a lid on it for as long as possible, see if we can find out who our victim is for certain. Eric, you said Louis's passport didn't have any biometric data on it?"

"No, I said the passport offices he… or his passport passed through, didn't. I'd have to check when his passport was issued. It's possible he has some of the early data on it. Are you thinking to identify him from it?"

"Yes, that's it exactly," Tamara said.

"It'll likely be useless if it hasn't been issued within the last ten years or so," Eric said.

"True, but worth checking," Cassie said.

"Cassie, have you got anywhere with the names George Melior gave us from the gym?" Tom asked.

"Annabelle Cook is quite possibly one of the dullest women I've ever come across," Cassie said, returning to her desk and picking up her notebook. "She lives in Thornham and when she's not at the gym or studying the ocean floor, she's busy making jam for the community hall bring and buy."

Tom arched his eyebrows and Cassie relented. "Okay, the bring and buy thing was a stretch but she doesn't do a lot. Her social media is dinner parties and community events… that type of thing."

"Anything for us to be interested in?" Tamara asked.

Cassie shrugged. "Her fitness trainer says she's close to Louis, but aside from that, no. Dull as dishwater."

"Well, it's a good job you're not looking to pick someone up then, isn't it?" Eric said dryly.

"She'd be safe," Cassie replied.

"What of the Bells?" Tom asked.

"Much more interesting," Cassie said, looking at her notes. "The Bells have both been acquainted with us, or at least our colleagues in neighbouring forces. Marcus Bell has several convictions to his name, for receiving stolen goods in his twenties and a later conviction for fraud. He received a two-year suspended sentence for that one and was lucky to avoid a custodial term. That was five years ago, and he's not appeared on our radar since he's been in Norfolk."

"What of his brother?"

"Stacy Bell… has a list of associates that would

make a gangster blush. He's been named in several enquiries but never found his way into an interview room, let alone a courtroom. The man must have nine lives or something."

"And what has he been linked to? Do we know?"

"He's been tied to all manner of black-market activity through his associations; importation of counterfeit goods, drug smuggling and distribution, mail fraud… the list goes on, but none of it has ever stuck to him personally," Cassie said, shrugging. "He's a low-level guy though, so I guess we've always gone after the bigger fish."

"That's organised criminal behaviour, but cash return focussed," Tom said, frowning. "Murder would be a significant step up for either of them."

"Motive is lacking as well," Tamara said. "It's lacking all round so far."

Cassie mock grimaced. "It'd be handy to know whose body we actually have."

"Point taken," Tamara said. "Have you checked in with the dive team out at the quarry?"

Cassie nodded. "I spoke to our enthusiastic constable, Daniel, just before we got into this discussion, and they've found nothing further. They'll keep at it, but no head and no hands so far."

"All right, we'll give them the rest of today and if we're no further along once we hear back from

Dr Paxton with his pathology report, we may need to change tack and contact the family."

Tom nodded. "In the meantime, I think we should pay the Bells a visit as well as Annabelle Cook."

Cassie raised her hand. "Please can I take the Bells? If I have to interview Madam Boredom, I might quit in protest."

Tom smiled. "I'll go and see her; you take Eric with you to see the Bells. So far, they're our most promising lead."

"Ugh…" Cassie said. "Not going well, is it?"

"I'll have to brief the Det Chief Super," Tamara said. "I think he'll be all right until this hits the press and then he'll get onto us."

"Yeah," Cassie said, "we can't have him looking bad, can we?"

CHAPTER TWELVE

THE SPACE along the water's edge at Burnham Overy Staithe, the small town located between the larger Burnham Market and Holkham, was near enough empty as Cassie parked the car. The only other vehicle was a small van, emblazoned with the logo of *Bell's Maintenance*. The tide was out and on the small beach off to their right and below them, many boats were sitting on trailers, lined up at the shallowest point for when the tide returned. Others were at anchor in the water and a few were beached waiting for the water to come back in.

Cassie and Eric got out of the car and looked around in search of either of the Bells. Calling their listed business number, a mobile, they'd heard the pre-recorded message that they could be found here at their registered premises, a small warehouse near to the water.

"Do you see anyone working down there?" Cassie asked, scanning the boats.

"I can see several people, but I've no idea if it's them."

A man stepped out of the boathouse, a black-and-cream-painted building on the other side of the road, clocking the two of them standing there in business dress and cast an eye over them. They must have stood out as not fitting in.

"Are you two looking for something?" he asked.

"Is it that obvious?" Cassie asked. The man nodded. "We're looking for Marcus and Stacy Bell," she said. "Have you seen them?"

He looked over his left shoulder. "Marcus is around the back, in the boat yard."

Cassie thanked him and they crossed the road and approached a wooden five-bar gate to the side of the boathouse. At the back of the building was a small field that had dozens of small vessels lined up side-by-side, most of them protected from the elements by blue tarpaulins. The gate was locked so they had to climb over it and then make their way into the yard following the sound of someone working, hoping it was Marcus.

Coming to stand before a sailboat sitting on keel blocks, confident that someone was inside, Cassie called up. "Ahoy the ship!" Eric shot her a quizzical look and she shrugged. "It's the most nautical I'm ever going to get."

A face appeared above them, leaning over to look down at them.

"Are you looking for me?"

His face looked thin, his features well chiselled but with sunken eyes. His skin was weathered and lined, and Cassie found herself wondering if this was the man they were looking for.

"Marcus Bell?" she asked.

"Depends on who's asking?"

She brandished her warrant card. "Police."

He seemed to recoil at that, but only momentarily. "Yeah, I'm Marcus. What do you want?"

"A word, if you wouldn't mind coming ashore?"

He stared at her for a second, unflinching and nodded. "Give me a second."

"We are ashore," Eric said quietly.

"I know that, Eric. I'm just getting into the spirit of things," she replied, lowering her own voice as she watched Marcus Bell descending the ladder. He missed the last two rungs, dropping to the earth with an exhalation and turning to face them. His eyes flickered between them, and Cassie was surprised to find she was taller than him.

"What's this about?" he asked in a flat tone.

"Is your brother about as well?" Cassie asked,

looking around and deliberately ignoring his question.

"No."

His tone was so abrupt it surprised Cassie, even though she was used to hostility from the general public on occasion, more so from those with negative experiences of the police, notably criminals.

"Ooookay," she said, smiling. "How well do you know Louis Taylor?"

He shrugged. "A bit."

Cassie and Eric exchanged a look. "We heard the two of you are friends, along with your brother, Stacy," Eric said.

He shrugged. "Like I said, I know him a bit. Why?"

"Because I'm asking, Marcus," Cassie said evenly. "Unless you've got something to hide?"

Marcus scoffed, then shook his head. His shoulders dropped and he seemed to relax his stance a little. "All right, I know him. He's a good guy. We work out together sometimes, grab the odd beer… so what?"

"There you go Marcus," Cassie said, beaming. "That wasn't too painful, was it? Now, let's try an easier one. When did you last see him?"

Marcus was thoughtful, then he looked around the assemblage of boats. "I've been really busy with work these past few days… and last week, so I've not been to the gym. I guess, it's been ten days to two weeks. I can't say for sure. What's he done?"

"Who says he's done anything?" Eric asked.

Marcus Bell narrowed his eyes and sneered at Eric's question. "Because you're asking?" He looked at Cassie, nodding towards Eric. "Is he allowed out on his own? Only, he doesn't seem too bright."

Eric bristled but he didn't rise to the jibe.

"Boat maintenance, isn't it?" Cassie asked.

"That's right."

"Business good?"

"Can't complain," Marcus said. "Keeps me out of trouble."

"Good to know," Cassie said. "Although, if you're so busy, where's your brother?"

"Gone away for a few days. We all need a break from time to time."

"That's true. When's he back?" Cassie asked, glancing briefly at Eric.

Marcus shrugged. "A couple of days, I should think. But I'm not his keeper."

"A couple of days, you say?"

"Yeah, but I'm not—"

"His keeper… yes, you said that. Where's he gone?"

"Didn't say."

Cassie laughed. "You know, for a man with

form, you're not exactly giving me the confidence to leave you alone, are you, Marcus?"

Marcus laughed himself. "And why would I care what you do? I'm legit now." He splayed his hands wide. "Look around you. I'm a busy man now. I don't have time for all that nonsense I used to be involved with."

Cassie smiled. "You know, I'd be a rich woman if I had a couple of quid for every time I heard an offender say that to me."

"Except you're not rich, are you? You're on a copper's salary… which is rubbish, yeah?"

"We get paid in the satisfaction garnered from sending scores to prison," Cassie said. Marcus's expression suggested he didn't care. "And trust me when I tell you, you don't want me on your case because I'm a nightmare." She glanced towards Eric who nodded.

"It's true, she is."

Marcus sighed. "What do you want to know? Anything to get you to leave me alone."

"That's better. Louis, tell me about him. What's he been up to recently?"

Marcus frowned. "I don't know what you're expecting me to say. I barely know him. Like I said, we have a drink, we work out in the same group. You're better off talking to that lass he likes."

"Which lass?"

"The one he knocks around with from time to time."

"Name?"

"Melanie something or other… I don't know her myself."

Cassie had been expecting him to name Annabelle Cook. Mentioning Lauren's ex-partner threw her but she didn't show it. "This Melanie… what's the nature of their relationship?"

"How would I know? I'm not his dating guru, am I?"

"But you've seen them together?"

He nodded. "Yes, a few times. I asked him about her once and he clammed up, so I guess he's nailing her."

"*Nailing her*?" Cassie asked. "Really? Does that pass for polite language these days?"

"I've heard far worse," Marcus said. "Said worse too."

"Melanie is a lesbian. Did you know that?"

"Is she?" Marcus asked, surprised. He grinned. "Fair play to the lad."

Cassie sighed. "I want to know where your brother is."

"Can't tell you what I do not know," he said, thrusting out his jaw. "Seriously, the entrance exams for the police must be really, really easy these days. I guess you just can't get the staff."

"When you speak to him, and I know you will

the moment we leave here, tell Stacy I want to speak to him."

"I'll do that," Marcus said, "but I can tell you now exactly what he'll say."

"That he'd love to do his civic duty and will be in touch immediately?" Cassie asked.

"Yeah… something like that," Marcus replied, grinning. "Or not."

"It would be in his interests to do so, Marcus."

"Whatever. Are you done here because I have work to do?"

"Yeah, we're done," Cassie said. "For now."

Marcus Bell turned away without another word and clambered back up the ladder and onto the boat without a backwards glance. Cassie and Eric made their way back to the car, the sound of calling seagulls whirling above their heads.

"He's a pleasant man," Eric said as they walked.

"Yes, and judging from their records, it's arguable that he is the nicer one of the two."

"You were surprised by mention of that Melanie. I take it you know her?"

Cassie looked over at him. "What, because we're all lesbians together?"

"No!" Eric said, affronted. "You told him she was a lesbian, so that means you must know her."

"Oh… yes… sorry, Eric. I shouldn't have snapped."

"Yes, well…"

Cassie stopped, reached out and gripped his forearm stopping him as well. He turned to face her.

"I'm sorry, Eric. I shouldn't have said that."

"It's okay, honestly," he said, accepting the apology. "But you do know her?"

"I do… a little."

"So, do you want to go and speak to her?"

Cassie shook her head. "Probably best if it doesn't come from me, and besides, I spoke to her this morning, and she didn't let on that she was particularly friendly with Louis. I mean, she said she knew him, liked him even, but nothing more."

"Do you think she was hiding something?"

"I sure do now, yes."

"All the more reason to ask—"

"Not now, no. But we will, Eric. We will."

CHAPTER THIRTEEN

Tom took the turning off the east road and onto Staithe Lane, just before entering the village of Thornham proper. The tree-lined road headed towards the old harbour on the coast, but he turned right, the road running parallel to the sea and drove past the Lifeboat Inn, a pub that had been serving locals for over five hundred years.

Annabelle Cook's address was in one of the most prestigious parts of the village. Marine biology must pay well, Tom thought to himself as he slowed the car, pulling up outside a massive brick-and-flint-inspired contemporary home facing the sea in the distance. Someone was sitting at a table on a first-floor exterior terrace, sipping at a glass of wine. Although it was cold, the sun was shining and the view across the marshes to the sea from that elevated vantage point must be quite special.

Walking up the short drive, Tom glanced up at the terrace before reaching the overhang of the porch. Of the woman there was no longer any sign. He rang the bell and waited, hearing the breeze whistling through the mature trees lining the property's boundary. The door opened and a woman looked Tom up and down, smiling warmly.

"Hello, may I help you?"

"Ms Cook?"

The woman shook her head. "No, but I can certainly fetch her for you. May I ask who is calling?"

Tom took out his warrant card. "Detective Inspector Janssen, Norfolk Police."

He assumed she was the housekeeper judging by her formality and extreme politeness. If she was surprised to have the police at the door, then she didn't show it.

"Please do come inside, Inspector," she said, welcoming him into the house and guiding him through into a front-facing reception room just off the entrance hall, itself an impressive double height area with a galleried landing above. "Ms Cook will be with you momentarily."

She excused herself and closed the door to the room behind her as she left. Tom was alone in the room which was larger than the entire footprint of the house he shared with Alice and Saffy. He didn't have to wait long before the door opened again. Annabelle Cook entered and Tom took her measure. She wore her dark hair to her shoulders, framing her finely chiselled features, high cheekbones and smooth jaw line, above her stylish attire. She greeted Tom with a warm smile.

"Detective Inspector," she said, shaking his hand with a delicate touch. "May I offer you some coffee or a cup of tea?"

"No, thank you, Ms Cook," Tom said, returning her smile. "I would like—"

"Annabelle, please," she said, offering him a seat on a nearby sofa. They both sat down. "What can I do for the police?"

"I'd like to speak to you about a friend of yours, if I may?"

"Yes, of course."

"Louis Taylor."

The mention of Louis's name startled her. "Oh… Louis. Whatever has happened?"

"You think something has happened to him?"

"No… not exactly," she said. Her eyes narrowed and she searched Tom's expression. "I thought he'd gone away… on holiday, so I'm surprised you mentioned him."

"He told you he was going away then?"

"Oh yes, absolutely," she said, nodding. "He

was going abroad, Spain I think, if my memory serves me."

"Spain?"

"Yes, I believe so. Madrid… I think or perhaps Barcelona."

"And when will he be back?" Tom asked.

"I thought he was going for a fortnight," she said, thinking hard. "So I guess he'll be back later this week. Why, what's going on?"

"Would you be surprised to learn that Louis never made his flight?"

She recoiled a little in her seat, staring at Tom. "Why ever not?"

Tom shook his head. "We don't know. He checked in online, but he didn't arrive at the gate. Nor is he at home."

"That's so strange," she said, her brow furrowing. "I saw him… it must be a couple of days before he left and he was looking forward to it so much. That doesn't make any sense."

"Can you tell me the nature of your relationship?"

Shaking off her expression of deep thought, she took a breath, pursing her lips before speaking.

"We… are friends."

"Good friends?"

"Yes, I would say so."

"And you met Louis where?"

"At the gym," she said, nodding. "We found that we have a shared interest in ecology, a desire to live within our environment rather than bending it to our will."

"I see, and you're a marine biologist, I understand?"

"That's right. I work with energy companies spearheading the green revolution, or at least that's what they call it in their company literature. It sounds good for the public." She looked down, adjusting her blouse at waist level. "Non-fossil-fuels-related business is the reality."

"Offshore wind and the like?" Tom asked.

She smiled. "Correct."

Tom glanced around the room. "Pay well?"

Annabelle laughed. "It should, but nowhere near enough to afford this," she said. They both turned as a man entered the room, casting a suspicious eye towards Tom. Annabelle gestured towards the newcomer. "My husband, Alex." Tom rose and Alex crossed the room to shake his hand.

"Alex Gillie," he said, his grip was like a vice, but Tom's was equal to it. Their eyes met and Tom had the sense he was being studied.

"DI Janssen," Tom said.

"A detective inspector, huh?" Alex asked, glancing at Annabelle as he released Tom's hand. "Whatever have you been up to, darling?"

She smiled at the comment but Tom thought it was artificial. Alex turned his focus back to Tom, shooting him an inquisitive look. His cheeks were red as if he'd been exercising, but he wasn't dressed for it, standing in his pale chinos, a pink checked shirt and a gilet. As Tom took his measure, he saw his eyes were bloodshot and a little sunken with dark rims visible beneath them.

"I'm here because of your wife's relationship with Louis Taylor."

Alex offered him a dismissive expression. "That weird guy from the gym? The… cleaner?"

Tom nodded.

"Well, I can't help you there, Detective Inspector. I barely knew the man."

"You said he is weird. Why would you think that?"

Alex frowned. "Because he is weird. He's obsessed with the environment… doing the *right thing* and so on. Weird."

"You'll have to excuse my husband, Detective Inspector," Annabelle said. "He judges something's worth in capital value… if he can make money from buying or selling it, irrespective of the consequences."

"Now that is a gross exaggeration, Annabelle," he said, wagging a finger at her. "We have green initiatives to offer and—"

"As long as they are profitable, yes."

"It is an old cliché, but money does indeed make the world go round," Alex said defensively. "All of your environmental guff bores the pants off me, but I'm well aware that there are changes afoot… and as the pendulum swings the rest of us will move along with it."

"Kicking and screaming," Annabelle said, with a trace of a smile.

"But we will move," Alex said before turning to Tom. "As for Louis, he's not exactly… someone who moves in my circles, if you know what I mean?"

"What is it you do, Mr Gillie?"

"Alex gambles with other people's money, don't you, darling?"

Alex exhaled, waving the comment away. "Please disregard my dear wife's left-leaning scepticism, Detective Inspector. I'm on the board of a wealth fund," he looked pointedly at Annabelle, "and we invest ethically on behalf of our clients. I'm semi-retired now… made a fair bit in the City and now I spend a bit more time away from the office, but I keep my hand in."

"Which means in reality he works only thirty to forty hours per week rather than living in his office. And as for ethically…" Annabelle said, raising her eyebrows. "Behave."

"Yes, ethically," Alex repeated, "where possible."

It was the last comment that Tom found most telling.

"Business is good?" Tom asked, making conversation. "I keep hearing that there is turmoil in the economy, and we all need to brace ourselves."

"A good fund manager makes money in almost any market," Alex said. "Trades have to happen, money still moves, and people still—"

"Get rich off other people's backs," Annabelle said.

Alex cocked his head, then looked at Tom. "You'd think the designer clothes and the new SUV pay for themselves, wouldn't you?" He grinned, shaking Tom's hand once more. "I'll leave you in my other half's capable hands, Detective Inspector. As I said, I barely knew Louis, so I'll be of no use to you. I have a few things to do in my study, so if you'll excuse me?"

He smiled and left the room. Annabelle watched him go, smiling as he passed, gently touching her shoulder as he walked by her. Despite their seemingly polar-opposite ideological views, Alex was still affectionate towards his wife. Tom felt they must have some interesting discussions across the sofa at the end of the day.

"You'll have to forgive my husband's bullish charm, Detective Inspector. His bark is far worse than his bite."

"They say that opposites attract," Tom said, smiling.

She nodded, returning his smile. "Beneath all of that brash exterior is quite a different man. Over the years I've been able to steer him towards charitable donations, helping impoverished communities both here and abroad. He's not really the poster boy for capitalist nihilism, but he does make a good fist of making everyone think so."

"I'm sure," Tom said. "Can I ask you something about Louis?" She nodded. "I'm getting a rather confusing picture of him. He worked as a part-time cleaner… and there is nothing wrong with that, but he seems far too educated for—"

"Such a job?" Annabelle said. Tom nodded. "It's true, Louis is not just a cleaner, as my husband sees him. And he's not weird either. He's a very decent man, with a lot of integrity. If you were to hear his views on modernity, the way we are shaping our environment to suit us rather than preserving it for our own future, you'd find him just as fascinating as I do."

"Were you aware that Louis hasn't been working through the agency for several months now?"

She seemed shocked. "Er… no, I wasn't."

"And yet he still attended the gym sessions and doesn't appear to have altered his life to take that into account. This foreign trip, for instance."

"What has he been doing instead?"

"I was hoping you'd be able to tell me," Tom said. Annabelle met his eye with a blank expression, her lips slightly parted. Then she shook her head, almost imperceptibly. "He never said anything to you?"

Again, she shook her head only this time more vigorously. "I've no idea. I'm sorry."

"That's okay. In many ways, Louis Taylor is proving to be something of an enigma to us."

"You never said what he's supposed to have done."

"I didn't say he'd done anything."

"Then you must be concerned about him," Annabelle said, fear edged in her tone.

"We would like to speak to him, it's true. Have you heard from him since he left on this trip?"

She shook her head. "No, but I wasn't expecting to."

"Tell me, have you ever been to his home? To Louis's house?"

"No, I haven't."

"You're sure?"

"I would remember," she said, raising her eyebrows.

"Of course," Tom said, watching her intently. Her demeanour didn't shift at all. "Do you know if Louis was seeing anyone?"

"Not as far as I know,' she said, "but he wouldn't necessarily tell me."

"Why not? The two of you are friends, after all."

"Good friends, but we don't live in one another's pockets."

Tom took out one of his contact cards as they both stood up, Tom making to leave. He handed the card to her and she examined it.

"Should you hear from him, or if you think of something that you consider relevant, no matter how small, please could you give me a call?"

"I can do that, Detective Inspector," she said, smiling. "I hope everything is all right."

"As do I," he said, making his way to the front door. She accompanied him, seeing him out. The door was closed before he made it halfway down the driveway and back to his car. Taking out his mobile phone, he called Eric.

"Hello, boss," Eric said cheerfully.

"How did the two of you get on with the Bells?"

"Stacy is out of town at the moment, but his brother was an absolute delight," Eric said. "Cassie, in particular, loved him."

Tom chuckled. "I'll bet." Reaching the car, he looked back at the house as he fumbled with his key fob to unlock it. Glancing up, he saw Annabelle reappear on the roof terrace, leaning on the railing and looking in his direction. He couldn't tell if she was watching him or admiring the view for she had a set of large, dark sunglasses on, shielding her eyes from the glare of the low winter sun. "Are you back in the station?"

"Just on our way," Eric said. "Be back in about five."

"Can you run a check on any vehicles registered to Annabelle Cook, please?"

"Of course. What are you hoping to find?"

"Apparently, she drives a BMW, and someone else does who visited Louis Taylor on occasions. I'm wondering if it's her."

"It could be someone else," Eric said.

"You've got something?"

"Louis was quite close to the receptionist who works at the accountants Louis was fired from…" The sound was muffled as Eric moved the mobile away from his mouth to ask Cassie something. "What was her name again?"

"Melanie," Tom said, noting a text message had come through on his phone. He glanced at it as he got into the car and his phone call transferred to the Bluetooth, now emanating through the car's speakers.

"Ah… yes, Melanie," Eric said. "Marcus Bell suggested they were an item."

"You'd better check her records with the DVLA as well then while you're at it. If Stacy Bell is out of town, there might be a reason why."

"Lying low, do you think?"

"Quite possible. Find him."

"Will do. Are you coming back to the station?"

"I'm calling in on Dr Paxton first," Tom said, rereading the text he'd just received. "It looks like he's finished his autopsy on the remains found in the quarry. I'll see you back in Hunstanton later."

CHAPTER FOURTEEN

Dr Paxton looked up as Tom entered his office, peering over the rims of his glasses. He smiled.

"Hello, Tom," he said, rising from behind his desk and peering past Tom as if half expecting someone to be accompanying him. "Flying solo today, are we?"

"For now, yes. How are you?"

"A little discombobulated… and rather more than a little perturbed by the puzzle you've had me decoding this past twenty-four hours, I have to say."

"It's unusual, I'll admit," Tom said, "and the more we look into it, the stranger it becomes."

"Now that is the sort of puzzle I like, Tom," Paxton said, "although, I prefer to have all the pieces available to me if I'm going to work on it. Do come with me."

They left his office and made their way through the building to the mortuary. Tom was hopeful that the post-mortem might give them something to work with. At the moment, they had scant details with which to forge a path in the investigation. Paxton pushed open the door, holding it for Tom to pass through. The temperature drop as they entered the refrigerated room where the bodies were stored was quite stark and Tom buttoned up his coat. Paxton went to a desk in the corner of the room, returning with a sheaf of papers in a manilla folder. He counted quietly as he moved along the bays, stopping at the third from the end and pulling the handle, a resounding clunk sounded in the tiled room, reverberating off the walls.

"How is young DS Knight?" Paxton asked, pulling the metal tray out which did so effortlessly.

"She's well."

"Do give her my regards, won't you?"

"Of course," Tom said. Dr Paxton and Cassie always seemed to be at loggerheads, but recently she appeared to have captured the pathologist's attention. There would never be a more unlikely pairing, even if Paxton was her type. He was far from it.

Unzipping the body bag, Tom recoiled from the smell. Dr Paxton noticed.

"Terribly sorry. I should have warned you to prepare yourself for the level of putrefaction," he said. "The quarry must be a haven for microbes, insects and general wildlife. I know it's been cold, but your man here, what we have of him, has been in the water for some time. However," Paxton said, narrowing his eyes and leaning over the remains, "I don't believe the poor chap went straight into the water after death."

"What makes you say that?" Tom asked with a hand over his mouth and nose, silently hoping this would be a short visual inspection.

"The stages of decomposition," Paxton said, looking at Tom and arching one eyebrow. "The human body passes through five stages, as I'm sure you know; the autolysis stage, more commonly referred to as fresh, followed by bloat, active decay, advanced decay, and finally the remains are skeletonised. Now, at this time of the year with air and ground temperatures in low single figures, or below, we would expect decomposition to be somewhat slowed. The initial stage of autolysis would take place over twenty-four to seventy-two hours, depending on the time of the year, so in this circumstance it would be towards the upper end of the scale. At this point the internal organs start to deteriorate in the course of the next three to five days and then bloating occurs."

"That's when the body begins to leak, doesn't it?"

"Quite right, Tom. You've been paying attention these past few years."

"I wish I didn't have to," he replied.

"Yes, well… I can understand that," Paxton said, casting an eye over the cadaver which he'd reassembled as best he could, although the limbs were still separated. "Bloating does exactly what it says on the tin," Paxton said, frowning. "The tissue and organs decompose causing gases to develop internally, swelling the body and giving a green tinge to the blood vessels and the skin itself. The gases continue to develop as the organs and indeed the blood within the corpse decomposes, turning the body from green to red, which you can see here."

"Unfortunately. What does this mean, Doctor?"

"Well, simply put, I think this fellow died… and was stored somewhere prior to being bagged up and deposited in the water."

"Are you certain of that?"

"As far as I can be. I know we all watch these cracking television programmes where a dashing pathologist, rather like myself, manages to pinpoint a person's death to exactly what was on the television that particular night, but sadly, I'm sure you'll be devastated to hear, that's not the case. We analyse, crunch data and use our experience."

"Can you walk me through it?"

"Of course," Paxton said, smiling. "Had this chap died and gone straight into the water, he wouldn't be as far along the decomposition process as he seems to be. As I said, the water temperature is very stable in the quarry. It is not a large lake, but it is deep. Once past the bank, the ground slopes away steeply. The depth of the water maintains a water temperature that varies little even in the height of summer. The shallows will warm through, but the deeper parts will remain cold. This is why we see so many deaths during the summer months of people taking dips in reservoirs or lakes. Hypothermia strikes when they are out in the deeper parts and they cannot maintain buoyancy, and they drown. It's very sad."

"So, you think our victim was put into the water how long after death?"

"Now that is a call I don't have the data to determine, Tom. I'm sorry to say. Who's to say where the body was stored, a fridge, freezer or out in the open, in an airing cupboard… you see my problem?"

Tom nodded.

"However, the body has passed into the third stage of decomposition, that of active decay. You can clearly see the tissues changing colour, and I was surprised to see the level of blood still within the body… or the parts of the body."

Tom looked at him quizzically.

"Well, the body has been dismembered – I'll come to that in a moment – and had that been done soon after death, then the blood would quite simply have drained out. Rather like what happens in an abattoir—"

"I'd rather not picture that, if you don't mind."

Paxton chuckled. "I often wonder if that was what drove our wonderful DCI towards her passion for veganism?"

"Perhaps," Tom said. "You were saying… the blood?"

"Yes, the blood wasn't drained. Believe me, if you start separating limbs shortly after death, you will end up covered in blood. Once this fellow was brought to me, and I completed my analysis, I would argue that a significant level of his bodily fluids remained. Although, at this stage of active decay, much of the fluids have dispersed into gases and decomposed… I would say that he died, the body went through the onset and the passing of rigor prior to being dismembered."

"Indicative of an unplanned homicide," Tom said quietly.

"Or a chaotic plan by a total amateur," Paxton said. Tom had to accept that either possibility could be true. "You'll see from these cuts," he leaned in, directing Tom to look at several places where the arms and legs had been removed at their respective joints, "that they were initially begun with a precision instrument. And when I say precision, I mean nothing more selective than a sharp kitchen knife, perhaps three to four inches in length, a filleting knife or similar. When that began to struggle with sinew and tendons… the butcher, and I use that term loosely because this person was not a professional by any stretch of the imagination, gave up with precision and control and moved onto more barbaric and clumsy tools."

"Such as?"

Paxton took a deep breath, his forehead creasing. "A small hand axe, perhaps. A little wood chopper or hatchet, for example. And not a sharpened one either. The blade was dull. They may as well have been using a hammer judging from the way some of this tissue has been pummelled into submission."

"Impatience, do you think?"

"That would be my guess. Like I said, an amateur having a go at being clever." He tutted. "Damned messy business."

Tom stepped back; the smell was making him feel nauseous now. Paxton beckoned him forward.

"Before you're put completely off your lunch, Tom. There is something else you should see."

Reluctantly, Tom came closer, and the doctor pointed out a half dozen incisions on the cadaver's torso. Tom looked at him quizzically. "Stab wounds?"

"Not deep enough," Paxton said, shaking his head. "Undoubtedly done with a blade, but not very deep. Deep enough to hurt… to terrify perhaps, and definitely to cause blood loss, but none of them mortal by any means."

"Torture?"

He nodded. "I would say so, but for what purpose, I've no idea."

"Do you have a cause of death?"

Paxton frowned, staring down at the remains. "I'm afraid not, Tom. I don't have enough to work with. What I can tell you is the tox screen came back negative for drugs, either pharmaceutically prescribed or illegal substances. Likewise with poisons, makeshift ones like bleach or more chemically constructed professional efforts, cyanide and the like. There was no alcohol detected in the blood stream. No damage to bodily organs either naturally, by way of a cardiac arrest or unnaturally through blunt force trauma, sharp objects or projectiles. Aside from the incisions I pointed out to you, there is no damage to exterior skin tissue, no abrasions or bruising, which likely rules out a struggle or a fight to the death." He raised his hands, fists clenched into a boxer's pose. "The lungs show no sign of water ingress prior to death, so he didn't drown… and my best guess would be, if you find the head… you'll likely find the cause of death."

"They're still looking," Tom said gravely. "What can you tell me about his identity, anything?"

"Well, he doesn't have his name stencilled on his body so he can be handed back to his owner in the morning assembly, if that's what you mean?"

"Sort of, yes. DNA?"

"I have plenty of that, but there are no hits in the database. I've sent it to my colleagues at the Ministry of Defence for them to run against their personnel records, just in case he's a serving military man, past or present who has been in trouble, they'll hold his records in that case, but if he's ever been arrested by you or one of your colleagues then it was prior to the mandatory acquisition of DNA."

"Or when it was still disposed of if you were not charged."

"Indeed. Obviously, dental records could be compared… if we had any teeth," Paxton said glumly. "For now, all I can tell you is this is the body of a white male, aged approximately thirty-five to forty-five years of age, with a margin of error plus or minus two to three years."

"That… narrows things down a little."

Paxton smiled. "Fear not, Tom. I have a plan. I've taken samples and sent them off to a friend of mine who works at a well-renowned university specialising in the research of stable isotopes."

Tom laughed dryly. "English, please, Doctor."

"It is a process where they can analyse the levels of carbon contained within a plant species. It's all about atoms and chemical changes. Basically, every plant on earth consumes carbon dioxide from the atmosphere and, in different parts of the world during the process of photosynthesis, the chemical elements of the carbon are altered by the volume of sunshine they're exposed to. This changes the make-up of the plant—"

"I'm losing the will to live here," Tom said, smiling.

"The point is, we should be able to tell where this chap originates from, or where he lived for most of his life based on what he was eating over the years. Archaeologists use this stuff all the time in their studies these days. It really is quite fascinating."

"That's... impressive. Are there any drawbacks?"

"If he moved around a lot, then the results will be inconclusive. However, if he stayed in one place or perhaps two for a lengthy period, then it will be very apparent."

"That's great."

"A head would be far more beneficial though, I have to say," Paxton told him. "This is a long shot, but it's all I have to offer you at the moment. At least you'll have a nationality and, if he is from somewhere exotic, then it will narrow your search."

"I'll take it, thanks," Tom said. It was such a reach that Tom was well aware of what they needed to do now, only he had to convince Tamara. Otherwise, their investigation was likely to stall.

CHAPTER FIFTEEN

TOM ENTERED the ops room to see Cassie and Danny Wilson standing around Eric's desk. Danny was explaining something, using his arms for dramatic effect. They didn't notice his arrival and he was upon them before they even knew he was there.

"…and this guy, he's right there, one hand on the steering wheel and the other is reaching behind his seat into the rear footwell," Danny said, "and I'm yelling at him to stop… and he's still reaching… I yell at him again, saying *mate, I'm going to haul you out of the car by your—*"

He saw Tom and stopped, Eric was looking up at him from his seat, waiting to hear the conclusion. Cassie however, turned to Tom and smiled awkwardly.

"Hello, boss."

Eric snapped upright in his chair, rummaging through some things on his desk to try and make himself look busy.

"Am I interrupting something?" Tom asked.

Cassie grimaced. "Nah, Danny was just on his third best anecdote… that's all."

DC Danny Wilson flushed and hurried away to his desk.

"Is Tamara around?" Tom asked.

"Not seen her for a bit," Cassie said. "She got summoned upstairs to see the chief just now and she's not come back yet. Hopefully, he hasn't handed her her P45."

"Don't joke, I think he's looking for a reason to demonstrate his authority."

Cassie laughed. "I don't doubt it. Whiny little man," she said, lowering her voice to ensure no one could overhear her just in case. She stared at Tom, reading him. "How did it go with Doctor Death?"

"Not good. He sends you his best, by the way."

"Me?" Cassie asked and Tom nodded. "I swear that man gets stranger by the week."

"I think it's sweet. You made an impact on him. Like a puppy who forces a new owner to like them… despite making a mess on the carpet all the time."

"Now, there's an image," Cassie said. "So, what does the good doctor have for us? Anything useful?"

Tom sighed. "No visible cause of death… some suspected evidence of torture and no means of identification. He's white and between thirty-five and forty-five… ish."

"Terrific. We don't have many of those living around these parts."

"Assuming he is from these parts," Tom said.

"What do you want to do?"

He shrugged. "I think we're out of options, don't you?"

"Go public?" Cassie asked, grimacing again, only this time it was genuine.

"I think so. What other choice do we have?"

"Things always get complicated when the public are informed. They want to be involved, start a panic… and then the press shows up." She shuddered. "It must have been so much easier being the secret police, back in the day. Act with impunity… arrest and detain at will."

"Yes, it all sounds so romantic." Tom frowned. "We'll need to obtain DNA samples from Louis Taylor's family too. You never know, they might be able to shed some light on why he lives the way he does."

"You're assuming he hasn't legged it off from them as well," Cassie said. "Remember, not everyone's family is as close as yours and mine."

"Fair point."

"Should we wait to clear this with Tamara?"

"Of course. But make a start on Louis's next of kin, would you? I'll draft a press release and by then, hopefully, Tamara will be back. Oh, one thing," he said.

Cassie looked over at him, "Yes?"

"Eric mentioned that Marcus Bell thinks Louis and Melanie had something of a thing between them."

"He did, yes. I don't see it myself, but I suppose he had no reason to lie."

"Do you think you could speak to her—"

"Me?"

"Yes, I appreciate your history with her is not great, but she seemed to warm to you earlier…"

Cassie snorted with derision, but Tom kept his gaze on her, and she relented. "Okay, I'll see what I can do. Perhaps Lauren and I could ask her out for a drink after work or something. Take a low-key approach and see what happens? From what I gather their relationship was pretty much done before I… before we, well," she shrugged, "you know?"

"Sounds like a plan."

"I just need to sell it to Lauren, which won't be easy," Cassie said, frowning. "Don't worry, I'll figure something out."

TAMARA APPROACHED the office of Detective Chief Superintendent Cole. His personal assistant smiled warmly at her and gestured towards the closed door.

"Go right in DCI Greave, they are waiting for you."

Tamara was surprised, wondering just who *they* were. She knocked on the door out of courtesy and pushed it open. Inside she found two men, both of whom she knew and one of them was a surprise. It was a face she hadn't seen in a long time. Taken aback, she knew her mouth was open, but she didn't know what to say.

"Tamara! You're looking well," he said, getting up from his seat opposite the Det Chief Supt and bounding across the small distance between them, offering her his hand. "It's been a while, hasn't it?"

"Yes, sir, it has… I'm sorry, I wasn't expecting to see you here."

"I don't doubt it," he replied, beaming.

"Detective Chief Superintendent Wells has come up from Norwich to see us today," Cole said, and Tamara could almost detect the irritation in his voice at the way she'd been greeted as she'd entered. Tamara looked between DCS Wells and Cole, nodding.

"A bit off the beaten path up this way for Major Crimes, isn't it?" she asked.

Wells smiled, inclining his head. "We go where we're needed."

"And that brings us to why I called you up here, Tamara," Cole said.

"Sir?"

Wells gestured for Tamara to take a seat and they all sat down, Wells fixing her with a stern gaze.

"Tell me, Tamara, what's your interest in Alex Gillie?"

Tamara held his gaze, filtering her thoughts to what this was all about in her mind.

"Alex Gillie?" She shook her head. "The name doesn't mean anything to me, I'm afraid. Who is he?"

Wells cleared his throat, frowning. "He's not come up in any of your investigations?"

Tamara shook her head. "No, I don't believe so."

Wells exchanged a glance with Cole who seemed annoyed by something and sat forward, resting his hands on his desk before him. "Tamara, I think you should be very clear about this."

Tamara felt affronted. Wells adopted a more conciliatory approach.

"Tamara, this is important."

"I appreciate that, sir, but the name really doesn't mean anything to me."

"Then perhaps," Cole said, "you should have a

tighter control on your team, DCI Greave. Tom Janssen visited Alex Gillie's home earlier today."

Tamara tried to mask her surprise. She must have reacted though because Wells seized upon it. "Where was DI Janssen going today? I presume you are up to speed with your team's caseload?"

"Yes, of course. Tom was visiting the friend of someone we are trying to trace," she said, avoiding giving out details. If Major Crimes were hovering around Alex Gillie, then she wanted to know if it could be in any way related to their investigation.

"But not Alex?" Wells asked, his tone lightening.

"We are still establishing the friendship circle," she replied, noncommittally.

"Is this to do with the human remains found out at the quarry?" Cole asked.

Wells' eyes darted to Cole and then drifted back to Tamara.

"Yes, sir," Tamara said. "It is. Tom was visiting Annabelle Cook, who we believe was a friend of the person this case appears to be revolving around."

"Revolving around?" Cole asked. "Do you mean to say you are yet to identify the remains?"

Tamara tilted her head, and nodded, reluctant to admit it for fear it could be used against her. She was not wrong.

"DCI Greave... We are well on into this investigation now and I'm sure we will need to release information to the public very soon. I hope we have more than a list of casual acquaintances to run with by then."

Tamara bristled but remained tight lipped.

"I'm sure Tamara has things in hand," Wells said, smiling warmly at her. She appreciated the support. Wells had been something of a mentor to her in her time working over in Norwich. "Don't you, Tamara?"

"Yes, firmly," she said, returning his smile.

"Yes, well, I sincerely hope so," Cole said, sitting back. His eyes remained fixed on Tamara, and she found his scrutiny a little off-putting.

"So..." Tamara said, "what's Major Crimes' interest in my case?"

Wells turned the corners of his mouth down. "None whatsoever."

"There's no link between Alex Gillie and my dead body then?"

"None that I'm aware of and I very much doubt it." Wells raised an eyebrow. "What's your working hypothesis?"

Tamara smiled. "I don't believe in the hypothesis approach. If you form one, human nature sees you seek out evidence to support it rather than seeing the situation in the round."

"Honestly, DCI Greave," Cole said, shaking his

head. "Sometimes I wonder how you attained your level?"

Wells glared at Cole and then looked at Tamara with a softened expression. "I'm afraid I very much agree with your approach, Tamara. A blinkered view will only ensure you will miss things, often vital things, and that's where mistakes or stalled investigations occur."

"You taught me some things, sir."

"I'm pleased I managed to impart my wisdom onto you," he said, grinning. Cole flushed and Tamara saw the humiliation in his expression. No doubt she'd pay handsomely for it in the coming hours or days but, for now at least, she would enjoy it.

"Best teacher I ever had."

"Let's not get carried away," Wells said, smiling and clearly flattered by the compliment.

"What is Alex Gillie to you, sir?" Tamara asked, chancing her arm. "Does he run a side line in disposing of human bodies?"

"No, certainly not," Wells said. "Nothing like that."

"So, what is your interest?"

Wells gently smacked his lips, glancing at Cole before answering. "He is a peripheral figure in an ongoing operation, and that's all I can say at this time. We would prefer it, however, if you and your team gave him a wide berth." He fixed his eyes on her. "Do you think you could do that for me, Tamara?"

"I'm sure, DCI Greave can steer a path well away from your man Gillie, can't you, Tamara?" Cole said forcefully.

Tamara looked at both of them in turn. "Once we've been able to establish what happened to our victim, as well as why, then I'm sure we can take these matters into consideration—"

"Tamara, I don't think you fully appreciate the delicate position we find ourselves in—"

"No, you're right, I don't," Tamara said, through a smile. "But you must appreciate my position. I am dealing with a murder investigation and until I—"

"DCI Greave!" Cole barked at her.

"Until I know the who and the why," Tamara continued, undeterred, "then I cannot give any assurances as to where my team will and will not go," she said, primarily taking aim at Wells. "However, I will bear in mind your case and try to keep our presence to an absolute minimum."

"Tamara—"

Wells held up a hand, stopping Cole from issuing what was no doubt likely to be a severe reprimand. "I understand completely, Tamara, and I am grateful for your consideration." He seemed unhappy with the agreement but was clearly keen to take a professional approach to it. "May I ask that if you plan to revisit Gillie, or his partner Annabelle Cook, that you run it through my office in the first instance?"

Tamara's eyes narrowed at the mention of Annabelle. "I will certainly try, but investigations can move at pace and there may not be time."

"I understand," Wells said flatly. His jovial demeanour at sharing a discussion with a former colleague had dissipated somewhat now.

"I'm sure, DCI Greave will be in touch with your office as soon as she is aware of the need, should it arise, to speak with Mr Gillie or... his partner?"

"Annabelle Cook," Tamara said, looking sideways at Wells. His left eyelid flickered as she said the name, an involuntary movement at hearing it or just coincidence, she wasn't sure.

"Yes," Cole said, "this Cook lady, is she relevant to anything?"

"Remains to be seen, sir," Tamara said. "Is she relevant to your operation?" she asked Wells pointedly. He shook his head. "So... if there's nothing else, sir?" she asked Cole and then arched her eyebrows towards Wells with the same, unspoken question. He shook his head. Cole dismissed her with a flick of his hand. She made it to the door before anyone spoke.

"Tamara... I want a full briefing at five o'clock today," Cole said, "on all aspects of the investigation and where you are taking it. Irrespective of what your former line manager may think of you, so far I am disappointed with the progress in this case." He glanced at Wells, almost daring him to speak up for her. On this occasion, the visiting DCS didn't comment, sitting in his seat with an impassive expression. Not that Tamara had expected him to come to her defence even once, let alone twice. "Carry on DCI Greave."

She nodded towards him. "Yes, sir. Thank you." Backing out of the office, she pulled the door to behind her and took a deep breath.

"Rough meeting?" Cole's personal assistant asked.

Tamara smiled, and shook her head, making her way out of the office and into the corridor. She knew better than to speak ill of a senior officer to the one person they spent most of their working day with. Heading back towards the ops room, she couldn't help but wonder what Major Crimes were doing in her neck of the woods along with what the nature of their relationship with Alex Gillie was.

CHAPTER SIXTEEN

Tamara found the team waiting for her back in the ops room. Reading their expressions, she knew that the investigation wasn't progressing as well as they'd hoped. She beckoned Tom over to her and ensured they were out of earshot before filling him in on the meeting she'd had upstairs.

"So, what is their interest in Alex Gillie, do you reckon?" Tom asked.

"He's... let me get this right... a peripheral figure in their case."

Tom arched his eyebrows. "What case?"

"There's no way I was going to be cut in on that," Tamara said. "One thing I will say though, is that DCS Wells heads up the Major Crimes division, jointly operating between Norfolk and Suffolk. There's no way on earth he's come all the way out here to steer us away from a *peripheral figure*, whatever he meant by that. Gillie will be anything but."

"Great. Do we do as they ask?"

"Like hell, we do," Tamara said, with a mischievous smile. "If they choose to dial us into their case, then maybe I'll consider it, but until then we crack on with our own investigation. One thing though," she said, lowering her voice.

"Yes, what's that?"

"I have the sense that Cole is just itching to make an example of someone," she said, concerned. "Whether it's deserved or not."

"Duly noted. We've had the results back from pathology," Tom said. Tamara met his eye expectantly. "No joy. Whoever that is in the quarry, their DNA isn't in the database. Paxton has an idea about running some chemical scan to ascertain the person's likely origin, but…"

"That's needle in a haystack stuff," Tamara said. She looked at Tom and knew what he wanted to do next. "Okay, contact Louis Taylor's next of kin and advise them that…" she rubbed at her eyes, "…that he's missing, and we have come across a body that we need their help to identify."

"And the press?"

She nodded. "Yes, we'll need to make sure we stay ahead of the curve on this one. We don't want idle speculation and with the children finding the remains I'm, quite frankly, stunned that we've kept a lid on it thus far." She turned her attention to the information boards. "I need to brief Cole at five o'clock with everything we have. Something tells me that whatever I go to him with will not be enough."

Tom sighed. "Then we'd better get a result sooner rather than later." He called Cassie over. "Cass, this angle of Melanie having a relationship with Louis Taylor. Based on her withholding that information this morning, I'm afraid that if we bring her in formally, she'll just deny it."

"I agree," Cassie said. "From what Lauren used to say about her, she's quite uptight… doesn't respond well to pressure. She swings both ways though, so it's not out of the question for Marcus Bell's suggestion to have some truth to it."

"Are her and Lauren still friendly?" Tamara asked.

"I think so, yes," Cassie said. "It's me she has a problem with."

"Well, we need to find out what she knows about Louis because if she left out her relationship with him, then there's a reason and I want to know what that is."

Cassie bit her lower lip, thinking. "I could maybe get Lauren's help, if you don't mind."

"Would she help?"

Cassie shrugged. "She's not going to be up for

being an informant or betraying confidences or anything like that, but if we can get Melanie out of the office and into her comfort zone, then maybe she'll open up. Keep it informal."

"I'm okay with that," Tamara said, "as long as you don't blur the lines."

"Professional at all times, boss," Cassie said, smiling. She looked between them both and Tom nodded. Cassie walked away, scooped up her mobile from her desk and went to make a call.

"Are you sure this is the best way?" Tom asked. "I mean, Cole is gunning for one of us to take a fall. It's obvious."

"Ah… let's not worry about Cole. The man has a stick up his backside. It's always going to make him grumpy."

Tom smiled. "All right, but let's not give him an open goal to aim for though, yes?"

"Agreed."

"I'M REALLY NOT sure about this."

Cassie examined Lauren's face, feeling bad for having put her in this position. It was one thing to think this was good for their case but involving her partner without considering her feelings made her doubt the decision. She'd always worked hard to keep her work and private life separate, social engagements aside. She'd learned from bitter experience that bringing loved ones into what she dealt with on a day to day basis seldom ended well.

"It'll be okay, I'm sure," she told her, adopting as reassuring a tone as she could, raising her glass to her lips. The bar was quiet with only a handful of patrons present. Looking out of the windows and over Hunstanton's waterfront, she could see a rain cloud on the horizon starting to obscure the massive offshore wind farm that was usually visible. "When did you last see her?"

"Mel?"

Cassie nodded.

"Last month. We had a drink."

"You never mentioned it."

Lauren shrugged. "Didn't I?"

Cassie heard nonchalance in her tone but it was artificial, perhaps diversionary. She looked at Lauren trying to read her but she didn't meet her eye, instead Lauren glanced towards the door just as it opened and Melanie walked in, scanning the room. Lauren waved and Melanie made her way through the seating area and approached them. The smile on her face faded as she clocked Cassie siting opposite Lauren, momentarily hidden behind a support pillar.

"Oh… I should have known," Melanie said, scowling at them both. Lauren was defensive, reaching up and touching Melanie's forearm gently.

Melanie shook her hand away. "Here was me thinking you actually wanted to catch up."

"I did… I do," Lauren protested. "I'm worried about you."

Her tone had changed and Cassie felt a pang of jealousy, but she shrugged it off.

"Melanie, Lauren isn't lying. She is worried about you," Cassie said. "So am I."

Melanie softened, smiling at Lauren but when her gaze turned towards Cassie, the scowl returned. Cassie found herself questioning the validity of this approach. She stood up.

"Look, genuinely we are concerned about you." She lowered her voice, although there was no one within earshot. "After I saw you this morning, I had the feeling you were worried… about Louis and…"

"And my job," Melanie said. "I'm really worried about my job." She looked around the bar, fearful. "This is a small town… and good jobs are really hard to come by."

"I know," Cassie said, "and I appreciate you coming here—"

"Well, I wouldn't have if I'd known I was being ambushed."

"I'm sorry," Cassie said, glancing at Lauren who lowered her eyes to the table, wringing her hands in her lap. "It's my fault… it's just I thought you might have something to say about… about Louis that you didn't feel you could say in your workplace. Am I right?"

Melanie looked at her, pensive. She nodded.

"I'm really sorry if I'm making you feel cornered, and all of this can be off the record if you prefer it. I'm really just trying to find out what's happened to Louis."

At mention of that, Melanie's eyes narrowed and she begrudgingly pulled out a chair and sat down next to Lauren. Cassie retook her seat. Melanie looked at her.

"Do you think something has happened to him?"

Cassie considered keeping the details to herself but if Melanie was going to open up then Cassie had to make the first move. "Honestly, we don't know. He was booked on a flight to Panama via Madrid, but he never made the flight."

"Panama?" Melanie asked. Cassie nodded. "I thought…"

"You thought what?"

Melanie frowned deeply, her eyes searching the room as if looking for someone. Reassured, she turned back to Cassie. "I knew he was going to Spain, but Panama? Whatever would make him go there?"

Cassie cocked her head. "Good question." She sat forward, noticing her own glass and that Lauren had almost finished hers. "Would you like a drink?" She looked at Lauren. "Maybe you could get us all a drink?"

Lauren was put out at the blatant attempt to remove her from the conversation, but Cassie persisted, and Lauren got up from the table with a huff and headed towards the bar. Cassie watched her go until she was out of earshot.

"Melanie, I understand that you and Louis have been seeing one another. Is that true?"

Melanie looked around, her eyes lingering on Lauren, standing at the bar but still keeping an eye on them while she ordered a round of drinks. "Yes, we have been seeing each other, on and off." She shrugged. "It's nothing serious but… yes. Why?"

"Then it follows that if he was going to confide in anyone what he was doing, it would likely be you. Right?"

"I guess," Melanie said. "But… I don't know why he would be going to Panama. I haven't heard from him since he left… and now you're here at work asking all these questions." She shook her head. "I don't understand."

"We met your boss, James, earlier as you know. He really doesn't like Louis, does he?"

"No, he doesn't."

"He said he had Louis fired because he was stealing—"

"No! That's not true," Melanie snapped. "Louis is not a thief. He's a genuine, lovely guy." She looked across the bar at Lauren who was in the process of paying for the drinks. "You know, I stopped dating men a few years ago. They all seemed to be so utterly useless, narcissistic and selfish."

"You'll get no argument from me."

"But Louis is different. He's caring… decent and honest," Melanie said, her eyes glazing over as she looked out over the water. "There's no way he did the things Mr Newell said he did. What do you think has happened to him, to Louis? It's all so… strange."

Cassie had no intention of telling her they suspected he'd possibly been murdered, dismembered and his remains dumped in the quarry. However, she also didn't want to lie to her.

"That's what I'm trying to find out."

Lauren returned with the drinks, the three glasses all pressed together, setting them down on the table. She put one in front of Melanie. "Your usual," she said, smiling. Melanie thanked her. She slid another across the table in front of Cassie but said nothing before sitting down. Seeing Melanie looking tearful, she reached out and took her right hand, squeezing it supportively. Cassie felt that same tell-tale flicker of emotion, but buried it deep, surprising herself. She'd never considered herself to be a jealous person. Perhaps she had something to work on after all.

"Tell me, how did James react after our visit this morning?"

Melanie leaned in, lowering her voice and speaking conspiratorially. "He wasn't happy *at all*. I mean, he was agitated all day after you left, snappy and irritable. He'd been in a good mood until you turned up."

"Cassie has that effect on people," Lauren muttered.

Cassie ignored her. "Any particular reason why?"

She shook her head. "He didn't say anything specific. What did you talk to him about anyway? It was like you'd flicked a switch in him."

Cassie shrugged, catching Lauren's dark look in the process. She knew her well enough to know that she was concealing something. After all, Lauren always beat her in a late-night hand of poker.

"Louis was fired because of James," Cassie said.

"Yes, for stealing," Melanie said, "although I never bought that. Like I said, Louis isn't a thief. He's a decent guy."

"Then why did James have him sacked?"

Melanie shrugged. "I don't know."

"What did Louis say to you about it?"

"Not much. He just said that some people feel threatened by others… and he didn't want him around." She looked sideways at Lauren, forlorn. "James said he wouldn't prosecute, or get the police involved, because he didn't want the reputational damage to the business among his clients and whatnot… but Louis swore blind he didn't steal anything." She laughed but it was a dry sound without genuine humour. "What was he supposed to have stolen anyway, a ream of paper or done some unauthorised photocopying? It was all very strange."

"But it didn't seem to bother Louis?"

Melanie's brow furrowed. "I wouldn't say that. He was angry at first, but after a few days he seemed to calm down and brushed it off. As long as he was working, he was fine."

"Where did he work after that?"

"Oh, other jobs through the agency," Melanie said, raising her glass and sipping at her drink. Cassie studied her, rolling her lips. She caught Lauren watching her intently, almost asking the question. She returned a look to suggest she didn't ask what was on her mind. Lauren looked away. Melanie put her glass down. "Look, I really love my job. And I need it. I mean, really need it. The money's good and it's all year round, weekdays. I don't want to lose it."

Cassie nodded. "I understand, really, I do. I'm not looking to cause trouble for you."

Melanie smiled gratefully.

"Has Louis fallen out with anyone else recently that you're aware of?"

"No, not at all. Why do you ask?"

Cassie shrugged. "Just trying to build a picture. What about his past, does Louis ever talk to you about that?"

"No, not really. I asked, but he said his family have all passed away. Not that he had a large family," she said, smiling awkwardly. "I think that's why he's been a bit of a loner."

"Right," Cassie said. "That figures. And his job, was he happy being a cleaner?"

"There's nothing wrong with that. It's honest work."

"I never said there was, I'm just curious… Louis being such a capable man."

Melanie was thoughtful. "I don't think he is ambitious, that's all. A person is more than just the work they do, right? So much more."

"That's true," Cassie said. "I like to think I'm much more than a person who wades through human garbage day after day." She half expected Lauren to smile at that but she sat opposite, still clutching Melanie's hand, stone faced. "Why are you so concerned about speaking to me, Mel?"

She scanned the bar again, slowly, seeking out anyone she recognised. Comfortable, she looked directly at Cassie. "Mr Newell, James, specifically instructed all of us this morning that we are not to speak to the police without first agreeing legal representation. He said a solicitor would be provided by the company… I don't understand any of this. What is going on?" She implored Cassie with her eyes, but there were no answers she could offer her.

"I don't know, Mel. I really don't," Cassie said. "But I'll do my best to find out."

Melanie withdrew her hand from Lauren and reached across, gripping Cassie's as she reached for her glass. "I meant what I said, I really need this job… but I want to know where Louis is."

Don't we all, Cassie thought to herself.

Melanie looked around furtively. "Listen, I need to get back to the office. I've not finished my work for the day and if Mr Newell comes back in, I think he'll blow his stack at me not having done everything."

"That's no problem," Cassie said. "Newell went out, did he?"

"Yes, around lunchtime. I'm not sure if he's coming back. There was nothing scheduled, and he had two afternoon appointments that I had to move."

Cassie nodded.

"Can you keep me posted… you know, if you hear anything about Louis?"

"Yes, I'll see what I can do," Cassie told her, offering her a sympathetic smile. Melanie touched

Lauren's forearm as a parting gesture, got up and hurried out of the bar. Lauren took a deep breath.

"Is that what you expected?"

"What's that?" Cassie asked, momentarily lost in thought.

"Did you get what you wanted?"

"Time will tell."

CHAPTER SEVENTEEN

TOM PASSED the press release to Tamara to give it a final read through. She would be taking it to her briefing for DCS Cole to approve prior to releasing it to the press. Cassie had just returned from her trip out to speak with Melanie and Tom was keen to hear what she had to say, although by Cassie's initial reaction to their questions he figured there wasn't a smoking gun, so to speak. Cassie came to join them just as Tamara finished reading the text. She looked at Tom.

"That's good. Unless Cole has any reservations, that's what we'll run with. How did you get on, Cassie?"

"Here I was thinking the water out at the quarry was murky enough, but Melanie has just stirred up some more mess to cloud things."

"Really?" Tom asked. "What did she say?"

"She is adamant that Louis didn't deserve to be fired by James Newell. Certainly not for stealing at any rate. Although, she has been in an on-and-off relationship with Louis for some months, so… the views of a lover can be…"

"Suspect," Tom said.

"Yes, quite," Cassie agreed with a nod. "However, she hasn't got any other motive for why Newell might treat Louis that way. And Louis himself didn't offer up a reason either. Initially he was angry but was able to let it go shortly afterwards. That's all by the by, though. The main thing that threw me is how little she knows her supposed boyfriend."

"Care to explain?" Tamara asked.

"Well, as far as Melanie knows, Louis continued working out of the agency after James Newell had him fired, and we all know that hasn't happened. Further to that, Louis told her he was flying to Spain but failed to mention the onward flight to Panama. She's completely in the dark about his plans or how he makes his money. She also thinks he's practically an orphan… and we know that isn't true." She laughed dryly. "I mean, she also thinks he's decent, honest… and a lovely guy. Melanie isn't the first woman in history to be duped by a lover, but… he's done a proper number on her."

"So, Louis Taylor is something of a shady character after all," Tamara said. "Maybe it's Melanie who has been hoodwinked and James Newell's instincts were correct after all?"

"Plenty of people seem to think he's a decent guy though," Tom said.

Cassie arched her eyebrows. "People see what they want to see. He is also quite friendly with the Bells, and they are a couple of lowlifes."

"Sir?" Danny called, looking over his shoulder, a landline phone pressed against his shoulder as he sought to get Tom's attention. "There are some people in the lobby asking for you."

"Who is it, do you know?" Tom asked.

He nodded. "It's the Taylor family, and it sounds like they've decamped to Hunstanton en masse."

Tom made his way downstairs and out into the lobby. Four people were waiting for him, three standing and another, a woman, was sitting in the corner. They all turned to him as he stepped through the door, looking expectantly at him.

"Good afternoon," he said. "I'm Detective Inspector Tom Janssen and I'm the one who initiated contact with you." The small group made their introductions; Louis' siblings, a brother and sister, had made the trip along with his mother and uncle. It was the uncle who appeared to take the lead.

"Mr Janssen," he said, offering his hand. Tom took it and they shook. "I'm Isaac, Louis's uncle.

We… we must admit to being surprised by the call earlier today." He looked at his assembled family. "We've hoped… prayed for this day for many years… although," he seemed pained, "we didn't expect it to come quite like this."

Tom's eyes narrowed. "I'm sorry, I don't understand."

"Louis has been missing…" Isaac said, glancing at his sister, "for nigh on seventeen years. We always hoped to receive word of him or perhaps from him, but… to learn that he has been here in the UK… is quite a shock."

There was no one else in the lobby besides the clerk on the front desk and he was paying them little attention.

"Forgive me, but I wasn't aware of Louis being a missing person," Tom said.

"Well… we contacted our local police station years ago… and asked them to look into it, but they said it was nothing to do with them. They directed us to the FCO, you see."

"The Foreign and Commonwealth Office?" Tom asked. Isaac nodded. "Did Louis go missing abroad?"

Isaac frowned. "We assumed so, yes." He glanced nervously at the family. "At least, so we thought."

"You'd better come through," Tom said, "and you can tell me about it."

Ten minutes later, Tom had them seated in the far corner of the refectory. The kitchen staff were clearing everything away, most officers should have been and gone by now. It would only be those on late turn and night shift who would be passing through and, even then, only to use the vending machines. Cassie had joined them, and she brought a tray laden with cups of tea and a few snacks she'd been able to rustle up.

"Sorry, it's not much," she said, setting the tray down. They all offered murmurs of gratitude, aside from Louis's mother, who looked shellshocked at being in a police station on the Norfolk coast.

"Can you fill us in on what you know about Louis's movements?" Tom asked. It was left to Isaac to explain, he seemed to be the patriarch of the family. He cleared his throat, then took a sip of tea from a cup passed to him by his nephew.

"Louis was… an absolute star… a wonderful son, caring and compassionate. He was a star pupil too. Did you know he sat his A-Levels a year ahead?" Tom shook his head. "A very bright lad, a real gift for languages and also for maths. Fluent in Spanish and Italian, he really had his pick of universities…"

"He went to the London School of Economics, didn't he?" Tom asked.

"That's right, yes. He flew through the course… landed a job on a graduate programme at an investment bank. But he wanted to see a bit more of the world before he got onto the treadmill."

"So, he went on the backpacker's trail?" Tom asked.

"Yes, he did… he planned a round-the-world trip taking in every continent, aside from Europe, after all he was well versed in European affairs, and he set his sights on spreading his wings further afield. He went missing on that trip, you see, so that's why we're so surprised that you called."

"Did he keep in touch with you while he was away?"

"Yes," Isaac said, "but more with his mum and these two reprobates." He looked at his niece and nephew who both smiled.

"He would call," his mother said, it was the first time she'd spoken beyond a cursory hello, "once a week, every week, to let us know where he was and where he would be heading next."

"You've got to remember," his brother Noah said, "that social media was a new thing around then. I think wi-fi was new as well. Louis didn't even have a mobile phone, it was phone cards and payphones at that time."

"But he did keep you informed?" Tom asked.

"Always. He was good like that," his mother said. "He knew I would worry otherwise."

"And when did you last hear from him?"

Isaac frowned, thinking hard. "It was late

2007… in the run up to the new year celebrations in Thailand, wasn't it?" he asked the family. They all nodded. "He'd been staying in the north of the country, around Chang Mai, and was due to travel south. He had the idea of spending much of the period of festivities among the party islands. Seemingly, in Thailand they celebrate new year along with us and then they often join in in the Chinese celebrations through February and again in their traditional time of Songkran, in April."

"Was he quite a partygoer then?" Cassie asked. The siblings both laughed. "Sorry," Cassie said, shaking her head, "was that a daft question?"

Isaac held up a hand apologetically. "If you knew Louis, you would understand. He was very sociable, but he wasn't what you would call a party animal or anything like that. He saw… alcohol… recreational drugs, as a spectacular waste of time." He shook his head. "No, Louis was all about the experience of life, the variety of culture and difference among us. He sought it out. That's one of the reasons he was so into his languages."

"But he planned to work in the City?" Tom asked.

Isaac shrugged. "He always said a successful decade in the City would set him up for the rest of his life. He was a planner, Louis… had everything worked out down to the last detail."

"What was his last communication with the family?" Tom asked.

"That was with me," his mother said. "He called to say he was catching a train south to Bangkok where he had arranged for a room in a hostel just off the Khaosan Road…"

"We've since learned this is something of a Mecca for backpackers who pass through Thailand." He looked at his sister, her eyes lowered. "But we never heard from him again."

"You said you approached your local police station?" Tom asked.

"Yes, of course," Isaac said. "We didn't know what else to do. No one expected to hear from Louis that week, but with Chanukah approaching – we often spend it together as a family and we did expect to hear from him. It was the first time he wouldn't have been with us."

"And the police sent you to the FCO," Tom said. "Were they helpful?"

"Yes," Isaac said. "They listened to us… and made a few calls. I don't think they were overly concerned, although we were. Seemingly, backpackers dropping out of sight for a period isn't all that unusual. However, they did contact the authorities, checked hospital admissions and that sort of thing… to see if Louis had been involved in an accident." He spread his hands wide. "There was no trace of him. They assured us that he would likely surface once the holiday season subsided… as if he'd forgotten to call us."

"But he didn't," Tom said.

"No… days passed, and they became weeks and without any word from him, we called our contact at the FCO and… I must admit, they were very good with us, but there was still no sign of him."

"What about the Thai Police, did you try them?" Tom asked.

"Of course. I flew out there," Isaac said, "along with Noah, and we tried to retrace his steps. Louis had told us the name of the hostel he was due to stay in and we went there. Louis had checked in as planned… stayed two or three nights and then left with a small group of people he'd been hanging round with." He shook his head. "They didn't know where they were going. Again, they were very helpful. It was a place run by two young Israeli lads who'd completed their military service and were branching out into business."

"I thought I read somewhere that it was difficult for foreigners to own businesses and property in Thailand," Cassie said.

"Like many other things in Thailand, I've subsequently learned, it is complicated." Isaac frowned. "In some business areas you will need a Thai partner and you'll always need a licence to trade. It can become a bit… murky, shall we say. The amount of things I've had to get my head around in this search for my nephew over the years has been a struggle at times."

"And you went to the police?" Tom asked.

"We did, yes. They were… helpful, to a degree," Isaac said. "Louis was documented as he arrived in the country, his passport was stamped by immigration, and he'd arranged the ninety-day visa. After that, they have no record of him either being arrested, which would have been very unlike Louis, or being involved in an accident. We employed a local guide who helped us to contact the hospitals in the city to see if they had admitted anyone who was unconscious or who had perhaps lost their memory. That didn't get us anywhere, so we started to expand the search to include adjacent towns and so on… and we kept that up until we'd exhausted our options."

"And you turned up nothing," Tom said.

Isaac looked forlorn. "No… there was no sign of him. Since then, we've added Louis's name to overseas registers for missing persons, contacted charities and religious groups who offer spiritual retreats… we've even joined backpacker meet-up forums in the hope that someone would know Louis and will have seen him somewhere. Anything to give us a place to search."

"Did anything ever come of it?"

"Yes… we've had people come to us in the past.

Most of the time they've been genuine, trying to help, coming forward with sightings or people they met who they thought might be him." He shrugged. "None of them ever panned out. Then there are the ones who try to take advantage, claim to know where he might be, but need a bit of money to help locate him." He sighed. "We fell into that trap a few times over the years. I like to think we're a bit savvy now."

"Louis's name didn't come up in our database," Tom said.

"No, it wouldn't," Isaac said. "I guess that was a mistake on our part, but we never thought to register him at home. I mean, if he was in the UK then he would have come home, wouldn't he?"

Tom inclined his head. "One would think so, yes, if..."

"If he wanted to?" Isaac asked. Tom nodded. "How long has Louis been living near here?"

Tom sensed the trepidation in his tone.

"As far as we know, he's been in the area for roughly the last couple of years."

The family collectively gasped.

"Two years?" Isaac asked.

"Yes, it would appear so."

"Doing what?" Noah, Louis's brother asked.

"He's been doing agency work for a large part of that time, contract cleaning," Tom said, reading the shock on their faces. "Recently, we're not sure where he's been working though."

"I-I don't understand," Isaac said. "I don't understand this at all."

"That's why we need your help," Tom said, "all of you."

"This body… the one we were told about," Isaac said. "You think this is Louis?"

"We don't know that," Tom said. "Identification was found nearby that suggests it is possible that the remains are your nephew's, but it is also possible that he is not related. However, we have been unable to locate Louis so far."

"Can I see him?" his mother asked. "I want to see my son after all these years. I want to know if it is him."

Tom took a deep breath, glancing at Cassie. Only she knew the reality of the situation.

"I'm afraid, Mrs Taylor, that that is not possible at this time," Tom said. "The remains that we have found are… incomplete."

"Incomplete?"

"Yes, we are still searching but at this time a visual identification will not be possible."

Her eyes gleamed and her daughter put an arm around her shoulder, supporting her.

"Does Louis have any identifying bodily marks that might stand out, on his arms, legs or his upper body?" Tom asked. "It may prove helpful." The family exchanged looks and collectively shook their heads. "That's okay. Would you be willing to provide DNA samples that we could then use for comparison?"

"Yes, of course," Isaac said. "Anything we can do to help."

Tom glanced at Cassie and she rose from her seat, heading off to get the DNA sample kits. It wouldn't take long to swab the family and then those samples could be taken straight to the lab where staff were already primed to work through the night on the comparison analysis.

"Where are you staying tonight?" Tom asked. "Have you made arrangements?"

Isaac shook his head. "I've no idea. We didn't think that far ahead to be honest. We just jumped in the car and drove straight here."

"I'll have one of my team help to arrange something for you, if you'd like?"

"Thank you, Detective Inspector," Isaac said, looking at the solemn faces of his family. "We would appreciate that. We don't intend to leave here until we know whether we can take Louis with us."

CHAPTER EIGHTEEN

Tom opened the front door to find Russell, their Jack Russell Terrier, lying at the foot of the stairs. He lifted his head from his paws, ears pricked as he looked at Tom before seeming to sigh and lower his head again. The dog looked depressed.

"Well, that's a welcome," Tom said, dropping to his haunches to scratch behind Russell's ears. His eyes looked up at Tom but that was the only reaction. Rising, Tom closed the front door, slipping off his coat and hanging it on the newel post. Voices carried from the kitchen and Tom remembered his father-in-law was coming for dinner and despite his best efforts, and a stern reminder from Alice, it had indeed slipped his mind. "Once more unto the breach…" he told himself, taking a deep breath and walked into the kitchen.

"Hello, everyone!" he said cheerfully. "Sorry for running a bit late, but…"

"Duty calls," Ian, his father-in-law said, smiling from his seat at the far end of the dining table. Ewelina, his partner, sat next to him and she shot Tom a broad smile. Alice was busy clearing the table of the dirty plates and although she smiled at Tom, he could see she was annoyed. What he didn't know was if that was aimed at him, her father, or Ewelina. Perhaps all three of them.

Alice came by him, plates in hand, and she leaned into him to enable him to kiss her cheek affectionately. "Everything all right?" he asked quietly.

"Dinner was lovely," she said, continuing on and setting the plates down on the surface above the dishwasher.

"Mine was a little overdone," Ian said, patting his stomach, "but other than that, it was a splendid attempt."

The cutlery shrieked as Alice forcibly put a fistful of knives and forks into the cutlery basket of the dishwasher. "Attempt," she repeated. Internally, Tom grimaced.

"Not a slight on you, love," her father said, "likely to be the thermostat on the oven. You should have that looked at, Tom," he said, nodding in Tom's direction.

"Yes, these cheap Chinese brands are not the

same quality as we are used to here in the west," Ewelina said, smiling at Ian. He patted the back of her hand. Tom pursed his lips, glancing at Alice and seeing the tell-tale flicker of her left eyelid… which only happens when she is borderline incandescent. She forced a smile.

"We'll do that, won't we, Tom?" she said, raising an eyebrow.

"Oh, absolutely," he replied. Looking around, spying the half-empty plate opposite Ian, he wondered where Saffy had got to. Glancing into the living room, he couldn't see her. "Where's Saffy?"

Alice slammed the dishwasher door closed. Tom wished he'd not asked.

"In her room," Alice said lightly. Too lightly.

"Is… she okay?" Tom asked.

"Oh yes, she's fine," Alice said in a tone that he recognised. Saffy wasn't fine, at all.

"Should I go and see her?"

"I'd give it a few minutes, if you know what's good for you," Ian said, jovially. Tom glanced at Alice, and she nodded. "Quite highly strung that one, isn't she?"

He seemed awkward, shifting his weight in his seat. Ewelina looked down at the table, still smiling. Alice was seething. Tom thought better of asking if she'd set aside a plate for him, but Alice must have read his mind.

"Are you hungry?" Alice asked. "I have food for you."

"I am but I can sort that in a minute." She smiled at him, grateful. "So, what's the news with you two?" Tom asked, crossing the kitchen to the dining table.

"Well, funny you should ask—"

"Dad's getting married!" Alice said, smiling broadly. "To Ewelina."

Ian burst out laughing. "Well, I'd certainly hope so." He put an arm around his betrothed, drawing her to him. She smiled bashfully, looking up at Tom and raising her right hand to show him the engagement ring. Continental European tradition is to wear the ring on that hand, opposite to what is commonplace in the UK.

"That's… a stunning ring," Tom said. "Quite large."

"Expensive, I'll bet," Alice said.

"She's worth it," Ian said, taking Ewelina's hand and kissing it. Tom thought Alice was likely to vomit as he saw her cringe in the corner of his eye. Everyone else missed it, fortunately.

"When's the big day?" he asked.

"Oh, we haven't set a date yet," Ian said.

"But it will be soon," Ewelina said, "and we will be married on the beach in St. Kitts."

"Very nice," Tom said. "St. Kitts is beautiful."

"It will be," Ian said.

"Wait for it," Alice mumbled, heard only by Tom, or ignored by the others.

"We were just telling Alice," Ian said, "we'll have the ceremony over there but make sure we come back to the UK for a party that you and everyone else who can't make it will be invited to."

"And… there it is…" Alice whispered.

Tom understood. "Right, a party sounds great. I'll look forward to it."

"Yes, I hope you'll understand, Tom, but we're not planning on inviting children to the ceremony." Tom pursed his lips, glancing at Alice but quickly away again as she continued her enthusiastic clearing away. "It's just that we'll be filming the event and children… running around—"

"Shrieking and making noises…" Ewelina said, shaking her head, "will ruin the occasion for us."

"Ah…" Tom said.

"I mean, you and Alice are obviously welcome to come over," Ian said, looking from Tom to his daughter and back again.

"Hmm… busy," Alice said loudly. Tom cleared his throat.

"Well, we'll have to see," he said.

"Definitely busy," Alice replied, wide eyed and tilting her head. "Besides, Saffy would hate to miss out. And being there without her would… what's the word children use, Ewelina? Suck. Yes, that's it. It would really, really suck—"

"Yes, well..." Ian said, grimacing and looking at Tom and silently pleading for help. Tom almost imperceptibly shrugged to imply there was little he could do. Ian's shoulders sagged.

"Oh... and do tell Tom about the pearls of wisdom regarding Saffy," Alice said pointedly to Ewelina who avoided her gaze with such confidence that it appeared she hadn't registered the naked sarcasm Alice's words were laced with. It was possible something had been lost when crossing the language barrier, but the accompanying expression surely wasn't. Ewelina looked at Tom sympathetically.

"Your daughter... I don't mean to speak out of turn but she does appear to suffer with attention deficit disorder. She is quite a lovely girl but in my experience, my professional experience, she does show all of the hallmarks—"

"Professional experience?" Alice asked. "I thought you worked in fashion."

"It is true, I do make-up and hair styling for modelling shoots... in many places, all over Croatia, but I am also fully trained in a new discipline."

Alice's father nodded fervently. "Ewelina is a certified therapist now."

"Certifiable, definitely," Alice said. Tom gave her his sincere *that's not helping look* but Alice ignored him.

"Alice, darling," Ian said, "Ewelina has been

working very hard for her qualification. You shouldn't belittle it."

Alice took a breath and nodded. "Okay, I'm sorry. I didn't mean to be dismissive. What therapy are you certified in?"

"Crystal healing and aromatherapy," she said triumphantly.

Alice dropped her hands to her side and glared at Tom. "Crystal—" Walking towards the hall shaking her head, she picked up the dog lead from the worktop and spoke over her shoulder as she left the room. "I'm taking the dog out. You lot can clear up."

Tom grimaced and he saw Ian bite his bottom lip.

"She left quickly," Ewelina said. "I know she's your daughter, Ian but that's very rude."

Ian patted her hand but didn't comment. He looked at Tom. "Would… er… you like a hand clearing up?"

"No, don't worry. I can take care of it."

Ian checked his watch. "Look at the time. We need to get away anyway. I promised Ewelina we'll go for a walk along the seafront, show her a traditional English seaside promenade."

They both stood up, Ewelina excusing herself to go to the bathroom. Ian came to stand alongside Tom.

"Congratulations on the engagement," Tom said, shaking his hand.

"Thank you, Tom. I don't think Alice is enamoured with the idea, I must say."

"She'll come around, don't worry."

"You think so?" he asked hopefully. Tom raised his eyebrows, unsure of what to say. "I thought so too but it's kind of you to say." He looked around, hesitant. "About Ewelina… she doesn't mean to offend. Where she's from, the culture is very much about speaking your mind. It's something we could maybe learn from in this country."

"I don't think you'll want Alice to speak her mind on this one, Ian. I really don't."

Ian screwed his nose up and bobbed his head. "Yes, you're not wrong."

"It'll blow over," Tom said. Ian smiled. "In a year or two."

Both men laughed just as Ewelina entered the room. She glanced between them, clearly wondering if they were laughing at something she would disapprove of. Satisfied it wasn't related to her, she looked for her handbag and gathered it, then held her hands wide towards Ian.

"Oh yes, your coat. One moment," Ian said, hurrying into the hall to get her coat from the cupboard beneath the stairs. He returned moments later and she allowed him to help her put it on. She smiled at Tom, leaned in and kissed both his cheeks.

"Thank you for dinner," she said. "We will see each other again soon?"

"Of course," Tom said. Ewelina led the way and Ian shook hands with Tom again and followed her. Tom escorted them out and waited until they'd got to their car before closing the door. Taking a deep breath, he was startled to find Saffy sitting at the top of the stairs watching him.

He climbed the stairs and she shifted across to make room for him to sit down alongside her.

"Hello, munchkin."

"What's wrong with me?" she asked.

Leaning away from her, he looked back with a questioning look. "Who says there's anything wrong with you?"

Saffy sniffed, resting her chin on her hand glumly. "She did," Saffy said, pointing at the now closed front door. "Ewelina. She says I have *attention dedicated disorder* or something like that."

Tom sat upright, putting an arm around her and she leaned into him, resting her head on his body. "Do you care what she thinks?"

"Yes. If there's something wrong with me."

"Do you think there's something wrong with you?"

"I didn't before, but now I'm not sure."

Tom exhaled through pursed lips.

"That's your pony noise. That's what you do when you're thinking about what to say, but you haven't worked it out yet."

"Is that right?" Tom asked. "You know, you're a lot smarter than you look."

"Nah, it's what Mum told me."

"Ah… I probably need to up my game a bit then."

"Yes. You're quite obvious."

Tom laughed. "Is that right?" He turned his body so he could look into her eyes. "Now listen to me. What other people think about us isn't important. It's what we think of ourselves that is. Do you understand?"

"Yes."

"And if an adult says something, it doesn't mean that it's true," Tom said. "Oftentimes, adults say things that aren't true—"

"So Ewelina was lying?"

Tom's brow creased. "Not necessarily, no." Saffy fixed him with a puzzled look. "Sometimes adults think and say things without considering other people's feelings, and sometimes they say things they are not qualified to say but will say them as if they are fact. When in reality, they are only opinions. Do you see?"

"And everyone has opinions, right?" Saffy asked.

"That's right. Everyone has an opinion, and

they are entitled to have them, even if they are not correct."

Saffy was thoughtful. "So… I can disagree with them if I want to?"

"Yes," Tom said. "Of course, you can. That's your right too. All I would say is that you consider the opinion, perhaps research it for accuracy before challenging or disagreeing with it first. That way, you can have a reasonable debate on the subject and it shouldn't lead to conflict."

"That makes sense," she said, smiling.

"Good."

"So Ewelina said that I have that thing, but it's not true?"

"Or possibly, you might say inaccurate, depending on what the facts are."

"Do I have it, what she said?"

"Not as far as I know," Tom said, looking into her eyes. "I'm not qualified to assess that and neither is she, but I can tell you what I see."

"What can you see?"

Tom took her hands in his. They were still so small, even though she was growing at a rate he found frightening. "I see a bright, intelligent, charming young lady… and no matter what, you are exactly who and what I expect to see. You're honest, mostly," he said, smiling, and she withdrew a hand and bashed him on the arm, "and you are yourself. I wouldn't change you for the world." He leaned forward and kissed the top of her head. Saffy was beaming. "And I don't care what Ewelina has to say about it."

"Mum's angry, isn't she?"

Tom nodded. "That's an understatement."

"Mum calls her the wicked witch of the east."

Tom barely managed to stop himself laughing. "Does she?"

"Yes, she says someone should drop a house on her."

Tom laughed. Saffy joined him and they hugged. The front door opened and Russell bounded through first and, seeing them sitting at the top of the stairs, raced up to them, launching himself into Saffy's arms, his tail twitching furiously, lead dangling down behind him. Alice came next. She glanced up and smiled.

"Have they already left for home… or the hotel, whatever?"

"Yes, almost straight away."

"Ah, shame," Alice said. Saffy laughed and Alice looked wounded as she took her coat off. "I meant it. I would have liked to say goodbye. Anyway, young lady, it's way past your bedtime—"

"That's just your opinion, Mummy. It doesn't mean it's true."

Alice stopped, looking up at her daughter. "Is that so, young Sapphire? Unfortunately for you, I make the rules around here and I want you to go and clean your teeth, get into bed and I'll be up to tuck you in in a few minutes."

Tom leaned into Saffy, lowering his voice. "Remind me to talk to you about when to pick your battles and which ones are worth fighting." He winked at her, and Saffy sighed.

"Okay," she said, gently easing the dog away from her and getting to her feet. She gave Tom another hug. "I love you," she said.

"I love you too, munchkin."

Saffy hurried off, no doubt feeling Alice's watchful eye on her back. Tom descended the stairs, Alice training her eyes on him.

"Do I have you to thank for yet another outburst of indignant defiance?"

He sniffed. "Yeah, that'd be me." He looped his hand around her waist and pulled her to him. She put her arms around his neck, and he kissed her. "But she no longer hates herself, so that's a positive."

"Definitely a positive," Alice said. "Can you believe what Ewelina said? I mean… I'll take it from a professional but I'm not taking it from someone who practises Indian Head Massage."

"Aromatherapy," Tom said, "and crystal healing."

"Whatever… it's woo-woo," Alice replied, "and crystal healing? Don't get me started on that."

Tom inclined his head. "The NHS spend money on new-age stuff all the time."

"Yes, acupuncture, reflexology and practices like that. It's holistic, not new age, which I think is beyond nonsense. I've never once seen my colleagues issue a prescription for three amethysts under your pillow and call me in the morning. Have you?"

"Fair point."

The bathroom light clicked off signalling Saffy had cleaned her teeth and was making her way through to her bedroom. Russell came back downstairs to have his lead removed and promptly ran back up, disappearing onto the landing, no doubt going to sleep on Saffy's bed much as he usually did.

"Come on, let's go into the kitchen," Alice said. "If she hears us talking she'll only see it as an invitation to join us."

"I'm so sorry I was late back."

"Oh, don't worry," she said, dismissing his apology. "How is work anyway?"

"Early days and it's all a bit confusing I must say," Tom said as they walked into the kitchen. "Don't worry about all this, he said, waving a hand at the uncleared table and counters. "I'll sort it."

"What's the issue?"

He leaned against the counter, folding his arms across his chest. "Well, first off we still haven't identified the victim. We have an idea of who we think it is but no one has reported him missing. He was due to leave the country and fly to Europe for a holiday, but we believe he was flying onto Panama. No one else knew that. Not even his girlfriend."

Alice frowned. "Sounds like he was up to no good, to me."

"Yes, but what was he doing and how was he paying for it? He wasn't working recently as far as we know, and before that he was doing agency work, minimum wage mostly."

"Secret visits to South America?" Alice asked. Tom nodded. "Sounds like he was smuggling."

"What's that?"

"Smuggling. You know, drug mules," Alice said. "I was watching that documentary on it a couple of weeks back; you remember that night when you were late home."

"I'm often late home."

"Yes, that's true but it was about those girls who flew out to… Peru, I think it was. They got caught trying to fly out of Lima with cocaine on a flight to Spain. They were convicted and spent three years in prison before they were transferred home. You must remember? One was from Scotland and the other, Ireland."

"Oh yeah, I do now you mention it."

Alice shrugged. "Decent money… if you get away with it."

"And years of pain if you don't," Tom said.

They both looked up, hearing footsteps on the creaky floorboards of the landing.

"I'd better go and see to her," Alice said.

"Don't be too hard on her."

"I won't. I'll stay with her for a bit, make sure she's okay after what Ewe—"

"The wicked witch of the east said to her?" Tom asked.

Alice flushed. "I should have kept that one to myself, shouldn't I?"

"Probably," Tom said, nodding sagely. Alice left and he set about clearing away the aftermath of dinner, Alice's suggestion fomenting in his mind. He couldn't help but think she might be right.

CHAPTER NINETEEN

David poured another glass of red wine, passing it across to Tamara, who accepted it with a warm smile. The Taylor family had provided their DNA samples which were dispatched to the lab before the family left for a hotel Eric checked them into. Tomorrow, they should have some answers to some of the questions they'd been struggling with. They'd collectively made the decision not to go public until they had their victim identified, if he did indeed turn out to be Louis. If not, their approach would be two-fold; approach the public to try and put a name to their victim and, secondly, to find Louis.

"Thank you for dinner," Tamara said to her partner, David. "It was just what I needed."

"You're welcome, although you should probably thank Otem, it was his recipe after all."

"You did well."

He grimaced. "I missed a few steps."

"I couldn't tell."

"And I missed some of the ingredients. I just hid them in the back of the fridge."

Tamara laughed. "I don't mind."

"You say that now but wait until you find some mouldy pomegranate seeds tucked behind your sauces."

The doorbell sounded, interrupting their laughter. "I'll go," Tamara said, levering herself up but David gently pushed her back into the sofa.

"I've got it."

She didn't argue as he set his glass of wine down on the coffee table, pushing off and hurrying into the hall. Instead, Tamara reached for the television remote control, tucking her legs up beneath her on the sofa and increasing the volume as she switched channel to catch the news headlines at the top of the hour.

"It's someone to see you love," David said, coming back into the room. Tamara checked the time on the television. It was ten o'clock. She looked up at David, escorting DCS Wells into the living room. Tamara was surprised, turning off the television and getting to her feet. Dressed in sweatpants, a baggy jumper and winter socks, she felt awkward.

"Sir…"

"Peter is fine when we're outside of work, you know that, Tamara," Wells said, smiling.

"He said you were friends," David said, unsure of whether he'd done the right thing letting him inside having seen Tamara's reaction.

"It's fine, David."

He seemed unconvinced but Tamara smiled warmly, adjusting her jumper as if that would make a difference.

"Honestly, Peter and I used to work together when I was based in Norwich."

"Oh, I see," David said, looking between them. Conversation faltered and Peter Wells pursed his lips, looking between David and Tamara. "I'll… um… give you two a minute," he said, crossing the short distance between himself and Tamara, picking up his glass of wine and leaving the room.

"Thanks, David," Tamara said. He waved a hand over his shoulder and walked through into the kitchen. She smiled at Wells. "Can I… get you a drink. A glass of wine perhaps?"

"No, thank you, Tamara." Wells craned his neck to check that David had left them, and Tamara followed his line of sight but there was no sign of him. "New man?"

She rocked her head from side to side. "Newish, yes."

"I saw Richard the other day," Wells said, referring to Tamara's ex-fiancé who she left shortly before they were due to be married.

"Oh, really? I didn't realise you knew each other."

"He's an occasional visitor to our lodge."

"Right," Tamara said.

"He's well."

"Good," Tamara said, although she wasn't particularly interested. That was a chapter in her life that was closed. She didn't feel the need to revisit it. "What are you doing here, Peter?"

"Of course, yes. Straight to business." Wells cleared his throat. "I couldn't say as much as I wanted to earlier. Your Detective Chief Superintendent Cole is... a character."

"He is that. He's new and has been tough to get to know and harder still to get onside."

Wells smiled. "Stick with it. He'll be fine once he sees what you're capable of."

Tamara hoped she'd get the time, but she didn't say so.

"Are you happy out here in the sticks, Tamara?" Wells asked. Tamara shrugged. She was very happy, but a man like Wells wouldn't understand. He was a career officer, and every move he made was calculated to benefit that career. Not that he would ever openly say so. "I'm still surprised that you left Norwich. We could have used someone like you in Major Crimes."

"Of course you could," Tamara said, offering him a seat before retaking her own and picking up her glass of wine. "Who wouldn't?" She asked with the hint of a mischievous smile.

"It's not too late, you know? You could come back with me."

Tamara snorted a laugh, almost choking on her wine.

"What's so funny?"

"Like anything is that easy when you're dealing with constabulary admin. I'd probably end up transferred to Greater Manchester or something. By mistake."

"There is that, yes." Wells smiled. "But things can be expedited."

Tamara laughed. "It's very kind of you to suggest it—"

"I'm offering, not suggesting."

"Well, in that case it is very kind of you to offer, but I'm happy where I am."

"Are you?" Wells asked. "I mean, are you really?"

"Ask me again if I don't get this case solved."

"Yes, it sounds a bit tricky. I'm sure you'll get to the bottom of it."

Tamara nursed her glass of wine, holding the

stem and gently turning it in her hand. "It might help if you shared your interest in Alex Gillie."

"Would it now?"

"It might," she said, smiling.

"I told you earlier, Alex is a—"

"Peripheral figure… yes, I remember." She sipped from her glass. "Here's the thing though…"

Wells sat forward in his seat, resting his elbows on his knees, smiling. "Tell me, what is the thing?"

"You knew, before I did, who my DI was speaking to today." She sat back, lifting her legs onto the sofa once more and adopted a relaxed pose. Wells made to speak, but Tamara held up her hand and he fell silent. "Which is a result of two possibilities. One, Alex Gillie is working for or with you." Wells fixed her with an unreadable stare. "Or two, you have a team watching the house."

Wells raised a solitary eyebrow, silently asking if it was his turn to speak. Tamara gave him an open-handed gesture and he smiled.

"One of those things may very well be true, or something similar," he said. Tamara rolled her eyes at his obtuse reply. "And if you wanted to come to work with me at Major Crimes, then I might be able to fill you in."

"We both know that wouldn't happen overnight… and I need to know now if it is related to the disappearance of Louis Taylor."

"Who's… Louis Taylor?" Wells asked.

"Now that," Tamara lifted her glass and saluted him with it, "is a question on everyone's lips tonight. What's your interest in him?"

Wells laughed. "I don't know him. Did I always have such little credibility with the team, or is it just with you?"

"Just with me," Tamara said. "I think it stems from the Christmas party when you hit on me over a tray of vol-au-vents."

"Ah… I thought you might have forgotten about that."

"Forgiven, yes… but it's never forgotten, Peter." She tapped the side of her head with two fingers. "You never know when you might need to call in a favour."

"You wouldn't," he said, smiling nervously. "I mean… you wouldn't, would you?"

She chuckled. "No, of course not. I'm just winding you up. Do you still want me to come to work in Major Crimes?"

"Yes, absolutely."

"That's lovely, but the answer is still no."

He laughed. "Well, when you change your mind, give me a call." He stood up, Tamara moving to do likewise. "No need. I can see myself out." He made his way to the door. "Oh, and keep your team away from Alex Gillie, and his wife Annabelle, while you're at it."

"Now you're moving the goalposts," she said.

He stopped at the doorway, turning back to look at her with a stern expression. "It's my game. I can change the rules any time I choose to."

With that, he left. Tamara listened and heard the front door open and then close as DCS Wells left the house. David appeared at the doorway into the kitchen, glass of wine in hand.

"What was all that about? Not that I was listening."

Tamara frowned, patting the sofa next to her and encouraging him to sit down. He did so.

"I think that was a friendly reminder to stay out of his way."

"Oh… are you inclined to do so?" David asked.

"If he wants me to keep away from someone who may or may not be relevant to my case, then it's definitely someone I need to look into further."

"Won't that get you into trouble? Might it be better to do as he asks… until you know for sure?"

"Nah, where's the fun in that?" Tamara asked, touching her glass against his. David shook his head. "Cheers."

CHAPTER TWENTY

PC DAVID MARSHALL walked into the ops room, his eyes searching the room and upon spotting Tom, he hurried over to him. Tom was deep in conversation with Cassie and the constable loitered within Tom's eyeline to get his attention. Tom nodded to him.

"Good morning, sir. I'm sorry to interrupt, but I heard in the briefing yesterday that you'd be interested in anything odd going on around a property on Church Street?"

"Yes, the annexe to the rear, but it's the tenant we're focussed on. Why do you ask?"

"I'm just coming off night shift," Marshall said. "We had a call out there a few hours ago. The homeowner... Gary—"

"Yes, I know him. He's the landlord."

"Yes, well... he called in an attempted burglary."

"Of his home or the annexe?"

"The annexe. He disturbed the person trying to break in and scared them off. His wife called us. We were on the scene within minutes but didn't see anyone."

"Did they get into the house?"

Marshall shook his head. "We didn't find any signs of forced entry. It seems like the owner was on to them pretty quick."

Tom's brow creased as he thought hard. "What time was this?"

"The call to us was logged just before half-past three."

"Gary was up late."

Marshall shrugged. "Happens a lot when you get older. My old man tells me he's up three times a night these days."

"All that to look forward to then," Tom said. PC Marshall laughed. "Did they give you a description?"

"Generic. Male, he thinks. Dressed in a hoodie and dark clothing. Your stereotypical cat burglar." Marshall raised his eyebrows. "I'd have thought he was imagining it but for the car."

"The car?"

"Yeah, he was specific about that. The witness ran out into his back garden, he saw someone running down the street and they got into a white car. A hatchback, he reckons, but he didn't get the plate."

"Make of car?"

"No idea. He wasn't wearing his glasses, you see. The car sped off with no lights, only turning them on at the end of the street."

"All right, thanks, Sheriff," Tom said, referring to the constable by the nickname everyone in the station used. Marshall left. Cassie looked up at Tom from her desk.

"White hatchback? Wasn't it a white car that the kids saw out at the quarry?"

Tom nodded. "Speaking of cars, did you do that search on the DVLA's database?"

"I did," Cassie said, moving some things about on her desk and producing her notes. "Annabelle Cook has no cars registered in her name so, clearly, she either uses cars belonging to her husband or registered as company vehicles. If they're company cars, then they'll be registered to the business." Using the tip of her pen, she tapped at the top of her handwritten notes. "Alex Gillie has a half dozen vehicles registered to his private limited company, which Annabelle Cook is also a director of."

"Any of those vehicles happen to be a dark-coloured SUV?"

"Funny you should ask," Cassie said. "Yes,

there is a blue BMW X6. It was registered to them from new last year. There are also two other businesses that Alex Gillie is listed as a director of, but I haven't run them through the database yet. Do you want me to?"

"Hold that for now. Annabelle could be the visitor that Louis's landlord has seen. What about Melanie?"

"She has one car registered to her and it's a red Ford Focus."

"That's not very interesting."

Tom's mobile rang and he glanced at the screen. It's the lab," he told Cassie as he answered. Cassie beckoned both Eric and Danny across. Whatever the results of the DNA testing were, it was going to impact their investigation. Tom listened, asked a few questions, and then thanked the lab technician for the call, confirming the hard copy of the results would be emailed across. Hanging up, he scanned the expectant faces, all waiting to hear. "Well, well, well," he said glumly.

TOM THANKED the hotelier for escorting him through the building and out into the small courtyard garden at the rear. Surrounded by a brick and flint wall encompassing them on all sides with only a gated access to the track running parallel to the main road out front, Tom found Adela, Louis's mother, sitting alone at a small table beneath an overhanging beech tree. Despite the walled courtyard being protected from the harshest extremes of the coastal breeze, the wind did still rustle through the shrivelled brown leaves clinging to their branches in defiance of the season. Marcescence, no doubt aided by the tree growing in the lee of the four-storey building, sheltered from the prevailing wind.

She looked up and smiled at Tom as he came to join her.

"May I sit down?" he asked.

She nodded. "Hello, Detective Inspector."

"Tom, please," he said, smiling. She returned his smile and nodded.

"Tom," she said politely. "I'm terribly sorry that I was so uncommunicative yesterday, but it was a lot to process."

"No apology is necessary, I assure you. Forgive me for coming to see you so early, but I thought you would rather hear from me directly instead of over the telephone."

"Thank you," she said, lifting her coffee cup to her lips. It was cold today, much colder than it had been of late and it appeared that winter was finally here. Despite this, Adela was still sitting outside, albeit wrapped in the thick outdoor coat and no doubt multiple layers beneath. She must have seen

Tom shiver, feeling the cold and she smiled as she put the cup down on its saucer. "You will have to forgive me for sitting outside. You must think me mad."

"No, not at all."

"I have been awake for much of the night," she said, removing her sunglasses and setting them down on the table. She looked drained, dark patches surrounded her eyes which themselves appeared sunken and hollow. "Do you have children, Tom?"

"I do," he said. "A little girl. She's..." he was about to explain Saffy's adoption but decided against it. She was his daughter. There was nothing else to say. "She's delightful."

"How old is she?"

"Nine," Tom said. "Going on eighteen."

Adela smiled warmly. "That is a good age. Worship her, Tom. Don't let anyone tell you any different because one day... and you never know when that might be, it could all end. It is... almost overwhelming to have to comprehend the death of your own child, let alone the way it occurs."

"It's not Louis," Tom said. There was barely a flicker of a reaction from her. She stared at him; blank faced.

"Please can you say that again?"

"The DNA comparison tests confirm that the human remains we have found are not those of your son, Mrs Taylor. There are no familial markers when compared with the samples you all provided to us yesterday."

He saw her chest heave beneath the heavy coat and her shoulders dropped. Lowering her head, she raised both hands to her face, closed her eyes and almost silently began to cry. Tom heard movement behind him, and the other members of the family came out into the courtyard, led by Isaac and then Louis's siblings, Noah and Abigail.

"It's not him," Adela said, and they were all relieved. Noah smiled and embraced his sister, whereas Isaac came past Tom to place a supportive hand on Adela's shoulder. She smiled up at him. "It's not Louis."

Isaac looked at Tom. "Then where is he? Where is Louis?"

"I'm going to do my best to find out, I can assure you."

Tom parked his car in the shared drive in front of Louis's home. Cassie was already there, waiting for him. Gary Bowers was standing with her and by the look on her face, he'd been quite chatty. Cassie shot Tom an *it's about time you got here* look, which made him smile, although he internalised most of the reaction.

"Good morning, Mr Bowers," Tom said. "I understand you had a late-night visitor?"

"We did. I saw him off though, quick smart. It's coming to something when people are trying to rob you in your sleep."

"It was the annexe they were trying to get into, right?"

He nodded. "I think I got to them before they could break in."

"Mr Bowers has given us his spare key," Cassie said, holding it aloft, "but he wanted to make sure you knew… how courageous he was."

"Well, it's not that so much—"

"You were incredibly brave, Mr Bowers," Cassie said sternly. "A model citizen. Have you ever considered becoming a police community support officer?"

Gary Bowers softened his defensive posture, smiling at the compliment.

"We always need people like you," Cassie said. The man swelled with pride. Tom caught Cassie's eye with an expression that suggested she was laying it on a little thick and she broke the eye contact. "Anyway, thank you for your help, Mr Bowers. We'll make sure the key comes back to you after we lock up."

Bowers looked between them, seemingly disappointed that he was no longer needed but he relented, nodded and headed back into his garden towards his house.

"That was uncalled for," Tom said.

"Probably, but you weren't here for the first three iterations of how he was woken during the night, headed to the bathroom and then went full Delta Force down the garden path in his pyjamas."

Tom smiled. "Okay, fair enough. You've had a look around outside?" He asked as he donned a pair of nitrile gloves. Cassie did the same.

"Yes, Marshall was right. There's no sign of forced entry. The old boy must have been right. He scared them off."

"Or he saw him leaving rather than trying to gain entry."

Cassie's curiosity was piqued. "Then whoever it was must have had a key or been proficient at picking locks?"

"Picking locks isn't all that difficult once you know how," Tom said.

"I see I still have a lot to learn about your past, Boss."

Tom smiled. "However, I agree," he said, taking the front door key from her and inserting it in the lock, "it's far more likely that they used a key, if I'm right."

The door opened and a familiar sight greeted Tom as they entered, careful not to disturb anything and treating it like a crime scene. Tom scanned the interior hallway, seeing nothing unusual. Everything looked much as it had done when he was last here. The kitchen appeared untouched. There was an odd smell lingering in the air but that was likely caused by food going bad or the waste bin needing to be emptied. Aside from the stale air, Tom found the living room the same way.

"Do you know if they were carrying anything when they ran away from the house?" Tom asked.

Cassie thought hard. "No one said anything, as far as I can remember. We can always ask Mr Bowers… as long as we don't need to be anywhere until later this afternoon."

Tom laughed, resuming their search. The bedroom was unchanged, as was the bathroom. Tom was left with the realisation that their initial assumption must have been correct. Whoever had been here had been rumbled in their attempt to gain entry, abandoning it and leaving empty handed. He sighed, deflated.

"What do you want to do?" Cassie asked.

"I think we…" Tom stopped where he was, looking back into the living room.

"What is it?"

He made his way along the hall and stepped into the living room, staring at the floor. Cassie came to stand alongside. "Have we missed something?"

"The bag," Tom said, pointing at the sofa.

"What bag?"

"Exactly. It's not here."

Cassie shot him a puzzled look as Tom turned back into the hall and had a more thorough look around. The kitchen was the same, the bedroom and bathroom apparently untouched. Standing in the hall, Tom spotted some grey powder, scattered centrally on the carpet in the hall. Moving closer, he dropped to his haunches and found some wispy strands of a compacted material. It looked like black and grey candy floss, but he doubted it was spun sugar. It was mineral wool or glass fibre loft insulation. His eyes drifted to the ceiling and a small loft hatch above him, halfway along the narrow corridor. Paying it close attention, he noticed that the hatch cover was slightly askew, and not sitting flush to the rebate holding it in place. It hadn't been put back properly. He pointed to it silently. Cassie backed up, staring at the hatch, both of them listening intently.

Tom made his way into the living room, picked up a dining chair from the table in the corner and brought it back, all the time moving as quietly as he could. Placing the chair beneath the hatch, Tom put one foot on it and Cassie reached out, gripping him by the forearm. She whispered, "Are you sure about this?"

He nodded and she backed off. Tom stood on

the chair and gently pushed the hatch cover up and slid it away into the depths of the loft space. Using the torch function on his mobile, Tom stood up, making himself just tall enough to poke his head through the hatch. Unable to see as well as he liked, he used the back of the chair to climb up, levering himself up into the loft with his upper body strength. Cassie braced the chair for him, to stop it from toppling over.

"Be careful," Cassie said.

Tom angled his mobile around the loft, illuminating the dusty, stuffy space. All he could see were vast cobwebs and rolls of unfurled glass fibre insulation laid between the ceiling joists. "There's nothing up here," he said, "aside from the water tank and a lot of spiders."

"I hate spiders," Cassie said.

Tom was about to come back down when he hesitated, turning the light onto one corner where he could see the insulation had been disturbed, as if it'd been pulled out from its place, pushed aside and not put back. Ducking his head back down into the hall, he pointed in the direction he'd been looking. "Cassie, can you go through into the living room there and see if there's any wiring or a water leak or something in that far corner?"

'Yeah, sure," Cassie said, making her way through. "No, nothing," she called. "What are you expecting me to see?"

"I'm wondering what is going on over there. Some of the insulation has been pulled up and I can't fathom why."

"Does it matter?" Cassie asked, coming back to stand beneath Tom.

"It does if someone had something hidden up here."

"Hidden? Such as what?"

"I don't know, but someone has been up here rooting around for something."

"Who?"

Tom lowered himself back down onto the chair before reaching up to put the hatch back in place and got down from the chair. He looked at Cassie, inclining his head. "I'd wager only one person knows what was here and where to find it."

"Louis?" Cassie asked.

"Or someone he told."

"You mentioned a bag?" Cassie asked.

"Yes, when I was here the other day there was a backpack here. It had clothes and toiletries inside." He looked around. "It's not here now."

They found Gary Bowers waiting for them as they left the annexe. Cassie locked up and handed the key back.

"This person you saw leaving the property, Mr Bowers," Tom asked. "Were they alone?"

"I think so," he said. "I didn't see anyone else."

"And were they carrying anything?"

"Like what?"

"Anything at all," Tom said, not wishing to plant thoughts in his mind.

"No, I don't think so, but it was dark, and I didn't have any glasses on."

"And the car that sped away, did you see this individual get into it?"

"I did, yes."

"Which side? The passenger side or were they driving?"

"Oh..." Bowers said, unsure. "You know, come to think of it, I didn't actually see him get into the car, but he must have."

"One more thing, have you been into the property in the last couple of days or removed anything from it?"

"No, not at all. Why would I do that?"

His response was so genuine that Tom believed him. Cassie did too, by the look on her face. Tom thanked him and they got into their car. Cassie looked across at Tom.

"The car might not be related to it."

"I know," Tom said, disappointed.

CHAPTER TWENTY-ONE

THE TEAM ASSEMBLED for the mid-morning briefing in the ops room. Tamara took the lead with Tom sitting off to her left.

"Right, quick recap. The DNA comparison tests tell us that our victim isn't in fact Louis Taylor, which leaves us with a fresh line of enquiry; where is Louis and, also, is he a suspect in the death of the as yet unidentified human remains. The answer to that will depend on who's asking. Within the team we must keep an open mind and, to that end, yes, he has to be a suspect. Anyone from outside the team asks then we have no comment at this time. Clear?"

A general murmur of agreement sounded from the group.

"Tom, the alleged break-in attempt at Louis's house next, please."

Tom smiled. "I believe that Gary Bowers, Louis's landlord, is credible in seeing someone around the annexe at the back of his house. Cassie and I can back up what uniform thought when they attended in the early hours, the property shows no sign of a forced entry. That leaves us with two possibilities, that the person or persons unknown were disturbed before they could get inside or that the person had a key and possibly had already been in before their presence was noted."

"Is this likely to be Louis himself?" Eric asked, raising a hand.

"That's possible, Eric. It's equally possible someone else has his key and was coming to the property at his behest or trying to find something he has in his possession. I noted a backpack missing from the property that was there when I first went in the other day. Let's not jump to conclusions, but someone has been in there. The landlord swears blind it wasn't him and no one else has a key. My cursory inspection of the bag and it was just that, very brief, is that it contained travel clothing. Nothing much, just the essentials to travel light."

"As if he was going away?" Tamara asked.

"That's it. I assumed it was for his holiday, the

one he never made it to the airport for, but who knows?"

"If it is Louis," Tamara said, "then he's definitely hiding out. To return to his home in the middle of the night for a few clothes is risky—"

"I think there's more to it than that," Tom said. "I think whoever went inside climbed up into the loft to retrieve something. It's likely that is what they were after and the clothing bag was perhaps an additional item."

"Whatever it was must have been important to them."

"Important enough to hide in the loft space and to risk being caught returning for it."

"Are we assuming then," Cassie asked, "that they did it during the night to avoid our attention… or someone else's?"

Tom spread his hands wide. "Someone has disposed of our victim and although we don't have a cause of death, we can presume they met their end by unnatural means, until we're told otherwise. Where are the search team with finding the rest of the body?"

Cassie shrugged. "Today is the last day. If they don't turn anything up then the search will be called off."

Tom was annoyed. He looked at Tamara who shook her head. "Not my call."

"Cole?" Tom asked and Tamara nodded.

"You can't blame him. It's been two days," Tamara said. "If they were going to find the rest of him, then they should have by now. Manual search, repeated sonar passes... all found nothing. They may have dumped the rest of the body somewhere else entirely, just in case."

"The removal of the head and hands could only be to make identification harder," Tom said. "Therefore, it's likely the victim is known to us, either as a former criminal or someone who is wanted by us or listed as a missing person."

"Louis is missing..." Danny said, "sort of."

"But he was never reported as missing on the register here in the UK," Tom said.

"Although not everyone would have known that," Cassie countered. "In any event, it doesn't matter because it's not Louis. The family testing proved that."

"Right, we need to notify the Border Force to put Louis's name on a watch list. He was trying to leave the country a fortnight or so ago and he never made it. Maybe he had to pick something up from home in order to do so. A passport, cash... something."

Tamara frowned. "But he had ten days or more to do that before we were even involved. "If he's hiding from someone, then it wasn't us. There has to be someone in his circle who he's avoiding... possibly someone he's killed."

"What if whoever killed our victim is also after Louis?" Cassie asked. "I mean, from what we've heard about him, he doesn't sound like the murderous type. His bathroom is way too clean to have been used as a shambles anyway."

Tom nodded. "There has been time to clean it. Maybe we should send a forensics team around to see if the victim could have been dismembered at Louis's place?"

Tamara thought about it. "That will be hard to keep quiet if we do it."

"Where are we with going to the public?" Tom asked.

"We were waiting on the DNA testing. Now I'm waiting on Detective Chief Superintendent Cole to give me the green light. He wants to run it past Major Crimes, seeing as their case apparently takes precedence over ours."

"What's it to them what we do?" Cassie asked.

"Cole wants to ensure that such a high-profile murder case won't affect their activities. It's ridiculous, but it's where we are."

"The secrecy may help us," Tom said. "Louis doesn't know we're on to him… for anything. Not yet anyway. The moment we name him as a person of interest he'll be in the wind. And he's been pretty good at laying low thus far."

"Speaking of travel plans," Cassie said, looking up from her desk. "I've just had a look and there are a couple of interesting things about his flights out of the UK and on to Panama. Something we didn't notice regarding his booking; it was one way. Now, he could have got a great deal on that flight and thought he'd do the same from the other end when it came time to come home but, usually, I'd argue that one way implies you're not coming home."

Tamara and Tom exchanged a glance. Tom considered Alice's suggestion about drug smugglers employing couriers. They often chose random flights rather than having a mule book a return flight. Sometimes they would have bribed customs officers on particular shifts or locations and would arrange flights accordingly. "Perhaps it wasn't his call."

"Perhaps," Cassie said. She tapped a printout lying on her desk. She stood up and passed it to Tom. "Although, before we were just looking at Louis and that there," she said, pointing at the list in Tom's hand, "is the full passenger manifest the airline sent through for the flight to Madrid. Do you recognise anyone else who was due to be on that flight?"

Tom scanned the list of names. Tamara came to look over his shoulder, doing the same.

"There!" Tamara said, pointing at an entry. Tom frowned as he belatedly saw the name and realising why they hadn't picked it up before.

"That's someone we've been told to steer clear of."

Frustrated, Tom looked at her. "So, what do we do?"

"We need to get to them away from the house where we won't be seen."

Tom smiled. "Then it's a good job we know where we need to be."

THE SMALL GROUP were huddled in the tiny reception area exchanging words at the end of the session. Tom and Cassie waited patiently in the car, observing them from a distance. The small industrial park had a no through road, with farmland to one side and the rear with the local high school grounds on the other. Should anyone pay them any attention, it would be obvious they shouldn't be there. However, no one seemed perturbed by the nondescript car parked at the side of the road to one side of the parking area. They watched as the group came out, waving goodbye to one another and making for their cars.

They watched as Nicholas Craft got into his car, Marcus Bell into his SUV and their quarry crossed to the far side of the car park further away from the entrance than the others. This worked in Tom's favour because they departed before Tom and

Cassie needed to make their presence known. This was intended to be a discreet conversation after all.

"Here we go," Tom said and with that cue, Cassie and Tom got out of the car and walked casually across the car park. Approaching the car from the rear, Tom approached the driver's side while Cassie went to the nearside. The lone occupant had put their gym bag on the passenger seat and was adjusting their seatbelt readying to leave. Tom knocked on the window, startling the driver. The window was lowered, and a surprised face looked up at him.

"Good evening, Mrs Gillie," he said, sternly, "or do you only go by that name when you're travelling abroad?"

Annabelle Cook stared at him, her lips parting. She glanced across at Cassie, standing at the opposite door.

"I think we need to have a chat, don't you?" Tom said to her.

Annabelle, composing herself, nodded and glanced around. The car park was almost empty now. Only George Melior and his instructors were still present. All the other units, as well as the coast guard units behind them, were locked up for the night.

"Not here," she said, barely above a whisper.

"Follow us," Tom said, striding back to his car

and signalling for Cassie to join him. Reluctantly, she fell into step alongside him.

"What if she legs it?"

"Where's she going to go?"

Cassie, still unhappy but powerless to do anything about it, got into the car whilst keeping a watchful eye on Annabelle in hers. She needn't have worried. Annabelle started her engine and pulled out behind them as soon as they moved off. Instead of heading into town, Tom turned left and made the short drive from Hunstanton to Heacham, leading Annabelle to the large car park located between the caravan parks and the rear of the beach huts beyond the promenade. It was November. The caravans were all secured for the winter, as were the huts and even the holiday homes lining the promenade were largely unoccupied at this time of the year. The only people who would see them were the occasional dog walker or jogger out for an evening run.

They all got out of their cars, Annabelle searching the darkness encompassing the car park as if she'd driven into a trap.

"You can trust us. No one beyond my team knows we're here," Tom said, "or even that we are talking to you."

Annabelle's expression was dark, no, more than that; she was fearful.

"Yes… well, that's what you think," she said.

Tom heard the fear in her tone. When he met her the previous day, she'd been measured, presenting an image of herself she doubtless wanted Tom to see.

"What are you frightened of, Annabelle?" Tom asked.

She shook her head with a rueful laugh. "If you had any idea… at all, then you wouldn't need to ask." Looking around, her gaze lingered on the shadows at the far end of the car park. Her breathing quickened and she looked towards the sounds of the waves crashing against the nearby sea wall. "Can we take a walk?"

"If that would make you more comfortable," Tom said.

They crossed the access road, more of a track lined with compacted sand and soil, slipped between the brightly painted beach huts among the dunes and came upon the promenade. The tide was at its peak and despite the wind being stiff but not brutal, the waves were connecting with the sea wall and rebounding rather than cresting the concrete defences.

They stood side by side, looking out over The Wash. The cloud cover was thick and apart from hearing the water, all they could see were the whitecaps atop the breakers as they swept towards them. Annabelle folded her arms across her chest, drawing them tight around her body, feeling the chill of the night.

"Why were you travelling to Madrid?" Tom asked.

Annabelle was pensive, keeping her focus on the water in front of her.

"Annabelle?"

She broke her gaze from the landscape, lowering her eyes briefly before turning to Tom. "You've no idea how hard it is… to walk away from everything and everyone you know. To start again."

"You were leaving your husband?" Tom asked. She momentarily glanced sideways at him, nodding almost imperceptibly. "You were leaving with Louis?"

"Not in the way that you think, Detective Inspector."

"In what way am I thinking?"

She fixed him with a stare, taking a deep breath before exhaling in a controlled manner. "Louis is a wonderful human being. You shouldn't think any different, irrespective of what anyone else might say." She closed her eyes, gathering her thoughts. Tom allowed her the time, expectant of finally getting some answers to make sense of all this. "I was to fly to Madrid with Louis. He speaks Spanish, fluently… and he'd made arrangements for us there."

"What sort of arrangements?"

"Somewhere safe to stay… a place to hole up until onward travel could be arranged."

"Louis was scheduled to fly on to Panama," Cassie said. Annabelle confirmed it with a slight nod. "But you were not on the passenger manifest for that flight."

Annabelle pursed her lips but said nothing.

"Were you planning to follow on?" Tom asked.

Annabelle shook her head. "In all honesty, I don't know. Louis… was arranging things. He said it was better if I didn't know. That way, I wouldn't let it slip out to anyone in conversation or be tempted to tell someone."

"Tell them what?"

"That I was leaving."

"There are easier ways to end a marriage," Tom said, immediately regretting the words as soon as he'd uttered them. He knew nothing of her situation and any experienced police officer was well aware that for some women to leave their husband could cost them a lot. Potentially, even their life.

"You don't know Alex…" she said, her eyes gleaming in what little light was offered them from a partially obscured moon. "He's a man who is used to getting what he wants. It doesn't matter what the cost is, to him or to others. He is not a man to say no to." She fixed Tom with a steely gaze. "Alex is not a man you can just walk away from. Ever."

"Is he violent?" Tom asked, assuming he was.

"On occasion," she said. "He controls my life… my every move. Who I see, where I can go… even what I supposedly *choose* to wear." She laughed but it was without genuine humour. "I've been able to keep working, to a degree, and I even managed to get him to agree I could go to the gym to improve my health, so that we would have a better chance of…"

"A better chance of what?" Tom asked.

Annabelle blinked tears from her eyes. "A better chance of… me falling pregnant."

Tom allowed the silence between them to grow, Annabelle gathering herself as Tom thought through his approach. He hadn't expected this.

"Were you aware that Louis hadn't made the flight to Madrid?"

She shook her head. "Not until I arrived at the airport, no. I checked in… and I waited for Louis before heading through into security. I only had carry-on luggage… as Louis told me to do." She shrugged. "He never showed. I waited until the last possible moment and then… I had to come home."

"Did you tell anyone you were leaving?" Tom asked.

"No, absolutely not. As it was, I had to rush back. Alex was staying away in London that night and so he hadn't missed me. Luckily, I managed to resist the urge to send him a message announcing me leaving, otherwise... I don't know what would have happened."

"And he didn't suspect anything?"

She shook her head. "No, why would he? Everything was normal."

Tom desperately wanted to know if Annabelle was aware of the Major Crimes Unit's interest in her husband and his business interests but if he mentioned it he could blow their investigation apart, whatever that looked like.

"I asked you before, but knowing what I know now, I'd like to ask you again, Annabelle," Tom said. "What do you think has happened to Louis Taylor?"

She held Tom's gaze for a few moments, her expression unreadable. Then she shook her head. "I really don't know. I asked the others tonight at the class, and no one knows. No one has heard from him," she said. "Your interest is... alarming."

"Is there any way your husband could have found out about your plans, along with Louis's involvement?"

"I... don't think so."

"But if he did," Cassie asked, "what do you think he might do?"

"To me... or to Louis?" she asked.

"Both."

"To me... nothing," she said, putting her hand

against her belly. "Not while I am carrying his child."

"And Louis?"

She looked fearful once again. "I don't know how far he would go but I would be frightened. I don't know if Alex has boundaries at all. His moral compass… is skewed. But I don't think he will have harmed Louis."

"How can you be sure?"

She laughed. "Because he wouldn't be able to keep it from me. He would take too much pleasure in telling me about it. And he would tell me about it."

Tom let that sink in. "What do you know about your husband's affairs?" he asked.

"His business interests? Nothing at all." She looked glum. "His extramarital affairs… more than I'd care to. He makes little to no effort to hide them," she said, touching the corner of her eye with her left hand. "In fact, he goes quite far the other way, and lets me know about his conquests frequently. He wears my shame as a badge of honour."

Tom caught Cassie's expression in the corner of his eye. He shared her empathy.

"It is his shame, not yours," Cassie said.

Annabelle looked at Cassie, offering her an appreciative smile but she was still tearful. "It is my humiliation along with my weakness that he exploits though."

"The baby, is that why you decided to leave?"

"It is, yes. To bring a child into that man's orbit… to bring one up in such a controlling, abusive home… I will not do it, no matter what it costs me. I would rather we live on a shoestring, wandering from place to place than stay with him."

"And Louis was helping you?"

"Yes. I have money saved. Not much," she said, shrugging, "but enough to give us a start away from all of this."

"Why abroad?"

"It would take Alex a long time to find me. The plan was to keep moving for as long as I could. After that… who knows? But we would be free of him."

"There are places here in the UK, refuges that will help—"

"I don't doubt it, Detective Inspector," Annabelle said, "but they will not be able to keep him away from us. Alex is a banker who has made an absolute fortune over the last twenty years. The resources available to him are vast. Right now, he's still an investor but one who has his own foundation… have you any idea how much support he offers local businesses? How many politicians fundraisers he donates to on a regular basis? A man with as much money, and as many connections, as Alex has will never allow me to keep my child," she said, her voice threatening to crack. "He would drag me through the courts… no doubt pay psychiatrists to doubt my sanity, friends to testify as to my lack of ability to care for my baby. He would *never* allow me to keep the child. I had no choice."

"What will you do now?" Tom asked.

Her eyes watering, Annabelle shook her head. "Find another way, I guess. Somehow."

Tom took out one of his contact cards along with a pen, scribbling his personal mobile number on the reverse. Handing it to Annabelle, who took it and gave it a once over, he nodded at it. "Just in case you ever need some help," he said. "There's always a solution."

CHAPTER TWENTY-TWO

THEY BOTH WATCHED as Annabelle walked back between the beach huts towards where her car was parked, until she disappeared from view. Cassie sighed.

"Things are getting complicated now," she said.

"With Major Crimes, you mean?"

She nodded. "As if it wasn't already."

"She seems confident she's avoided her husband's scrutiny, pulled off a Houdini without him noticing."

"As far as she knows," Cassie said. "If he'd got wind of it, do you really think he'd let her know that he knows if he thought he could take care of it quietly? A controlling personality, who is very accomplished, can manipulate almost any given situation without coming across as unstable or erratic. Better to do things behind the facade, so to speak."

"You reckon Alex Gillie stopped Louis from making his flight?" Tom asked. He wasn't so sure. If Gillie had intervened to the extent of forcing Louis into hiding, then surely Annabelle would know about it. "Of course, we've made an assumption all along in this case."

"And that is?" Cassie asked, curious.

"That Louis is actually Louis."

Cassie fixed him with a stare, confused. "I don't understand."

"We thought it likely that Louis was our victim, but that was ruled out by a lack of a familial DNA match, right?"

"Yeah."

"And Louis has returned to the UK, but not contacted his family and by all accounts is living under the radar," Tom said. "What if the victim we have was passing himself off as Louis?"

"Say that again," Cassie said. "You think Louis might not be… Louis?"

"Exactly. We've got no pictures of him – the Louis Taylor we have living here in Hunstanton – as everything is from back before he vanished. Maybe he vanished a long time ago and someone else has been living his life. After all, we can only assume our victim's head and hands were removed to hamper identification. This might be why."

Cassie grimaced. "That's… depressing. It means we'd be even further away from identifying our victim or locating Louis. The real one, not Louis 2.0."

Tom took out his mobile and scrolled through his contact lists. He'd been provided with all of the Taylor family details just in case and none of them was willing to leave until they found out the fate of their missing family member, good or bad. Expecting the siblings to be more likely to have what he was looking for, Tom called Noah, Louis's brother.

"Detective Inspector," Noah said. "Do you have news?" He sounded hopeful and Tom was quick to ensure his anticipation was quelled.

"Nothing new to report, I'm afraid, Noah. We were hoping you could help us with something though. Do you have any photographs taken of Louis around the time he went travelling. I know you all said that he has no distinguishing marks, but—"

"I can do better than that. After the Foreign Office pretty much bailed on us, me and my uncle went out there, to Bangkok, and made our own enquiries."

"Yes, I recall."

"Yeah, well we had a guide and we hit all the haunts that are on the backpacker trail and all that. Largely… it came to nothing, but we did end up on internet chatrooms and forums which the backpackers, past and present, use to share info, pictures and find people they'd lost contact with. It was all a bit chaotic as I'm sure you can imagine, but we did get in touch with people who came across him."

"What do you have?"

"It was around then that digital cameras were becoming all the rage, before cameras were integrated into mobile phones." Tom thought how quickly things had changed. It's true, it wasn't all that long ago that phones were good for calls, texting, perhaps a calendar and a game or two that became the new craze of the day. "Anyway, one of the girls who was staying in the same hostel as Louis took a few pictures at a full moon party one night. It was a rooftop bash in the city. She had some great pictures."

"Do you happen to have access to them now?" Tom asked, glancing sideways at Cassie who seemed interested.

"Um… yes, I do. They're saved in the cloud, so I can download them. They'd be too big a file to email them over to you."

"That's okay, we'll come and transfer them onto a flash drive or something." Cassie nodded, indicating she'd be happy to go. "Would you be able to do that this evening, Noah?"

"Yes, sure. Is this… significant?"

"I'd like to say yes, Noah, but it's pretty much just routine," Tom said.

"Ah, right."

"We're still working on finding your brother, I assure you."

"Okay, thanks. I'll have the pictures ready as soon as possible."

"I'll send Detective Sergeant Knight over to see you shortly. Thank you, Noah. I appreciate it."

Tom put his mobile away, then he turned to face Cassie.

"Use the pictures to identify Louis?" she asked. Tom nodded. "I'll speak to Melanie. She'd be best placed to confirm who her on-off boyfriend is." She frowned. "What if… you're right and this guy isn't Louis at all? Where do we go from there?"

Tom shot her a wry smile. "Firstly, it's just a possibility rather than a theory."

"And secondly?"

He took a deep breath. "Let's cross that bridge if and when we reach it."

Cassie laughed. "We'll be up a creek without a paddle then, though, won't we?"

"Get yourself across to the hotel and pick up these pictures from Noah, then run them past Melanie, and we'll go from there."

CASSIE PARKED her car on Westgate in front of the hotel. Checking the time, she knew Lauren was expecting her home for dinner, so she called her to let her know she had a few things to do beforehand.

"Hi, it's me," she said as Lauren answered breezily. "Listen, I know I said I'd be home by now but I've still got a few bits to do. If you're hungry I'd say eat without me—"

"But I've already done the prep and I'm underway," Lauren protested.

"I'm sorry. I would have called earlier if I'd known," Cassie countered, "and I won't be too long. I've got to pick up a few files and… I have to speak to Melanie—"

"Melanie? Why?"

"Just show a couple of photos, that's all. It won't take long. I guess I could do that after we've eaten. As I said, I won't be—"

"Well… the thing is… Melanie is here."

"Excuse me?"

"At our place," Lauren said, her tone changing. "She is… having a tough time right now, what with Louis missing and there are some things going on at work right now. She… needed someone to lean on."

Cassie sat in momentary silence, listening to her partner breathing. "I see."

"That's okay, isn't it? I mean, you don't mind, do you?"

"Mind? No... no, of course not. Why... er... why would I mind?"

"That's cool. I just thought because of our past that you might, well, never mind."

Cassie felt a pang of jealously in her chest, although trying very hard to dismiss it, it only seemed to foment further. "Right, well... maybe she could eat with you then. It'd save wasting your efforts."

"Oh, okay... if you don't mind?"

There was that phrase again, *if you don't mind*. Cassie minded. She definitely minded.

"No, I can grab a takeaway or something on my way home. If Melanie wants to stick around with you until I get back, I can see her then."

"No, don't do that. I'll leave something here for you. You don't mind... about Melanie being here?' Lauren asked. It was clear by the way she asked the question; she knew Cassie was put out.

"Why would I?"

"Okay, I'll see you in a bit then."

"Yeah, bye," Cassie said, deliberately abrupt and hung up. Annoyed with herself for being so childish, she thought about throwing her mobile, but relented and put it in her coat pocket. "Well done, Cassandra. Feel free to join a grown-up relationship whenever you're ready," she told herself, cracking the door open and getting out. She was startled by the blast of a car horn, the screech of tyres as the driver swerved to avoid her door and then gesticulated at her as he drove past.

Cassie, hands shaking, got out and shut the door, bracing herself on the roof with a steadying hand as she caught her breath.

"Come on, woman. Focus," she told herself, rounding the car and walking quickly to the hotel.

Once inside she found the reception desk unmanned. Crossing the small lobby into the dining room, she could see the Taylor family sitting together and eating at a table on the far side of the room. Noah saw her and rose from his seat, wiping his mouth with a napkin which he put down on his plate and excused himself from the others. They all smiled at Cassie and Isaac nodded in her direction but without any further developments, no one else got up to greet her. Noah came across the room and Cassie greeted him. "I'm sorry to interrupt your meal."

Noah waved her apology away. "No need. I was finished anyway," he said, reaching into his pocket and producing a micro-SD card. "I know Detective Inspector Janssen suggested a thumb drive, but I didn't bring my laptop with me. The best I could do was to download them to my mobile and store them on the expansion port for the memory. I hope that's okay?"

Cassie took the tiny card from him, examining it in the palm of her hand. It would fit into her phone, so she wasn't concerned. "I can make it work, Noah, don't worry. You haven't got anything else on there you don't want me to see do you?" She asked, smiling and arching her eyebrows.

Noah flushed, smiling awkwardly. "I… don't think so," he said, "but the files are in an album called *Louis*."

Cassie laughed at his awkwardness. "I'm just kidding, Noah. I'll make a copy of that album and have this back to you tomorrow. Is that okay?"

He nodded and she thanked him. Noah returned to the table to sit with his family. Cassie walked to the lobby, loitering at the dining room door and casting a casual eye over them. They didn't see her watching them. They seemed like such a close family, comfortable to be with one another. Perhaps Louis's disappearance had brought them closer or maybe they'd always been so. Either way, Cassie felt for them and also wondered what would make a member of this group stay away from them for so long. Tom's theory came to mind and Cassie wondered if the Louis they were searching for was simply an echo of their past.

Leaving the hotel, she returned to her car. Keen to view the images, she hunted around in her bag for a narrow-pointed implement she could use to open the expansion port in the side of her mobile phone. Finding a random paper clip at the foot of her bag, she bent it and with a little difficulty using only the interior light of the car to aid her, she managed to eject the narrow tray and inserted the fiddly micro card into the slot before replacing it.

Accessing the drive, she scrolled past several albums until she came to the one titled *Louis*. There were twenty-two images in the file and she opened them one by one, moving swiftly through them, all night-time party scenes featuring numerous people dancing, laughing and apparently cheering something off camera, before reaching the end and going back to the first, only this time she examined them more closely.

Regretting not going through them with Noah himself, Cassie struggled to find Louis. There must have been thirty to forty people at the event and most of the shots were not poses, more chaotic images captured in the moment. One image caught her eye though, and she pinched the screen with her finger to enlarge a section. If it weren't for the Celtic tattoo on the upper arm, she would likely have crossed past it. However, it wasn't the tattoo matching the one on their victim pulled from the water of the quarry that caught her attention. It was the man standing behind him. Cassie stared at him, unable to believe the evidence of her own eyes.

"Well, I didn't see that coming," she said quietly, zooming out and staring at the full picture. Calling Eric, she drummed her fingers of her free hand on the steering wheel. "Eric, are you still in the office?"

"I was just shutting everything down. Dr Death has been in touch to say there's no joy with his... spectral analysis stuff, or whatever he called it. The best he could say was our victim was originally from Northern Europe, likely spending most of his life in the UK. Insights like that are worth waiting for, right?"

"Well, I have a little job for you."

"Little... at this time? Something tells me I'm not shutting everything down, am I?"

"No, sorry. You'd better call Becca and let her know you'll be late home."

"She's taken George to her mother's place for the night after his swimming lesson at the leisure centre, so it doesn't matter. I have an evening in front of the telly ahead of me."

"All right, sorry to ruin the grand plan, but here's what I want you to do..."

CHAPTER TWENTY-THREE

CASSIE PUT THE HANDBRAKE ON, switched off the headlights and pointed across to where a lone figure was tying the stern mooring line of a thirty-five-footer to the quayside. He hadn't noted their arrival, but it was close to eight o'clock now and activity at the water's edge was scarce at this time in Burnham Overy Staithe.

"That's our man," she said. Eric made to get out but Cassie stopped him with a gentle restraining hand to his forearm. They watched as he checked the rope at the bow, ensuring it too was fastened properly before he skipped back and climbed aboard. The below deck lights were on, and they saw a shadow move as he moved about. "Come on," Cassie said, getting out of the car.

Together, they walked along the quay, the odd

sound of a passing car or a dog barking carried from the nearby town, but they were pretty much alone down at the harbour. In summertime this area would still be teeming with sailors, tourists or hikers walking through the nearby marshes towards Holkham. Coming to the yacht, they stood on the quay.

"Ahoy the boat!" Cassie called in an exaggerated manner, smiling at Eric. He frowned, but she didn't mind. It amused her and that was her primary goal with her sense of humour. If others laughed as well, then that was a bonus. They heard movement on the stairs and a head appeared from the cabin, looking over at them. The tide was in and the boat was therefore raised up against the quayside. "Permission to come aboard?"

"Like hell," Marcus Bell said, coming up on deck and staring at them, hands on hips in a defiant stance. "Not without a warrant."

Cassie feigned surprise. "Something to hide, Marcus?"

"No," he said scornfully, "but this ain't my boat and so I don't get to choose who comes aboard. Besides," he said, pointing at her feet, "with those shoes on you'll mark the deck, and the owner of this particular boat will not be pleased."

"And who owns this boat then?" Cassie asked, casting an eye over it. She was impressed. It was one of the largest in the harbour at present.

"Got a warrant?"

"To know who the owner is?" Cassie asked and Marcus nodded. "No, of course not. That would be ridiculous."

Marcus's eyes flicked furtively between them. "What do you want, DS Knight. I'm a busy man."

Cassie glanced at Eric who reached into his coat and took out several pieces of paper. Moving closer, under the watchful eye of Marcus Bell, he offered them to him. Reluctantly, Marcus took them. His expression remained impassive, unchanged, as he went from page to page. Having studied them all, copies of the photos provided by Noah Taylor, he passed them back to Eric and sneered. "So what?"

"You've known Louis Taylor a lot longer than since he moved to Hunstanton and joined the gym," Cassie said, pointing to the pictures back in Eric's hand. "Partying with him in Thailand, so we see."

Marcus shrugged. "Is it a crime to be on holiday."

"You never said you knew Louis from back then."

"You didn't ask," Marcus said with a mischievous grin. "What does it matter anyway?"

"Because we're looking for him… and because someone is dead."

"What?" Marcus asked, the grin dissipating. "What are you talking about?"

Cassie saw Eric flash a glance at her, and she realised she'd overstepped the mark. "You met Louis in Thailand?"

Marcus considered his reply, his eyes searching both her and Eric, possibly trying to work out what he should permit himself to say, no doubt as little as possible. "What of it?"

"We've done some research through our travel records, Marcus. We know you flew out to Thailand along with your brother, Stacy. You weren't on a return flight; you both flew one way."

"Open-ended trip, wasn't it?"

"Only, you returned a month later, but Stacy… he doesn't appear on any flight for another two years." Cassie looked at Eric who read from his notebook.

"Stacy flew out of Singapore almost two years to the day after you returned home," Eric said, looking up. "We also checked our records at this end and he didn't return from your joint holiday in Thailand. He didn't pay tax, claim any benefit or appear on any Electoral Register anywhere in the UK, so where was he in those intervening two years?"

"Your records must be wrong," Marcus said. "It wouldn't be the first time the old bill made a mistake."

Cassie snorted. "It's not like Stacy is one of the Birmingham Six though, is it?"

"What do you want?" Marcus asked, sneering. "I'm busy."

"We want to know," Cassie said, "why Stacy was arrested by Thai Police during your holiday..." Cassie fixed her gaze on Marcus and he reacted almost imperceptibly to the mention of his brother's arrest. "What can you tell us about that, Marcus?"

He shrugged. "Tourists get arrested in Thailand all the time. It's a party place... so many drugs and alcohol flying around, loose women... it's easy to get caught up in something. Hell, even the police will sell you weed out there, then arrest you after you've paid for it. Different rules."

Cassie cocked her head, glancing at Eric. "Sounds like my kind of place." Eric smiled. "So, what happened to Stacy?"

Marcus sucked air through his teeth, but he must have figured it didn't matter so many years down the line, nodding slightly. "The hostel we were staying in... the owners were in business with some local guys. I guess they weren't paying their share of the bribes to keep business ticking along nicely. The place got raided... anyone carrying was swept up and thrown in a jail cell." He shrugged. "It's what happens."

Eric frowned. "Then you pay a fine and you're out in a few days." Cassie sent him a questioning look. He flushed. "So, I'm told. I mean... I wouldn't know."

"Yeah," Marcus said, his eyes narrowing, "something like that."

"And yet, two years?" Cassie asked.

"Like I said, your records must be wrong. It was a long time ago."

"You weren't there that night?"

"No," Marcus said. "We'd met these locals… girls…" he shook his head, smiling ruefully. "Shouldn't have got involved with their sort. Nothing good ever comes from it. Anyway, I was out for the evening. By the time I got back, the place had been properly turned over."

"And Louis?" Cassie asked.

Marcus shrugged. "No idea. I didn't really know him—"

"Oh, come on, Marcus," Cassie said. "If you're going to lie, at least do me the courtesy of making it a bit more elaborate… and convincing."

"It's true," he said, throwing his hands wide, "I never saw him again after that night. We weren't mates or anything. You're never mates with people you meet along the way in those kinds of places. You meet people, often horrible people you wouldn't give the time of day to normally, and you move on. That's how it works."

"You expect us to believe that?" Cassie asked.

"I don't really care what you do or don't believe," Marcus countered. "I mean, Louis and me… we're not exactly cut from the same cloth, are we?"

"On that we agree," Cassie said, looking him up and down. "So… what? Louis just turns up here a couple of years ago… and you're all friends together?"

"Like I said," Marcus argued, "he ain't really my sort of friend."

"So, he was Stacy's friend?"

Marcus flinched, pursing his lips.

"Where is your brother anyway; is he back from his little trip yet?"

"Nah, not yet," Marcus said, flatly. "When he comes back, you should ask him."

"We'll do that," Cassie said. She sniffed, casually looking around the quay. "He is coming back, isn't he?"

Marcus's eyes narrowed. "Yeah, why wouldn't he?"

"Just wondering, that's all. He's picked a great time to disappear. Along with Louis Taylor… anyone else gone missing who seems to be involved with them?"

"That's your job, not mine."

Cassie smiled. "Yes, it is. You're right."

"Are we through here?" Marcus asked.

"For now," Cassie said. Marcus didn't wait, turning and making for the stairs to take him below deck. "Hey, Marcus?" He stopped, looking over his shoulder at her. "Funny thing, there's no record of Stacy being released from any jail in Thailand."

Marcus shrugged. "Weird, huh?"

"It is… seeing as the Royal Thai Police contacted the British Consulate and advised of your brother's arrest on drug-smuggling charges, along with their intention to put him on trial. But… nothing. No more mentions, nothing official at all. It's like he just vanished from the system. Weird, huh?" Marcus held her eye for a moment before looking away.

"See you around, DS Knight," Marcus said before descending below deck and disappearing from view.

Cassie watched him go and then turned to Eric, signalling for them to leave.

"Is that it?" Eric asked.

"For now, yes. What do you want to do, arrest him for attending a party years ago?"

"He knows so much more than he's letting on," Eric said, hurrying to keep pace with her as she walked back to the car.

"Undoubtedly, Eric," she said, without breaking her stride, "but what he is keeping from us is another question entirely."

"So, what are we going to do?"

"Keep digging, Eric. We put the pressure on, keep dialling it up a notch and sooner or later something is going to give. It always does."

"Should we be looking for Stacy?"

"Yes, let's get his name and description out

there. He's not away on a trip. He's not showing his face for a reason, and I'm betting it's related to all of this."

Walking back to their car, Cassie rang Tom but he didn't pick up. She decided to call Tamara, who did.

"Hey, Cassie," Tamara said. "Where are you?" The water was lapping against the sea wall, boats at anchor rising and falling on the gentle swell.

"I'm over at Burnham Overy Staithe with Eric. We've just had an interesting chat with Marcus Bell."

"Oh really, tell me more."

"It turns out he knew Louis back in Louis's travelling days, specifically when he was in Thailand. It turns out that Stacy Bell was arrested in Bangkok on drug possession charges…"

"Now that is interesting. What about Marcus?"

"He was there too," Cassie said, turning her back as they reached the car and leaning against it, looking back at where she'd last seen Marcus. "He went very quiet on it all when we mentioned it. He's hiding something and I'll bet his brother is too."

Tamara thought for a moment, putting aside whatever she was doing, food preparation Cassie thought by the sounds. "Find Stacy Bell."

"Way ahead of you," Cassie said. "Eric's already onto it. I think it's a possibility that Louis came to

Hunstanton because of his association with the Bells."

"To what end?"

Cassie shrugged. "I don't know but at the risk of sounding like a pitiful pastiche of a Geordie Bogarde, *of all the towns in all the world, Louis had to walk into theirs…*"

Tamara laughed. "Okay, get the word out. Are you done for the day?"

"Yes, I think so," Cassie said, glancing at Eric who was finishing his phone call. Eric nodded. The word was out to all local officers to keep an eye out for Stacy Bell. "I've tried to call Tom, but there's no answer. If you speak to him…"

"I'll get him up to speed, yes," Tamara said, suddenly sounding distant as raised voices could be heard in the background.

"Everything all right?"

"Yes, yes, of course. I'll speak to you in the morning."

CHAPTER TWENTY-FOUR

"Look who I found sitting in your driveway like a stray cat, all lost and lonely," Francesca, Tamara's mum, said as she hustled into the room with DCS Wells on her arm. He seemed awkward, but smiled at her as he freed his arm. Francesca hurried across the room and gave Tamara a kiss on both cheeks, which she never did unless they had company, or she was trying to make an impression.

"Mother," Tamara said, forcing an artificial smile while nodding at Wells. "Back so soon?"

He smiled sheepishly, glancing between Francesca and Tamara. "Well, I was in the area…"

"In the area?" David said, coming up from the cellar with a bottle of wine in his hand. He sniffed the air and that was enough to jog Tamara's memory and she swore, hurrying to the stove to stir the contents of a pan which spat hot tomato into the air as soon as she did so.

"Damn it!" she said again.

"Tammy darling," Francesca scolded her, inclining her head towards Wells. "We have company."

"*We* don't, Mother," Tamara said, annoyed at her lapse in concentration due to Cassie's phone call.

"Have you burned your tomatoes?" Francesca asked, disappointed.

"No, they're just as they're supposed to be. Mother, what are you doing here anyway? And you too?" she asked Wells.

"Well, I'm here because your father has a night out with the lads—"

"The lads?" Tamara asked. David smiled.

"Yes, the chaps from the bridge club. They head out for a curry together once a month. I was at a loose end, so I thought I'd pop round."

Tamara arched her eyebrows. "Without calling first, that's nice," she said pointedly.

"Well, you're not up to anything are you?" Francesca asked.

"Not now, no," David said under his breath. If anyone besides Tamara heard, they didn't acknowledge the comment.

"Besides, if I hadn't popped round, I would have missed this handsome gentleman's visit, wouldn't I?" Francesca said, crossing to DCS Wells and looping her arm through his and squeezing him. "It's been a long time, hasn't it, Peter."

"Not for some," David said quietly. Tamara elbowed him in the ribs.

"I didn't realise you two were so close," Tamara said, hands on hips, allowing David to try and rescue the contents of their meal.

"Oh don't be daft, Tammy. I remember Peter from the Christmas do… and your birthday surprise dinner that Richard threw for you." She raised a hand conspiratorially in front of her mouth, partly shielding her from Tamara's view as she whispered, too loudly not to be deliberate, "I always preferred you to Richard. I don't know why Tammy couldn't see that—"

"Mother! Comments like that will not make you any more welcome in this house." She glanced at David who pretended not to have heard it. Gesturing for Wells to come with her, Tamara walked towards the French doors onto the garden. Detaching himself from Francesca's grip, he followed her. Tamara closed the doors behind them to give them privacy. David seemed less than happy about being left alone with Francesca who immediately moved to his side, peering over the stove, no doubt readying herself to offer constructive criticism.

"What are you doing, Peter?" Tamara asked, folding her arms across her chest.

"That's funny, I was about to ask you the same question."

Tamara felt a flicker of anxiety in her chest, similar to being caught doing something you're not supposed to when you're a child.

"What do you mean?"

"I believe I was very clear the last time we spoke, Tamara," he said. "Alex Gillie and his associates are off limits to you and your team unless we give you permission to speak to them."

Tamara pursed her lips, nodding slowly. "I have no recollection of that agreement."

"I imagine your line manager will disagree. He promised me your full cooperation in our investigation—"

"And I'm investigating a murder here, Peter. I don't have the luxury of ignoring people who may or may not be associated to your targets. What exactly has put your nose out of joint tonight?"

"You know damn well—"

"I'm afraid you're going to have to tell me, Peter."

"Your DI and his sidekick ambushing Annabelle Cook this evening."

"Ah… so your team are following Annabelle Cook," Tamara said, seeing an involuntary micro expression flash across his face, "or are you following my officers?"

Wells shifted his weight between his feet, avoiding her gaze. "Annabelle is off limits to your team unless I specifically—"

"Who the hell do you think—"

"Right now, I'm the one person standing between you and a disciplinary investigation," he said, scowling at her. "Give me one reason why I shouldn't be straight onto your DCS Cole as soon as we are finished here?"

Tamara saw David hovering near the French doors, watching them surreptitiously while her mum picked at the food prep laid out on the kitchen island.

"Look," Tamara said, changing her tone and attempting to be more conciliatory, "if I knew the nature of your investigation then I might even be able to help. You know me, and I would vouch for every member of my team. They're good. Maybe we can help."

Wells shook his head. "It's too much of a risk. We've been working this for almost two years… and we're close, Tamara. Really close. I cannot allow some rural… allow your team to hinder my case."

"Don't underestimate them, Peter. My officers know what's needed—"

"That's as well, Tamara, but there is so much

riding on this case… not just for the team but for me personally as well. If it comes apart, then I'm the one who'll be holding the grenade when it goes off. Do you understand?"

"I do, it's like a high-stakes game of pass the parcel," Tamara said, feeling for him, "but I have my own case to solve. It can't be a coincidence… that I have a dead body who is linked to your—"

"Stop there, Tamara. There… is no link. None whatsoever." Wells stepped away from her, staring at her hard. "And your team will stand down. This is your final warning."

"That sounds ominous."

He fixed his gaze on her, possibly trying to determine if she was mocking him. She wasn't.

"I've asked you to do so from a place of professional courtesy, as a friend… and now as a senior officer. If you don't pull your team back, then I will ensure it happens… and you will not like the consequences of my doing so."

Tamara nodded but said nothing. Wells waited for more of a reaction; a curse, a counter argument or a flat refusal but Tamara said nothing. He gave her a curt nod and made to leave. He'd barely taken three steps before Francesca came to the door, throwing it open and stopping him from leaving.

"Peter, you must stay and have dinner with us," she said. David looked at Tamara, clearly incensed, but Tamara shook her head and he turned away.

"Thank you…"

"Francesca."

Wells smiled at her. "A very kind offer, Francesca, but I really must—"

"A glass of wine then?" she said persisting.

"He's on duty, Mum," Tamara said, coming to stand beside her. "Peter has to go, don't you?"

"It's true, I do," he said, smiling as his eyes darted between the two of them.

"Well, don't be a stranger," Francesca said breezily. Tamara gave her a gentle push back towards the house. Wells already had his back turned and was leaving by the path down the side of the house.

"Honestly, Mother, what are you thinking?"

"I'm just thinking about that dashing chap…" Francesca said, looking to where she'd last seen DCS Wells. "If you'll not make a play for young Tom then the least you could do—"

"Mum, I have a partner," Tamara hissed at her under her breath, glancing towards David who, thankfully, couldn't hear them.

"Yes, I know," Francesca said, "but he's… he's…"

"He's what?" David asked without looking up from putting the salad together in a bowl. Tamara shot her mum a dark look and at least Francesca had the grace to flush. Neither of them were sure just how much David had overheard.

"I was going to say… dynamic," Francesca said.

"As opposed to what?" David asked. Tamara figured he couldn't know the context of their conversation.

"Studious," Francesca said.

"Like me?"

Tamara was about to intervene to rescue her mother but decided against it. David knew what they'd been talking about after all.

"Well… study is… good," Francesca said.

"Would it help if I said I'm a mountain climber and a fully qualified parachute instructor?"

Francesca reddened further. "I think I should be heading off. You know how your father hates it when he gets home and I'm not there. He worries."

Tamara cocked her head. "Yes, he is a worrier."

Francesca smiled at both of them in turn, gave Tamara a quick hug and left as quickly as she could. David passed Tamara a glass of wine and returned to what he was doing.

"Mountaineer… parachute instructor?" she asked.

David smiled. "Forgive me, but she deserved it."

"I thought you were afraid of heights."

"I am," he said, smiling broadly. "You wouldn't catch me hanging off the side of a cliff face."

"Or jumping out of a plane?"

"Or jumping out of a plane," he said, nodding,

"but I'm not in an interview room or under oath tonight, am I?"

Tamara laughed, glancing at the sauce simmering on the hob. "How long do I have?"

"A couple of minutes, why?"

"I just need to make a quick phone call."

CHAPTER TWENTY-FIVE

HAVING DROPPED Eric back at his house, Cassie set off for home. Eric had invited her in but she was keen to get back to Lauren. She kept telling herself that it didn't matter that Melanie had sought out her ex for support, and that it was indeed Cassie herself who'd brought them together in this scenario, there was still a nagging doubt in her mind as she put her foot down on the accelerator.

The lights were on in the little cottage that they rented on the edge of the Holkham Estate. It was a pretty Arts and Craft period inspired house, only two bedroomed, but secluded in a wooded area almost wholly encompassed by fields. They'd sold their flat in the town, cashing in on the rising property prices and Cassie was happy to move out into the countryside. Even though they'd never be able to afford to buy a place like this, it was a corner of their own wilderness away from the madding crowd. At least for a while until the desire for take-away food and convenience came back to bite them.

Melanie's car was parked alongside Lauren's and the curtains were drawn which she found odd. They rarely bothered. It wasn't as if anyone could see in from the main road beyond the copse to the front of the house and they had no neighbours who overlooked them. The nearest neighbour to them lived a quarter of a mile down the road on the out-skirts of the next village.

The front door was locked and inserting the key she found there was another already in the lock on the inside. She pressed the doorbell, irritated. Trying to see through the front window, she couldn't. The curtain was obscuring everything in-side. No one came to let her in and swearing under her breath, she made her way around the outside of the house to the rear. There were no exterior lights mounted to the side of the house and she caught her footing on the paving as she made her way through the back garden. The rear door into the old scullery was unlocked and she entered, walking into the kitchen and flicking on the light.

"I'm home. Sorry I'm so late," she called but no one answered. "I had to visit someone with Eric, but I'm done for the night now."

The kitchen was in a bit of a state, which wasn't unusual when Lauren was cooking. Why use only a couple of pans when you can empty every cupboard and make use of every utensil possible? The aroma of spices hung in the air and Cassie felt her stomach rumble at the thought of eating. She hoped they'd saved her something. Opening the fridge, she was disappointed not to find a covered plate set aside for her as Lauren usually did when she was late home from work.

The lights in the little dining room off the kitchen were on, the table set with half-eaten plates of food, a nearly empty bottle of wine and two glasses, themselves almost empty, alongside the plates. Cassie felt a pang of concern, looking around the room and then attuning her hearing to any sounds coming from upstairs. She couldn't hear anything. Taking a deep breath, she stepped into the hall, heading for the stairs. At the foot of them, she stopped and listened again, anger rising. The landing light was on and she recalled seeing the light on in their front-facing bedroom, the one she shared with Lauren as it was the larger of the two.

Putting a foot on the first tread, fearful of what she'd find upstairs, she hesitated as a shaft of light from the living room caught her attention. Moving towards it, she eased the door open to reveal a scene of chaos. The room looked like it had been blitzed by a madman. The room was small, but the contents of their sideboard had been emptied onto the floor, the drawers themselves cast on top of the paperwork. The sofa had been upended, the rear lining slashed and torn away to reveal the lining and the frame.

"What the..." she said, uncomprehending. Backing out of the room, she hurried to the staircase. "Lauren, what the hell is going on here?" No answer. Worried now, she made her way up, pausing as she set foot on the landing. The only light coming from upstairs was leaking out from the door to their bedroom. Cassie approached cautiously, glancing into the spare room, but seeing only the storage boxes in the gloom of the interior. The bathroom door was open, no one was inside.

Reaching the bedroom, Cassie took a breath before pushing it open. The room was also in a state. Their wardrobes had been emptied out and strewn across the bed and the floor. Cassie couldn't see the carpet and didn't know where to step as she entered. The chest of drawers beneath the front window had also been emptied, all of their belongings scattered on the carpet.

"Lauren?" Cassie whispered, but there was no sign of her. They must be outside somewhere, gone for a walk to calm down. Something like that. Cassie took out her mobile, dialling Lauren's number. Hearing it ring, she stopped, listening. It wasn't outside, but downstairs. Turning, Cassie made her way out of the room and hurried back to the ground floor, picking up the pace as she went and following the sound of the mobile ringing. Entering the kitchen almost at running pace, the ringing grew louder. Hearing a sound to her left, by the head of the cellar entrance she caught sight of movement in the corner of her eye. Turning to see, she felt a sharp pain in the side of her head. She stumbled to her right, off balance, her mind reeling from the force of the impact. Another blow, this time to the back of her head. She staggered forward, falling and landing prostrate on the tiled floor.

Pushing herself up with her hands, aware of a figure approaching behind her, everything seemed to move in slow motion, her own movements were laboured, and her thoughts jumbled. Vaguely aware of hands on her jumper, she tried to push back as she was hauled to her feet but either all of her strength had escaped her, or the figure was too strong because every attempt to get away only resulted in her straining but gaining no advantage. It felt futile.

Feeling herself dragged to her left, they passed into the dining room and Cassie was thrown across the table, sending plates and glasses of wine crashing to the floor alongside her. She heard a scream. Was it hers or someone else? She couldn't tell. Her head was spinning, her vision blurred. A dark shape came to stand over her and Cassie raised her left hand to shield her face only to have it slapped aside. A fist flew down, striking her on the face below her left eye and she slumped to the floor, barely conscious.

Firm hands grasped her under her arms, dragging her along the ground, her heels catching on the door jamb as they passed into the kitchen. She wanted to shout, scream, call for help but was unable to mount any form of a defence. Panic threatened to overwhelm her and then she felt a moment of peace, her fears allayed before everything went dark.

Cassie awoke to darkness, the strong smell of oil and the sensation of nausea. Worrying she was about to vomit, she tried to move but found herself bound at the wrists and ankles as well as struggling to breathe. She was on the move, at some pace too, feeling the vibration through the floor and the creaking of ageing suspension mounts as they traversed the uneven road surface. The floor was metal, uneven and pitted. She was in a van of some sort. There were no windows. The rear doors were fully panelled but as her eyes adjusted to the gloom, she gauged she was in a Transit or similar.

The van took a turn to the right, and it must have been off a main road because the van slowed and the vibration worsened, the van bouncing along, Cassie feeling every pit and hole in the surface in her back and legs. She tried to free herself, but she was secured with gaffer tape, so much so that she wondered if she'd ever have been able to tear it even if her hands were free. Liquid had run from her nose, likely blood, and was now drying and partially blocking her nasal passages making it harder to breathe. She felt perspiration on her face, her hair was matted and damp to touch.

Her memory of what happened was sketchy, and thinking only made her headache worse. The reflex struck again and fearful that if she puked she'd drown on her own vomit she tried to pull the tape from her mouth, but it was wrapped around her head in several passes. There was no way she could free it. Seeking to quell the threat of panic bubbling beneath the surface, she forced it down into the pit of her stomach and did her best to regulate her breathing.

The van came to a dead stop, but the engine remained ticking over as she heard a door open, the hinges protesting as the driver got out.

"You're late!" a male voice said. "Where have you been?"

"I ran into someone," another voice said. The second one sounded familiar, but she couldn't place it, muffled as it was by the metal encasing her. The van shifted slightly as someone got back in and the driver's door closed. The van was put in gear and moved forward. Were they entering a compound or something? Moments later she heard the handbrake clamp on and the engine noise ceased. Her heart was beating as she could hear footsteps on shingle walking the length of the van, moving to the rear. Cassie closed her eyes, pretending to still be unconscious.

The van doors were unlocked and yanked open, Cassie seeing exterior artificial light flood the interior of the vehicle behind her closed eyelids. It was still night time then. She couldn't have been out for too long. Someone clambered into the back of the van and she could hear him breathing as he leaned over her. He smelled too, much like the van, of oil or some such chemical she couldn't quite determine.

"Who the hell is this?"

"Information. That's what she is," Marcus Bell said from nearby. "Or at least, she'll have it."

"Who is she?"

"Don't worry about that," Marcus said, getting into the van and wasting no time in giving Cassie a swift kick in the leg. She wasn't expecting it and gasped in pain. "Useful, I'm sure but a terrible bloody actress."

Marcus grabbed Cassie by the space between

her bound wrists and hauled her around to face the rear, before dragging her to the tailgate. She mumbled a protest; such sudden movement made every aching muscle burn with fire.

"Not so cocky now, are you?" Marcus said, pulling her over the lip and allowing gravity to do the rest, depositing her unceremoniously on the ground at his feet in a heap. She glared up at him, but this only made Marcus Bell smile as he grasped a fistful of her hair, snapping her head backwards so that he could stare into her eyes. "If I were you, I'd start being a bit nicer to me," he said, broadening the smile into a malevolent grin. If she'd been able, Cassie would have spat in his face.

"She's got spirit, whoever she is," the other man said, coming to stand alongside Marcus. Cassie didn't know him but he didn't chime with who she'd expect to be associated with someone like Marcus. He was older, well dressed and didn't appear to be enjoying this as much. "Where did you find her?"

"At Melanie's girlfriend's house, snooping about," Marcus said. "Probably looking for the same thing as me."

"Speaking of which," the man said, ignoring Cassie's plight, "did you find it?"

There was a tension in his tone that hadn't been there before. Marcus glanced at him but said nothing, confirming what he must have feared. That moment of respite from their attention gave Cassie the chance to look around. They were by the water, in a boatyard somewhere. There were vessels tied up nearby but she couldn't see any nearby buildings or landmarks. She guessed they were still in Norfolk, something she was thankful for. Had they travelled further afield, then she'd be concerned, far beyond her current position, which wasn't great. An understatement befitting of her usual thoughts.

Marcus saw her looking around and gave her another kick. Cassie groaned but caught the other man's disapproving look. He didn't have the same stomach for violence. Something she was grateful for.

"Come on then, gorgeous," Marcus said, reaching down and hauling Cassie up by her bound wrists and manhandling her as she shuffled forwards. The rope at her ankles was loose enough to keep her upright but moving was difficult, not that Marcus seemed to care. When she stumbled, he allowed her to fall before repeatedly kicking her to get her to her feet as quickly as possible. They made their way across open ground, soil underfoot, baked in the summer and frozen in the winter, towards a boat shed less than thirty yards away. It may as well have been thirty miles judging on how long it took them to get there.

"You could always cut her feet loose."

Marcus scoffed. "No, not this one." He glanced past Cassie at his associate. "She'll be off like a rabbit. Once we're inside, maybe. She'll not be running then."

Cassie found that comment threatening. What was she going to find inside? She feared then for Lauren. By the time they reached the boat shed, Cassie was effectively being dragged, Marcus growing weary of her falling over, the top of her feet were bouncing off the uneven surface as they walked. Neither man seemed at all concerned about anyone seeing or hearing them, so Cassie figured they were in an isolated spot.

The door to the shed was hanging from a runner and it was drawn aside far enough to let them pass. The interior was lit from fluorescent strip lights hanging from the rafters overhead. They went to a small office partitioned off in the far corner. Venetian blinds were pulled down and closed to hide the interior from prying eyes and when the door was opened, Cassie wasn't surprised, but still saddened, to see Lauren tied to a chair in the centre of the room. Melanie was alongside her. Lauren seemed horrified to see her brought in and thrown on the floor, probably due more to the state of her, battered and bruised, than for anything else. Cassie looked up at her, doing her best to smile despite the tape to try and reassure her, at least a little.

Both Lauren and Melanie had been crying and

both looked as if the two of them had been roughed up, a realisation that both angered Cassie and boosted her resilience.

"What the hell have you done?"

Cassie rolled onto her back to see James Newell stride into the room, pointing at her on the floor. He looked shocked and surprised.

Marcus shrugged. "Had to be done."

"Had to be done?" James said, incredulous. "You kidnap a sodding police officer and tell me it *had to be done*. Are you an idiot?"

Marcus bristled but it was the other man whose face dropped. "She's the police?"

Newell nodded emphatically. "Yeah, CID… and this bonehead has brought her here."

"What was I supposed to do?" Marcus argued, gesticulating wildly with his hands. "She was at the house… snooping. Would you rather she found it instead of me?"

"I'd rather you didn't bring a detective sergeant to our little gathering, Marcus, you moron."

Marcus squared up to him, getting well into Newell's personal space and staring him down. James Newell relented, his expression and stance softening, an acknowledgment he'd bitten off more than he could chew.

"Don't speak to me like that," Marcus growled. "Because I don't know how well you can swim."

The threat worked and James backed off but

stopped short of an apology. "I just don't think it was too wise to bring her here, that's all."

"Yeah, well… needs must and all that," Marcus countered. "Let's wait and see what the boss says when he gets here, shall we?"

"You kidnapped a policewoman," the other man said.

"Oh shut up, Craft, for crying out loud," Marcus said, barely looking at the man as he dismissed him.

"Yeah… I know… but she's with the police—"

"Seriously man. Shut up," Marcus said, glaring at him. "Did you think this was going to be all easy money and a few nights on the water? This is where you earn your money, mate."

"I didn't sign up for any of this… kidnapping… torture—"

"Well, it's a bit late for that now, isn't it?" Marcus sneered. "Because you're in it, up to here," he added, raising his hand to his throat. Then he dragged it across his neck as if making a cutting gesture. "And you'd better shut up because I can sail, even your boat. Understand?"

The threat was clear, and Nicholas Craft fell silent, but was distinctly rattled. Marcus stepped over Cassie and grasped Melanie's cheeks firmly between fingers and thumb, squeezing hard. "And you are going to tell us where our money is, or you and your friend are going swimming." He leaned into her face menacingly. "Can you swim, Melanie?" he asked with a dark grin, "because if you can't, I'm happy to offer you a crash course."

Lauren was hyperventilating, tears falling. Marcus turned on her, an action that only made her worse. He grabbed her by the hair and yanked her head towards him. "What's up, love? Not what you had planned for your romantic evening together? Sorry to interrupt it."

Cassie spun herself around, swinging her legs up and lashing out with her feet at Marcus, catching him unawares, she connected and he almost fell. The action brought a laugh from James Newell and Nicholas Craft but their humour dissipated when Marcus set about kicking and then stamping on her at his feet. The beating felt like it was never going to end, the shouts and screams from whom, Cassie didn't know, seemed to grow faint as tunnel vision set in. And then the beating stopped.

Maintaining consciousness, almost numb to the pain now, Cassie's gaze drifted up to Marcus who was standing over her now. She realised he had a hand down to her left, just beyond her vision, and he was holding her hair. He was saying something, but she couldn't hear him or understand the words. Whatever he was saying, it couldn't be good news for her.

CHAPTER TWENTY-SIX

Tom unlocked the front door to his house and entered. Russell came to investigate who was there and snorted in disgust, turning and walking slowly back into the kitchen. Tom smiled. "Now, there's a greeting," he said quietly. "Makes it all worthwhile."

"What's that?" Alice said from the living room. He ducked his head around the corner to find Alice and Saffy sitting together on the sofa with a blanket drawn across them. Russell appeared in the background from the kitchen, water dripping from his mouth, glanced at Tom before scampering across the room and leaping up onto Saffy's lap. She moved the blanket aside and the terrier disappeared beneath the material, snuggling into his owner.

"Nothing, just talking to myself," he said. The girls were watching cartoons and Tom went into the room, leaned over and kissed Alice's forehead before patting Saffy on top of her head. She looked up at him and smiled. "Everything okay here?"

"Uh-huh," Alice said, grinning as the characters did something amusing. Saffy roared with laughter. "How was work?"

"Good," he replied. "I'm going to take a shower."

"Your dinner is in the fridge."

Tom nodded, but they were engrossed in the television, and he retreated to the hallway just as his mobile rang. It was an unknown number.

"DI Janssen," he said, answering while slipping his coat off one shoulder.

"I need to see you."

Tom hesitated, recognising the voice although she was whispering. "Annabelle?"

"I need to see you," she repeated.

He glanced at his watch. "Okay. When?"

"Now?"

The intensity of the comment, almost a demand, struck him. "Is everything all right?"

"I can't talk on the phone. I need to see you."

Tom pursed his lips, taking a deep breath. "Where?"

"I'll meet you at Hunstanton lighthouse. Just you. Nobody else."

Tom considered that. He didn't like it, but he'd never felt threatened by Annabelle Cook. It was likely to be more about keeping herself safe than anything else. "Okay, when?"

"Twenty minutes."

"All right, I can—"

The line went dead. He checked the connection and saw she'd hung up. He held the mobile to his lips for a moment, thinking. Poking his head around the door frame again, he caught Alice's attention. It must have been his expression, because she broke away from the television, sitting forward.

"What is it?"

"I know I've just got home, but I need to go out again."

"Is everything okay?"

"Yes, yes, of course." He frowned, sensing she didn't believe him. "I'll not be long."

"Stay safe," Alice said, clearly concerned that Saffy was beside her, but the little girl was still transfixed by the actions of a giant mermaid on the screen.

"I'll call you before I'm about to come home," Tom said, winking at her. Alice was concerned but she said nothing further.

Tom left the house, walking to his car. He thought about calling Cassie or perhaps Eric, but he figured they'd have clocked off for the day and he didn't feel it warranted calling them back into work just for a clandestine meeting with Annabelle. He got into the car to make the short drive to the coast and the lighthouse on the cliffs on the outskirts of the town.

Tom parked his car on the main road with both the old lighthouse and the new one in clear sight. He couldn't see Annabelle, or anyone else for that matter. The car park that ran down the hillside to the beach was in view and there were a handful of cars there amongst the space for several hundred, but at this time of night it was only the odd dog walker using the beach or twenty-somethings hanging around with their lowered cars and out-landish sounding aftermarket exhaust pipes who were present.

The wind was brisk, the clouds obscured the moon and stars, but it wasn't raining. Despite this, Tom drew his coat around him and thrust his hands into his pockets as he crossed the road and walked towards the lighthouse. Momentarily considering Annabelle wasn't going to show, he allowed him-self time to contemplate what she wanted. Perhaps she had considered their suggestion about using the refuge network to leave her husband, but if so, surely, she could have conveyed that over the phone. There had to be more than this.

Turning his collar up to the wind, he waited, casting an eye out over the water. The sea was get-ting rougher with the increasing speed of the wind.

He wouldn't want to be far from shore tonight, he was certain of that.

"Thank you for coming."

Her approach startled him and as he turned, he looked around for her car or sign of where she'd come from. He couldn't see it. She must have been standing in the shadows, perhaps on the other side of the lighthouse, maybe waiting to see if he had done as promised and come alone.

He smiled. "Good evening, Annabelle."

"You came alone."

It was a comment and not a question. He shrugged. "You asked me to."

She nodded. "I know, but with my track record of trusting men… I wondered if I'd miscalculated."

He took that as a compliment.

"Well, I'm here," he said. "So why am I here?" Annabelle seemed very nervous, wringing her hands in front of her and furtively looking around. "Are we expecting someone else?"

She shook her head. "Will you walk with me?"

He gestured for her to lead on, and she moved to her right, Tom falling into step behind her. "What's this about, Annabelle?"

"I'm afraid I've not been entirely honest with you, Detective Inspector."

Tom found his curiosity piqued, as well as his irritation, but he masked it. "That comes with the warrant card, so don't feel too badly about it."

She turned to face him, stopping him with a gentle restraining hand on his forearm. "Everything I told you is true…"

"But?"

"But…" she took a deep breath, releasing her grip on his arm, "I do know where Louis is."

Genuinely surprised, Tom inclined his head. "And are you going to share that information with me?"

She avoided his gaze, embarrassed. "Alex and I own a number of holiday properties along the coast. They're above the usual standard… you know, luxury houses."

"I see."

She resumed their walk. "They're largely unoccupied at this time of the year, Christmas aside, so no one is going to look for him there."

"And who is looking for him?" Tom asked.

"Besides you?" she asked.

"Louis was in hiding long before I came to his door," Tom said. "And something tells me he's hiding from someone scarier than me." She nodded without meeting his gaze. They were alone, walking along the cliff-top path, but that didn't stop Annabelle from continually checking. It was as if she was planning her escape routes in any possible eventuality. "Are you going to tell me where he is?"

"I will," Annabelle said, turning on him, "but you have to promise to help him."

Tom involuntarily let out a laugh. "How can I promise to help someone when I've no idea what he's done?"

"He's only done what he had to do to help me."

"Then tell me where he is."

"I don't know that exactly."

"But you just said—"

"I know where he was… and where he will be, but not where he is right now."

Tom frowned. "You're not making a whole lot of sense, Annabelle."

She raised a hand to stop him talking. "There's so much you don't understand, Mr Janssen. So much."

"Try me," he said, exasperated.

"Alex for one thing," she said, shaking her head. "You don't know what he's up to."

"I know he's of interest to some of my colleagues—"

"You know what they want you to know," she said, smiling ruefully. "But what you don't know is that he's working with your colleagues."

"Excuse me?"

"Alex is working with them," she said, shaking her head. "Only, what you and they don't know, is that he's playing both sides. He's taking you for fools… and he's getting away with it."

Tom stepped in front of her, barring her path. "What are you saying?"

Now it was Annabelle who looked frustrated. "Alex managed to get himself into some hot water… You see, he never planned to bring these people into his business. They came to him when his reputation in the City was riding high. They were legitimate clients with real money. He didn't know… or at least, didn't check, who they were or where their money came from," she arched her eyebrows, "and he didn't realise just how much these people didn't like to lose money. That was the time he broke his primary rule which was never to try and trade your way out of a bad situation. He kept raising the stakes, adopting ever wilder positions. He only made his situation worse."

"He gambled on getting himself out of trouble?"

"Yes, he tried."

"And those moves went the same way?"

"Exactly. Then he was faced with two options, style it out and make good with future investments," she said, "playing the biggest game of life and death, Russian Roulette or…"

"Come to the police for help and protection," Tom said. He'd heard of similar occurrences from his time with the Met, but he'd never been involved in such a case himself.

"Only their protection comes with caveats."

"He had to roll over on his clients," Tom said.

"Yes... but that's not the end of it. Alex is... so unbelievably arrogant, he thinks he can find a way out of this without facing consequences."

"What do you mean?"

Annabelle ran a hand through her hair, taking a deep breath. "He thinks he can turn this situation to his advantage."

Tom narrowed his eyes. "In what way?"

"He thinks with the police at his back he has carte blanche to act at will, that he can play both sides and come out ahead."

"Annabelle, what is Alex doing?" She seemed suddenly reticent to say anything more but Tom knew she'd come this far. She must want to tell him. "You must trust me," he said. "I can't help if I don't know what is going on."

She relented, nodding slowly. "Before, when things started to go wrong, Alex first raised funds from people he knew. Clients he had strong relationships with. The more money he could bring in, the easier it would be to hide the losses—"

"Like a Ponzi scheme."

"Exactly. By the time those sources began drying up, he already knew the type of people he was in hock with but... Alex being Alex, he pivoted, turning that to his advantage too."

"What people?"

Annabelle met his eye; she was at the point of no return with him now and she knew it. "Cartels."

"Drugs?"

She nodded. "He was helping them to wash their money through the financial system." Tom shook his head. "It's not as difficult as you think. Some of the biggest names in the global financial system stand accused of allowing these groups to use their systems to manage their money. After all, they can't keep the money from what is the fourth largest business sector in the world, larger than the entire global textile industry, under their mattresses, can they?"

"Just what is Alex doing?" Tom asked.

She shrugged. "He's done what he is good at; exploited his connections for profit, and he's doing it right under the noses of your colleagues. Whether they are aware or not, I can't say, but they haven't stopped him."

"Because he is providing information on their business? That's a lethal game he's playing."

"I know… and that is why I need to get away from him… the business… even the money. As long as I am with him then I will have a target on my back. They will use me to get to Alex… not that he cares, but he may care about his child." She looked at Tom, her eyes gleaming. "I cannot have my child at risk. I'll do anything to avoid that."

Tom frowned. As much as he appreciated the

information, there was something odd about her coming to him now. There was an urgency around this action, and he was curious to understand it. Annabelle must have read his mind because he found her studying his expression.

"Why did you want to see me tonight?" he asked.

"Because Alex has overreached. He's pushed the boundary too far and it could all unravel very quickly. You see, Alex used clients' money to build up this profitable side line… bringing shipments of drugs into the country along the Norfolk coast. He thought either the police operation would be concluded before anyone wanted their money back or he would have returned the money he took before they realised."

"But?"

"They want their money… and he doesn't have it. Alex has been stalling, hoping for his police handlers to gather what they need and act but what he's given them isn't enough, and they want to keep things going."

"And he can't pay the investors back," Tom said.

"That's right. Your colleagues won't help, but they can't know how deep in trouble he is because he's been going behind their backs."

"Either that or they don't care," Tom said. It was quite possible that the information they'd gleaned from Alex Gillie would help them in their investigations against the cartels and he was now considered dispensable. Alex would be one of many launderers around the world and his loss would likely see him replaced by another very quickly. "So… why tonight?"

"Alex left the house tonight hidden under a blanket in the boot of the housekeeper's car, driven by his minder."

Tom knew this would be to avoid the police surveillance team. "Where is he going?"

She shook her head. "I don't know for sure, but he is desperate. I've never seen him like this. He is scared. I think he's going to do something drastic."

"You're frightened, aren't you?" Tom asked her.

She nodded. "I think Alex has crossed a line and if someone doesn't stop him now, then…"

"What do you think he's doing?"

Annabelle was silent for a moment and Tom allowed her the space to gather her thoughts. "I lied to you before about Louis. I'm sorry, but I was helping to hide him from Alex." She laughed dryly. "He was in one of our own properties all along, right in front of him." Tom saw more than a hint of satisfaction in her expression, knowing she'd pulled the wool over her husband's eyes. "Louis knows what is going on, he… is involved and tonight, he is going to confront Alex."

"Why?"

"Because Alex is going to hurt the people Louis cares about. He hasn't up until now… he's been after Louis himself but seeing as he couldn't find him and, like I said, he's desperate. He'll do anything to get what he wants and Louis isn't the kind of man to stand by and allow it to happen."

"Are you talking about Melanie?" Tom asked.

"Yes, I believe so." She shrugged. "Who else can it be? I don't think Louis has been completely open with her about his past but he cares for her. I know that to be true, so much so that he has tried to keep her out of all of this."

Tom's thoughts went to Cassie, knowing she was going to speak to Melanie this evening. "When did Alex leave?"

Annabelle's brow creased in thought. "Three quarters of an hour ago… something like that. Maybe a bit more."

Tom had deliberately left his mobile phone in the car, keen not to let anything disturb them just in case him receiving a call spooked Annabelle.

"What exactly is Louis trying to keep Melanie out of?"

Annabelle averted her eyes from his gaze. "I'm capable of many things, Detective Inspector… but I won't betray my closest friend. You will have to ask him yourself."

Tom found himself irritated by her answer.

"Well, if I knew where to find him, then I'll be happy to."

Annabelle reached into her pocket and took out her mobile phone. She tapped the screen a couple of times and then passed it to him. He looked at the application currently open. It wasn't one he recognised. He gave her an inquisitive glance.

"When we were planning my… escape," she said, "Louis and me, he downloaded this app on a… throwaway mobile. I know that's not what's it's called—"

"A burner phone?" Tom asked.

"Yes, that's it. It's all pay as you go, unregistered, so that Alex doesn't know I have it. I only use it for… well, making calls I don't want Alex to know about. He has all my pass codes for my tech, my bank accounts and so on."

"But not this one?"

She shook her head. "No. Louis installed a piece of software that tracks other phone numbers via their GPS location." She pointed at the mobile in Tom's hand. "That app shows you where Alex's phone is now, and he always takes his phone with him."

Tom glanced at the screen. Using his fingers, he pinched the map and enlarged it. A small grey circle was on the move along the coast road. He angled the mobile towards her. "I take it he doesn't know he has this tracker installed on his phone?"

"No, I did it when he was asleep one night."

"And you were going to use it to give yourself the best possible opportunity to leave him?"

"Yes, as I told you before, when I knew he was down in London." She reached out and gripped Tom's hand. "Louis has given so much of himself to help me; I couldn't bear it if anything were to happen to him. You must help him."

Tom knew full well that any action he took would likely land him, along with his team, in very hot water with Major Crimes, but if Annabelle was right then they would have little choice unless they could get to Melanie, and possibly Louis, first.

"And Louis has the same information?" Tom asked, indicating the screen before him. Annabelle nodded. "I'll do what I can," he said, before leaving and making his way back to the car. He broke into a run; sensing time was of the essence. Retrieving his mobile from the glove box, he saw two missed calls displayed on the screen, one from Cassie and the other, Tamara. He tapped Cassie's name and called her back. The phone call rang out without the option of leaving a voicemail. Shaking his head, he dialled Tamara's number.

"Tom, I've been trying to call you—"

"I know, so has Cassie and you should know… I think we have a problem."

CHAPTER TWENTY-SEVEN

MARCUS BELL STOOD OVER CASSIE. She was conscious, aware of his presence but every fibre in her body felt like it was either numb or on fire. She wasn't sure which sensation she found preferable. Her left eye was closed, and she couldn't open it. Tentatively, she reached up with her bound hands and probed the flesh of her eyelid. It was damp to the touch and swollen, likely bleeding. Peering through her right up at Marcus, he made to strike her again only for the man James referred to as Craft to step across and place a restraining hand on Marcus's forearm.

Marcus brushed the hand away and Craft recoiled from him, fearful of drawing his ire to him. The name came to mind and Cassie recalled he was one of the group who attended the fitness classes, annoyed with herself for not realising sooner.

"I just don't think you should be laying into her like that," Craft said.

"What of it?" Marcus sneered, looking down at Cassie. She took the brief respite from the beating to check out Lauren. She was crying and had been doing a fair bit of it by the red blotches on her face. She always coloured like that, her skin patterns changing if she was deeply upset. Who could blame her? Melanie, sitting in a chair beside her, was equally distraught. She looked like they'd been heavy with her too, but Marcus had saved his best for Cassie, she was in no doubt.

"Maybe we should wait—"

"For what?" Marcus said, accusingly.

Craft shifted his weight, clearly uncomfortable with his position as the voice of reason. "Until Alex gets here. He'll know what to do."

"About what?"

They all turned to see two men entering the boat shed. The first was talking and Cassie guessed he was Alex, the second man following a couple of steps behind. The way he walked, along with his size, she pegged him for ex-military, and therefore probably a minder. Damn she really wanted to know what was going on. Marcus stepped away from her, his bravado tempered by the new arrivals.

"About her," Marcus said, indicating Cassie.

"And who is she?" Alex asked, coming to stand beside Marcus and observing Cassie at his feet. "Someone's made a right mess of her." He didn't seem particularly bothered by that realisation and Cassie took no comfort in him being present. He seemed nonchalant about her plight.

"She's police," Craft said, and Cassie detected a note of nervousness in his tone. Alex Gillie looked at him and then at Marcus.

"Which police?"

Cassie found that comment odd.

"Local," Marcus said. "I found her sniffing around that one's house," he said, pointing at Lauren.

"And she is?" Alex asked, casting an eye over the two women.

"She's pally with Melanie. Seeing as we've turned over Melanie's flat, car, her desk, and everything in between without turning up anything, we figured maybe she's using her own network—"

"I told you! I don't know what you're talking about," Melanie argued. She lowered her eyes when Alex glanced across at her.

"Well, we're soon going to know, aren't we?" Alex Gillie said, striding casually over to the two seated women. He pinched Melanie's face at her cheeks, forcing her lips to pout, pulling her towards him. She gasped, clamping her eyes firmly shut.

Leaning over her, his face was now barely inches from hers. "I want my money back."

"I… I… don't know what you're—"

"Don't lie to me!" Alex shouted at her, she flinched but such was the strength of his grip on her face, she couldn't pull away from him. Alex was threatening, an air of malice in his stance. "I know when women are lying to me… and I'll happily teach you a lesson if it will get me what I want."

"I don't have your money," Melanie whispered, barely audible. "I swear, I don't have it."

"I don't believe you, Melanie," Alex said. "My money has been going missing for months… and we thought we'd found our little tinker, working away out of hours, syphoning off a little bit here, a little bit there…" He shoved her head back, at the same time releasing his grip on her face. Melanie rocked back in her seat, Alex wagging a pointed finger at her. "And we dealt with him, didn't we?" The last question was asked as he glanced at Marcus, who nodded. "However, still the money is drifting away…" he made a gesture of fluttering fingers in the air before him, "like butterflies on a summer's day." He glared at Melanie. "How is that happening, do you think?"

Melanie was crying again now, shaking her head. "I don't know." Alex's expression changed, incensed. He lashed out at Melanie, slapping a flat hand across her face. Cassie felt the sting from her vantage point on the floor. Melanie shrieked.

"You're going to give me my money back," Alex said, "or I'm going to take it from your friend, one piece at a time. He moved to Melanie's left and stared at Lauren who, panic stricken, shook her head, pleading with her eyes for him to leave her alone.

"Please… I beg you… I don't know anything—"

Alex struck her in the face with a closed fist, Melanie yelped, and Cassie screamed in rage. Alex looked down at Cassie, a knowing look on his face.

"Touched a nerve, have I?"

Cassie glared at him. "Free me and you'll see."

Alex laughed. "I like this one," he said, dropping to his haunches alongside her, smiling warmly. "And it's probably a shame you're here because I have no need of you. Although, you do complicate matters." He glanced at Marcus. "Why is she here again?"

"I caught her snooping."

"Ah… that's right." He looked down at Cassie, shook his head and turned away from her, returning his focus to Melanie. He stood over her, resting his hands on the arms of the chair she was sitting in, his face very close to hers. He spoke calmly and in a measured tone. "I want my money, Melanie. Tonight. Not tomorrow. Not next week but tonight and if you are unwilling to give it to me, then I will make good on my word." He glanced sideways at Lauren and then down at Cassie. "One of your friends will die tonight. Perhaps both, but that depends on you."

Melanie, tears falling, shook her head. "I can't… I don't have it…"

"Then who does, Melanie?"

"I don't know," she said quietly. "I swear I don't know."

James Newell, up until now silent, stepped forward. "I believe her," he said, coming to stand behind the two women. Alex Gillie looked at him, arching one eyebrow. "I do," James said. "I don't think she has it."

"Well, seeing as she has been stealing it from right under your nose these past few months," Alex said, "forgive me if I don't have as much faith in your judgement as you do."

James's expression changed and he flushed. "I don't think she would know how to do it, that's all. Not without me noticing."

Alex stood upright, snapping his thumb and index finger, the action leading to a pointed finger. "You need to think less, James. That's your problem… you think you're a smart man because you can count but you're not. If you were working for me, I'd say you were over promoted, and I'd have you on a performance improvement plan. But as it is, you don't work for me and once this sorry little affair is concluded, you won't be working with me again."

James swallowed hard. "That's unfair…"

Alex laughed. "Is it? I think I'm remarkably calm about it, bearing in mind whose money is missing. Believe me, they won't be as calm."

James nodded, averting his eyes from Lauren and Melanie. Cassie assumed he was another who had little to no stomach for this sort of thing; white-collar criminals who thought they were a cut above acting in this way. Naive.

"Now, Melanie," Alex said, smiling warmly at her. "You and your boyfriend were helping yourselves to our investment fund… and squirrelling it away for a rainy day," he said, wiggling his fingers in the air. "Well, today you should consider it raining, and I want my money."

"I… don't have it," she said, fearful of his response.

"I'm tired of hearing that, Melanie," he said, shaking his head. Without looking at Lauren, he pointed at her. "Marcus, take one of her fingers, if you wouldn't mind?"

Marcus stepped forward, Cassie doing her best to swing her bound feet at him, but it was to no avail, she flapped around like a fish out of water. Marcus laughed at her attempt which only riled Cassie further. Lauren screamed before anyone touched her, Alex's minder coming to stand behind her and gripping her arm, pinning it to the chair and wrapping gaffer tape around her wrist to bind her arm to the chair. Marcus produced a knife from a sheath in his waistband, holding it proudly aloft as he moved on Lauren. She screamed, tensing and trying to wrestle herself free from the chair, but it was all in vain.

"Tell him, Mel, please… for crying out loud!"

"I don't have it, I don't have it!" Melanie screamed at Alex who shook his head.

"Shame," he said. "Your friend's going to be rubbish at the piano if this goes on a while."

Marcus placed his massive hands over Lauren's, pressing it down on the arm of the chair and Lauren screamed in fear as she felt the cold steel of the blade on her skin. "Any particular finger you'd care to lose first?" Marcus asked. "Or shall I just pick one?" He grinned at Lauren, clearly enjoying the terror in her face. "This little piggy went to market," he said, singing the children's nursery rhyme, "and this little piggy stayed at home…"

"Just like your brother," Alex said, shaking his head. Marcus looked up at him, a maniacal grin on his face. "He loves his work too—"

"Not so much these days," a voice called from the far end of the shed. No one had seen the newcomer enter and Louis strode forward into the light, absorbing the shock on everyone's face. Marcus released Lauren's hand, spinning on his heel and moving to intercept him, brandishing the knife as he came.

"You're supposed—"

"To be dead," Louis said. "Yes, I'm sorry to disappoint you. Your brother, Stacy, might enjoy his work, but he's not very good at it."

Alex exchanged a glance with his minder and the others in the room. Nicholas Craft smiled awkwardly, then caught James Newell staring at him and his smile faded. Cassie saw the curious mix of emotions wash over Marcus Bell and she'd have paid a fortune to know what he was thinking at that very moment. Alex, possibly sensing Marcus was about to react, raised a hand, indicating for him to stay where he was and allow Louis to come closer. "You have my money?" he asked.

"I have your money," Louis said calmly.

"All of it?"

"Minus a few sundry expenses, yes."

"I want it back, Louis. All of it."

Louis smiled, spreading his hands wide. "And you can have it, but you need to let all of these people go first."

Alex laughed, gesturing towards Melanie. Marcus Bell moved to stand beside her, his expression fixed, placing his knife at her throat. "I don't think you're in a position to bargain."

Louis remained steadfast, calm. "I disagree. You

need the money… because without it you're a dead man—"

"Which gives me nothing to lose," Alex countered.

"Nothing but your life, you have everything to gain from doing it my way. We do this on my terms… and then everyone has a better day. You know the police will see you all right…"

Marcus Bell looked sideways at Alex who maintained his impassive expression. Louis's comment wasn't overlooked by the others either. Nicholas Craft's eyes narrowed.

"What does he mean by that?" he asked.

"He doesn't mean anything by it," Alex said. "Nothing at all."

Marcus's eyes flickered between Alex and Craft, lingering on the former, looking less than convinced. By the look on James Newell's face, he had an inkling that something wasn't right. For a moment Cassie thought he was about to speak but then thought better of it. Marcus Bell, however, felt differently.

"What's he talking about?" Marcus asked.

"He's stirring… that's all," Alex said, looking across at him. "Don't let him get into your head. That's what he wants."

"How do you know what he wants?" Marcus asked. Alex, for the first time seemed less confident, and shrugged.

"Stands to reason."

"If you say so." Marcus's gaze lingered on Alex, but the latter pretended not to notice.

"All right, Louis," Alex said. "How did you see this going down tonight?"

"We'll leave them here," Louis said, nodding at Melanie and Lauren, "and once we're away and they are safe, I'll make sure you get your money."

"Where is it?" Alex asked.

"I don't have cash, obviously. I transferred it digitally… and that's where it's stayed, more or less. I'll tell you where it is… and you can go and get it, see it… do whatever you want, but that happens when we leave here. Not before. Clear?"

"You've got courage, Louis. I'll give you that," Alex said.

"Where's my brother?" Marcus asked Louis. "What did you mean before, when—"

"Not now," Alex said, chastising him. Marcus shot him a dark look but dropped it. Cassie wondered how long that relationship would last in its current form. She had to admit, despite the nature of her predicament and the pain she was in, she was also curious as to how all of this was going to unfold. She couldn't quite believe things had escalated so quickly and that neither her nor the team had seen it coming.

"We leave…" Louis said, "now."

Alex hesitated for a moment before pointing at

Marcus. "Make sure those two are secure," he said, intimating to Melanie and Lauren, then turned back to Louis. "When I have what I want, you can come back here and untie them."

Louis fixed him with a stare. "Agreed."

"What about her?" Marcus asked, looking at Cassie.

"She comes with us," Alex said. Louis looked down and met Cassie's eye, but he didn't object. Marcus cocked his head. "Insurance."

If Marcus had doubts, he didn't voice them. He took his knife and moved towards Cassie. Regardless of the sway Alex Gillie had over all of them, she still didn't feel comfortable with Marcus Bell coming at her with a blade in his hands. He leaned over Cassie, putting the knife between her bound ankles and cutting the rope.

"We can't have you shuffling out, can we?" he said with a mischievous grin. "We'll be here all night."

The breezy tone of his voice did little to allay her fears. She was still in deep trouble, they all were and she knew it. Subtly looking around the group, James and Nicholas seemed apprehensive but they stepped forward when summoned by Alex Gillie, nonetheless.

CHAPTER TWENTY-EIGHT

CASSIE CAUGHT Lauren's eye and did her best to relay a sense of calm, that everything was going to be all right. There was no possible way she could be confident about that and no chance of her conveying that message to Lauren or to Melanie for that matter. Instead, all she could do was smile. The action stung as her face was swollen, her lips split in several places and Cassie knew she must have cut quite a pitiful figure before those around her. Lauren didn't seem reassured and Melanie was openly crying. Cassie couldn't blame her. If her eyes weren't almost completely swollen shut, then she might be crying too.

"Gag those two," Alex ordered, and Marcus picked up a roll of gaffer tape, tossing it to Nicholas Craft who caught it adeptly. He wasn't pleased about the task but a stern look from Alex encouraged him to do as he was instructed. With an apologetic look on his face, he extended a length of tape from the reel and went to wrap it around Lauren's head. She resisted and Nicholas had to force her to keep her head still in an awkward headlock using his armpit. Lauren moaned but relented as the second pass of tape around her head stuck on the first.

Cassie, powerless to help, was hauled to her feet by Marcus who put himself between her and Lauren, blocking their eye connection and glaring at Cassie. There was so much venom in his expression and he held the knife aloft just in case she'd missed it, making sure she knew he had it and was ready, if not keen, to use it. She had no doubt he'd be capable of cutting her and the fear came to mind that her previously antagonistic approach to him might come back to bite her. With luck, Alex had as much control over Marcus as he seemed to think. If not, Cassie would have to think on her feet.

With Melanie also silenced, Alex signalled for them to leave and Louis backed out of the boat shed, unwilling to take Alex at his word and turn his back on him. Marcus shoved Cassie with a firm hand in her back and she stumbled forward, unsteady on her feet. They were numb, the rope had been secured so tightly that the passage of blood had been significantly restricted. She found balance an issue. Not that Marcus had any sympathy. He shoved her again and as she stumbled, he grasped a handful of her hair and pulled her upright. The short stab of pain that followed would usually make her yelp but she wasn't going to give him the satisfaction. Instead, she glared at him. Marcus smiled.

James Newell and Nicholas Craft brought up the rear, both men sporting uncertain expressions. Cassie couldn't think of two individuals who were less suited to such an endeavour as these were. Alex turned as he walked, looking back at them, loitering in the background.

"You two, get a move on. If either of these two," he said, pointing at Louis and then Cassie, "try to run, I want you to bring them down."

Nicholas turned pale whereas James Newell scoffed. "I'm an accountant. What on earth do you expect me to do?"

"I expect you to do whatever I say," Alex replied with such force that James immediately nodded. He then looked at his minder. "Make sure the car is ready."

The man hesitated, reluctant to leave his employer, but Alex felt in complete control of the situation and so his minder went towards the car parked on the far side of the yard.

"We'll go on foot," Louis said.

"Just stop right there, Louis," Alex said. The

group did as instructed. Cassie looked around. She couldn't see any buildings nearby, no one to raise the alarm to but there were boats moored nearby, so they were somewhere on the coast and couldn't be too far from people. If she could find a window of opportunity, a chance to run, then she'd take it. How far she'd get, she had no idea and the thought of leaving Lauren at the mercy of these people, Marcus in particular, filled her with dread but it was the only option she had.

Louis took another couple of paces before he also stopped, looking around them. "It's not far."

"You're leading us away from Melanie, I know," Alex said. "I understand why and I'm prepared to play ball in order to get what I want, but at the same time I have my limits. Where's my money, Louis?"

Louis held his gaze, looking pensive. His eyes flickered to Marcus who took another step towards Cassie. She felt the cold touch of the blade against her neck. No one spoke and the only sound was the breeze passing through the reeds at the water's edge, the creak of the boats rising and falling on the gentle swell and the water lapping against hull or nearby earthen bank.

"That's not the question that needs answering though, is it?" Louis asked. Alex grew impatient but Louis was undeterred. "Don't you think Marcus ought to know where his brother is?"

"Stop stalling—"

"No!" Marcus said, removing the knife from Cassie's throat and stepping forward. "I want to know where Stacy is."

"You don't," Alex said dismissing him with a flick of his hand. "Louis's trying to drive a wedge between us." He raised a pointed finger at Louis. "But it's not going to work."

"So, where is Stacy?" Louis asked, looking at Marcus. "Where do you think your brother is?"

Marcus was confused and he looked between the two men. Alex bore the hint of a smile, but one without genuine humour.

"What are you talking about?" Marcus asked.

"Ignore him," Alex said flatly.

"Tell him, Alex. Tell him what you sent his brother to do."

Marcus's eyes narrowed and he bit his bottom lip. "You sent Stacy abroad."

"Not now, Marcus—"

"You said he was in Amsterdam… but he's not answering his phone when I ring him."

"That's because," Louis said triumphantly, "Stacy isn't in Amsterdam, is he, Alex?"

"What?" Marcus asked, his anger and frustration growing.

Alex's expression changed; to Cassie he seemed concerned. It was a look she'd seen across the table in an interview room many times over the years when a suspect realised the interviewer had more knowledge than they'd anticipated and were in a somewhat perilous position. A situation they were unexpectedly in danger of losing control of.

"Tell him," Louis said forcefully. "Tell him how you're working with the police—"

"What?" Marcus asked again, only this time he stepped in front of Alex, entering his personal space. Alex took a step backwards, enough to break the spell of overarching confidence he'd up until now projected. "You're working with…" he looked at Cassie who did her best to shrug, unwilling to draw the man's wrath away from his boss, while also seeking her best route of escape. They were standing in open ground and she was unconvinced she'd make it very far if she made a break for it.

"He's winding you up, don't you see?" Alex said. Marcus was unconvinced.

"Tell him it's not true then," Louis said, almost mocking him. "Tell him you've not cut a deal to throw everyone else to the wolves while you walk away with a pat on the back and handshake from your mates on the force."

Marcus brandished his knife and Alex looked for his minder, who was already in the car some distance away and unlikely to know what was going on. "Alex… tell me where my brother is or I swear I'll cut you here and now and leave you for dead."

"Now… let's not be hasty," James Newell said, but a dark look from Marcus silenced him. Nicholas, drained of all colour, looked ready to throw up.

"Where is he?" Marcus barked.

"He's at the bottom of Ringstead Quarry," Louis said. Marcus spun on his heel to face him. "Or he was… until that lot pulled him out of the water." Louis pointed at Cassie. Marcus looked at her and Cassie nodded, happy to follow Louis's lead. He must have a plan tonight, she'd run with it until such time as she could make a break for it herself. "He sent Stacy after me, didn't you, Alex? But Stacy got more than he bargained for. He didn't know about your little deal with the police, and he wasn't too pleased to find out you were going to turn everyone else in and leave the way clear to you pocketing everyone else's share of the cash. He was shocked."

"And why should anyone believe anything you have to say, Taylor?" Alex asked, raising his voice. Cassie detected something new in his tone, fear.

"Because Stacy and I go way back… and because we have a shared knowledge of what it's like to be incarcerated. Believe me, neither of us want to face that again."

Marcus was more focussed on Louis now but keeping an eye on Alex as well. The latter was rooted to the spot but looking towards his car, possibly hoping for support. Marcus moved towards Louis, his fingers curled tightly around the handle of his knife.

"What happened to Stacy, Louis? Tell me."

"I offered to cut him in..." Louis said. "To make sure he got his share and yours as well." He looked past Marcus at Nicholas and James. "Not you two, though. Stacy didn't care much for the two of you." James silently seethed whereas Nicholas seemed more offended than anything else.

"Is this true?" Marcus asked, wheeling to face Alex. "Stacy wouldn't stand for it."

"He didn't," Louis said. "You know Stacy, as much as he was a calculating guy, he also had that hot streak... the one that could get him into just as much trouble as it could get him out of. He went to have it out with you, didn't he, Alex?"

There was no point in denying it, the truth was written across his face. Alex tried to remain impassive but he was a terrible actor. Louis, emboldened, slowly moved closer. He chanced a glance at Cassie, she saw and wondered what, if anything, he was trying to say with that look. It was fleeting and she was left none the wiser.

"What did you do?" Marcus asked.

"Marcus... Stacy is in the Netherlands. He's keeping a low profile and that's why he's not answering his phone—"

"Or it's because his phone is at the bottom of

the quarry lake," Louis said, smiling.

"Shut up!" Alex shouted, imploring Marcus with a strained look. "Focus, man. He has *our money* and we want it back. You can't trust a thing he says. He's a thief."

A car door opened, and Cassie saw Alex's minder get out, watching them with an inquisitive look. The moment Louis had the upper hand was about to pass. As soon as the minder returned to them, Alex would regain control, perhaps even be able to convince Marcus he was telling the truth. After all, as far as Cassie knew, Louis was indeed bluffing. Albeit he was very good at it.

Louis must have thought the same because he stepped forward and shoved Marcus off balance and into Alex. The movement took everyone by surprise. James Newell remained rooted to the spot and Nicholas, rather than stepping into the fray, backed off several steps.

"Run!" Louis shouted and Cassie took off towards the path running along the water's edge, giving any pursuer no choice but to chase her on foot.

Marcus let out a guttural roar of rage, pushed himself away from Alex and turned to confront Louis only to find him engaging and attempting to wrestle him to the ground. Despite Louis's slight appearance, he was strong and the two men grappled with neither taking an immediate advantage.

Marcus, still armed with his knife, attempted to bring it to bear only for Louis to take a firm hold of his wrist and stop him from using it.

Unfortunately for Louis, Alex Gillie moved forward and kicked out at Louis's left leg and with Marcus bearing down on him, he buckled and fell to the ground, Marcus driving his blade home between Louis's ribs, the first time almost by accident but then several times more with extreme force, grunting with the effort required for each blow but the actions were so frenetic, and Louis' fight back so fierce, that it was unclear if the blows were actually landing. Louis, for his part, didn't cry out, instead gasping for lungfuls of air as he fought his attacker with increasing desperation.

"Get her!" Alex shouted, pointing at Cassie. Marcus stood off the stricken Louis and set off after her. Cassie knew her lead was likely to be eaten away in moments, her feet were still numb, and her balance was off, pitching to both left and right as she ran. Waves of nausea hit her with almost every step and her head was thumping, the pain growing ever sharper the more her blood pumped.

Marcus closed the distance between them with ease, Cassie hearing his footfalls and his rasping breath as he chased her down. She'd barely made it to the edge of the boat yard before she felt someone slam into her. The next she knew she was falling through the air, but she didn't hit firm ground, instead striking water, and disappearing beneath the surface. The water, full of sediment and churn from the incoming tide, was dark and unaware of falling into water she'd failed to take a breath, the shock of the impact stunning her. For a moment, Cassie couldn't tell which way was up or down. Striking out with her legs, she hoped she was kicking for the surface, her lungs burning from lack of oxygen.

Surfacing, Cassie gasped for air before flailing in the water with her bound hands and sinking beneath the next wave, gathering a lung full of seawater as she went under for her efforts. Her strength fading rapidly, panic flared in her as her foot caught on something she couldn't see, something cold, hard and unmoveable. Was it an anchor chain or something hanging off a moored boat, she couldn't tell. She kicked at it, trying to free herself, looking up, longing for the safety of the surface but she couldn't free her foot.

Just as she thought she was done for, she was aware of a figure nearby, brushing past her in the darkness. Firm hands grasped her, pulling on her coat to try and haul her back to the surface but she still couldn't move. She flapped at the body with her hands, instinct clawing at them to save her. The hands let go and she wanted to scream at them not to leave her, but the figure disappeared into the gloom.

Reaching down, Cassie tugged at her foot, desperate to prise it free but feeling lightheaded, her fingers numbing due to the cold, she struggled to gain purchase and felt her resolve fading. Out of the depths, the figure returned, swimming down to her trapped foot. She felt pain in her ankle as they desperately pulled and twisted her leg to try and free it. She thought she'd never be free but then she was rising through the water. She tried to kick but her legs wouldn't work. Powerful arms wrapped around, and she was suddenly moving upwardly at pace.

Breaking through the surface into fresh air, Cassie gasped, feeling more hands reaching for her and dragging her up and out of the water. Unceremoniously hauled up onto the quayside and dumped on the ground, lying on her back, she didn't care if Marcus Bell, Alex Gillie or any of his makeshift crew was there to beat her again. She was safe, at least for now.

"CASSIE!"

The voice was familiar and yet distant, removed somehow. She felt someone pulling on her chest, the voice getting louder.

"Cassie! Can you hear me?"

She opened her one good eye, the other firmly swollen shut, the face peering over her was distorted, out of focus for some reason, detail and edges fading in and out. It looked like Eric.

"Wake up, Cass!"

He shook her violently. Too violently. She swung a hand up, knocking his arm away and Eric's face retreated from view.

"It's okay. She's okay."

"You'll not be if you don't stop roughing me up," she said bitterly. Her voice all but a whisper.

"Yeah, she's definitely okay," Eric said.

Cassie involuntarily coughed, her body going into spasm, she rolled onto her side, water escaping her mouth, expelled from her stomach or lungs, she couldn't tell. Rolling onto her back, flashing blue, white and red lights flickered in her peripheral vision. Someone came to kneel beside her, leaning over and opening her eye, directing a torchlight into it, momentarily blinding her.

"I'm all right," she said; knowing she was anything but.

"We should get her into the ambulance," someone said.

"I'm fine," Cassie argued, lifting her head and surveying those around her. Tom was by her side, water dripping from sodden hair which he swept back from his forehead, adding to the pool he was already kneeling in. Eric was standing over them both, he too was soaking wet. She looked both of them up and down. "Well, you two took your time about it, didn't you? You're so reactive when I'm not around to take the initiative."

Tom laughed and Eric frowned.

"I ruined a perfectly good pair of shoes coming in after you," Eric said. "Why on earth you thought it was a good time to go swimming, I'll never know."

Cassie smiled at the joke, instantly regretting it as her split lips cracked once again. The paramedic attending her used a pair of scissors to cut the tape binding her wrists. The sensation of blood flowing through to her hands felt good, albeit different as they throbbed.

"We'll get you to the hospital, Cassie," Tom said. She was about to protest but the stern look on his face told her it was unadvisable and she relented, nodding curtly.

"Lauren?" she asked, looking past Tom to the scene beyond. Marcus Bell was struggling on the ground with PC Marshall and a couple of other uniformed officers atop him keeping him in place. Alex Gillie was in handcuffs, standing stoically, arrogantly in Cassie's opinion, off to the right. Several paramedics were crowded around someone on the ground, but she couldn't make out who.

"She's safe," Tom said, indicating towards the boat shed. Tamara came into view leading Melanie and Lauren out, also escorted by DC Danny Wilson. "We got here just as you went into the water."

"Fashionably late," Cassie said, making Tom smile.

"We cut it fine, that's true."

Cassie snorted a laugh but ensured her face didn't crack. "How did you find me?"

Tom pointed to the still form of Louis. "He told Annabelle and she called me."

Lauren left Tamara's side and ran across to where Cassie lay, dropping to her knees and throwing her arms around her. Cassie returned the embrace as best she could but her entire body ached and the force of Lauren's hug hurt in so many places.

"We really should get you to the hospital," the paramedic said.

"Are you okay?" Lauren asked, looking her over.

"I would be if everyone stopped asking me that..."

Lauren looked at Cassie, withdrawing from her a little. Cassie apologised, raising a hand and Lauren offered her a strange look. It wasn't the response to her usual barbed character and dark humour. It was far more than that. There was something in Lauren's eyes that told her things had changed between them. Cassie couldn't put her finger on why she thought so, but in her mind it was there, nonetheless, front and centre.

Lauren looked over at Melanie who was hovering around the paramedics working on Louis. She was distraught and Danny was doing his best to allay her fears.

"That's Louis, right?" Cassie asked.

Tom nodded. "Marcus Bell stabbed him repeatedly before he knocked you into the water."

"He made his move to allow me to escape," Cassie said.

"Well, let's hope you get the chance to thank him for it." Tom looked down the road, hearing the approach of vehicles. "Aye, aye... things are about to get interesting."

Two cars arrived on the scene at speed, lights flashing. DCS Wells got out of his car, standing with his hands on his hips as he glared around at anyone who dared meet his eye. Tamara walked slowly towards him.

"I hope you've got a good explanation for all of this, Tamara," Wells said, snarling. He tilted his head towards Alex Gillie, lowering his voice. "And why is that man in handcuffs?"

"He's facilitated the abduction and torture of two civilians, one of my detectives and is a suspect in the attempted murder of another," Tamara said calmly.

"Release him," Wells ordered.

Tamara shook her head. "I will do no such thing."

Wells turned on her, stepping up and getting into her face. "Have you any idea what you've—"

"Almost certainly, I do yes," Tamara said with the trace of a smile. "But I won't sacrifice the life of one of my officers in order to keep your operation going. You'll have to make do with what you have and take the win where you can."

Wells glared at her, but accepted his influence over events was extremely limited. He raised a pointed, accusatory finger at her. "You've not heard the last of this DCI Greave."

"You'll be more than welcome at my debrief, DCS Wells," she said firmly. Wells retreated, signalling to his team to get back in their cars. Tamara appeared to take a deep breath as she turned and made her way over to them.

"He looked… unhappy," Cassie said.

Tamara cocked her head. "He'll get over it."

"You think so?" Tom asked.

Tamara scrunched up her nose. "I doubt it." There was an air of resignation in her tone. "But I'll stand by my decision, no matter what. I'd make the same choice again." She looked down at Cassie. "I'd ask you if you're going to be all right but I know that'd irritate you, so I won't. Two paracetamol and back in the office tomorrow, yes?"

Cassie shook her head, but she was grinning inside.

CHAPTER TWENTY-NINE

Tom waited in the corridor along with Tamara. He'd been able to go back to the station with DC Danny Wilson to ensure the arrested parties were processed and placed in cells prior to interview and, most importantly, to change into dry clothes he kept in the bottom drawer of his filing cabinet for just this eventuality. Happy to leave the process with Danny and Eric, he'd returned to the hospital to await news of Louis's condition. So much depended on his ability to resolve matters. That is, if he made it through surgery. They'd been waiting six hours now, three hours to allow for the surgery itself and another two hours for him to come around from the anaesthetic.

The consultant leading the trauma team stepped out of an office along the corridor, immediately met by Louis's family desperate for news. Tom watched closely, unable to hear what was said but assuming he could gauge how well the operation went by their reaction to the doctor's words. They seemed both shocked and relieved as he finished talking to them and continued on to speak with Tom and Tamara.

"What do you reckon that means?" Tom asked.

"He's alive… which is something."

The consultant approached with a grave expression.

"Detectives," he said, greeting them. "The good news is the surgery went well. If your man was a cat and had nine lives, I would argue he's used most of them up tonight."

"He'll recover?"

"Yes, in time. He lost a fair bit of blood and took some severe damage to the tissue in his lower abdomen but his assailant missed the vital organs. Blood loss was the greatest threat but you got him here in time."

"Can we speak to him?" Tamara asked. The consultant looked nonplussed. "We'll go easy, but we do need some answers."

"Okay, but he has just undergone extensive surgery… please keep it brief and try not to raise his blood pressure."

"It will be informal," Tom said. Anything Louis told them tonight would likely be inadmissible in a formal case anyway due to him being under the influence of medication and having undergone the operation. Even so, before they could look to press charges against Gillie and the others, they needed to know the extent of their actions. That being said, kidnapping a police officer would almost certainly be enough to hold them on remand in any event.

They made their way to the room; PC Marshall was standing guard. He opened the door and Tom nodded his thanks as they entered. Louis was awake, propped up on his bed, connected to a drip although he looked pale, his eyes sunken.

"Mr Taylor," Tom said. Louis moved his head towards them, grimacing slightly. "You've been leading us a merry dance this past week."

He smiled weakly. "It was… unintentional, I can assure you."

"We have some questions."

"I'll answer them," Louis said quietly, holding up a hand in supplication.

"I would like to read you your rights, Louis. After all, you are implicated in—"

"I know… and I have nowhere left to run to," he said, meeting Tom's eye. "Fire away."

"Tell us about how we ended up where we were tonight, Louis."

Louis laughed, grimacing with pain as his muscles flexed. He took a deep breath, leaning his head back against the pillow and gently resting his right hand on his bandaged midriff.

"The abridged version? Unless you want to be here until dawn," he said.

"As much or as little as you want to give us," Tom said, setting down his mobile with the voice recorder app switched on. Louis eyed it, but he didn't object.

"Alex Gillie has been running drugs into the Norfolk coast via the continent, using boats under the care of Stacy and Marcus Bell." He sucked air through his teeth, clearly in pain. "I could do with another shot of whatever they gave me earlier," he said, arching his eyebrows. He sniffed hard. "Nicholas Craft has been sailing his yacht across to Rotterdam… and then he meets the Bells off the coast, and they transport the drugs ashore. The product is moved down into London… using connections Alex has made through his investment company."

"Laundering drug money?" Tom asked.

"Among others, yes. I don't think he was too picky about where the funds came from."

"And how did you get involved in this?"

"Reluctantly."

"I hear that a lot in my line of work," Tom said, dryly.

"I'll bet," Louis said, adjusting his position in

the bed and trying to get more comfortable. "I came to Hunstanton looking for help."

"From?"

"Stacy, mainly. He owed me… and always said I should look him up if I needed help."

"How did he owe you?" Tom asked. "Does this go back to your travels in Thailand?"

Louis was pensive and for the first time, Tom wondered if he might not be forthcoming. He needn't have worried.

"I knew you'd find out sooner or later, so… yes, I first met Stacy and Marcus backpacking. It's what happens when you're abroad in an unfamiliar environment; you tend to congregate with who and what you know. Brits abroad and all that. Other nationalities do it too… safety in familiarity, you know? Marcus and Stacy got into a spot of bother with some Italians. I speak Italian, enough to get by anyway, and I helped smooth things over. Stacy nicknamed me Luigi, and we kind of stuck to each other after that. We were hanging out in the same places, and the brothers were good company. Fun to be around."

"You got into trouble though."

Louis nodded. "And I've been running from it ever since." He looked straight ahead, as if seeing something in the distance. "A few of us went on a trip… down river, organised by a local guide company. What I didn't know at the time was that it was a front, maybe not the company, maybe the staff were using it to smuggle stuff in or out of the country, I don't know." He sighed. "In any event, they used us as cover, only the police were waiting as we apparently crossed the border back into Thailand. Hell, I didn't even know we'd left the country, that's how much I knew about what was going on."

"They were smuggling drugs?"

He nodded. "And stashing it among our kit, you know? The guides could claim it was stupid tourists… up to no good… and the police bought it."

"You said Stacy owed you?"

"Yeah… I may have been naive, but Stacy… he'd been a mule for years… and a good one. He'd obviously never been caught and he knew what these guys were up to. It'd been his idea to take the boat trip. He knew these guys… knew what was going on. They didn't bust us at the boats… I guess the guides had paid off the right people – that's how it works over there – but us? No such luck. Stacy's people got it wrong… and the metro cops were waiting for us at the hostel." He stared at Tom and then looked at Tamara. "I thought that was the worst nightmare of my life… to be arrested and taken to the police station… jailed and then moved on to Bang Kwang Central Prison… more commonly referred to as—"

"The Bangkok Hilton," Tom said, referring to

the international nickname of the prison.

"And you should believe everything you hear about it… only imagine it a hundred times worse. It's maximum security… where all foreign prisoners are housed, along with the worst domestic incumbents the country has to offer. Even when I was passing through the gates, aware of the horror stories, I thought *they'll keep us separated from everyone else*… I mean, we're British, westerners… it'll be different for us." He shook his head, his eyes glistening. "It wasn't. The first cell we went to was built for twenty prisoners… and there were at least seventy of us. We slept on the floor… one toilet in the corner which was little more than a hole in the floor dropping into an open sewer that flowed out of the prison walls. We were given Thai prisoners to look after us, trustees of a sort, but all they did was fleece us for anything they could."

"Were you convicted?"

"I was sentenced to fifteen years… which was lenient, or so my lawyer told me. Stacy was known to the authorities. They were aware of his connections… and they wanted to make an example of him. He was sentenced to death. I was shocked… and Stacy… well, little fazed him, but when word came through to us… he knew then what he had to do. He had no choice, but he couldn't do it alone."

"Do what?"

"Escape, of course," Louis said with a slight

smile. "No one had ever done it before… escaped from the Bang Kwang. I mean, there were rumours that a European had managed it… but none of us knew his name or how he'd done it. It was more folklore than anything else. People had tried, don't get me wrong, but to do so and get caught…" he shook his head. "The punishments could be worse than death. There were two guys who escaped from a prison to the north… Chiang Mai, I think it was. Anyway, they were recaptured soon enough. Not by the police but by the prison guards. They saw it as an affront to them, to escape their prison and they were hunted down… returned to prison and then ruthlessly beaten and tortured… their legs smashed to pieces. They came to Bang Kwang in chains, shuffling along with their twisted legs looking like something out of a horror film. They had to set them themselves, you see? They were denied medical treatment." Louis shook his head. "It was horrific. But that was what the guards could do to you. The prisoners… were something else altogether. You could buy protection, if you had money. Stacy had friends and that helped us out for a time, but I didn't have money and the security wasn't always extended to me."

"Were you attacked?"

Louis's expression cracked as he recalled painful memories. He nodded.

"It wouldn't be so bad if they came at you one

on one, but…" he shook his head, smiling ruefully, "they don't. They're not daft, these guys. They come at you in a pack… like wolves and they go at you until you go down and if you go down, you're not getting back up."

"And that's why you tried to escape with Stacy?"

"If Stacy went then I knew two things were certain, my security, what little I had, would be gone and also that the guards would take their revenge on me, because I was his friend. But it wasn't only that that encouraged me. I was there one day, and this Thai lad ran past me… another lad chasing him with a knife… nothing homemade like you see in the films, but a proper knife. It was huge… almost like a machete. Anyway, he runs past me and another guy comes from nowhere and poleaxes the knife guy with a chair, just flattens him. Then he grabs the knife and sets about him… stabbing him, not in a frenzy, but in a calm, calculated way; his chest, stomach, arms, legs… everywhere. I was rooted to the spot barely five feet away, transfixed. A crowd gathered… and they're chanting *khā̀ kheā, khā̀ kheā*, over and over, and I had no idea at the time what it meant… but I learned later it was *kill him*. They were calling for him to die. It was entertainment, nothing more."

Louis stared into space. Tom and Tamara exchanged a look but said nothing.

"When it was over, the guards' whistles separated the crowd. They came in… kicked the body to make sure he was dead… and he was very, very dead… and they had him put on a trolley and wheeled away. Then, business as usual. It was normal. I knew then that I had to get out or I was going to die."

"Did you seek help from the consulate?" Tom asked. "Stacy's arrest was communicated to the British authorities, but there was no mention of yours."

Louis seemed puzzled. "I–I didn't ask for consular assistance. I couldn't. They would have told my family and I couldn't bring the shame to them. I thought… if I could get released, pardoned… win my case somehow, then they would never need to know."

"You thought that was possible?"

Louis shrugged, but only slightly, grimacing as he did so. "I was in denial, completely delusional. The trial took a year to come around and by then I had convinced myself that I could beat the case. I mean, I hadn't done anything. I thought the court would see that too, but they found me guilty anyway, regardless. Stacy felt bad… he promised to help me inside, to get me through it. It was his fault I was in there, after all. Of course, that all changed when we heard what they had in store for him. Death by firing squad." He shook his head. "It's barbaric. They tie you to a post and three guards point guns at you, the triggers are tied to a piece of cord, and they pull that rather than the actual trigger. No one knows who actually pulls the trigger that way." He winced, feeling pain in his stomach and looking down at where the wounds were. "It's a Buddhist thing apparently."

"Avoids responsibility for taking a life," Tom said.

"Yeah… something like that." He took a breath, exhaling slowly. "Anyway, Stacy had a plan. Stacy always has a plan. We prepared… it was months in the making. There were three of us. Me, Stacy, obviously, and a Danish guy we nicknamed Thor because he was massive. The plan was good, ambitious, but we thought doable. We had no choice, anyway, so why not go for it."

"How did it pan out for you?"

Louis grinned. "Yeah, it went well for a while and then… it fell apart. We were separated from Thor, and he ran into the guards just shy of the main gate. A big hulk of a blond European tends to stand out. There was a commotion, and we heard it reported later that a guard was killed." He seemed contrite then. "It shouldn't have happened but whatever went down, happened. A man died. Two, actually because they shot and killed Thor. Stacy and I slipped out amid the confusion."

"You walked out?"

Louis smiled. "Maximum security isn't the same in Thailand as it is here. No one would have believed one prisoner could reach the main gate without being seen, let alone three!"

"How did you get out of Thailand?"

"That wasn't as hard. Stacy had connections, as I said. Friends in the Chinese Triads, no less. They sorted him out with a stolen passport and we went our separate ways. I trekked up to the Burmese border and slipped across. There's no love lost between the Thais and the Burmese, so they weren't looking for me. It took me months to get home. I went across land, hitching where I could, grabbing the occasional train." He looked at Tom and then Tamara. "Like I said, I've been running ever since."

"Why did you come to see Stacy?" Tom asked.

"Money, of course," Louis said. "Have you any idea how hard it is to live in this country when you have to do so under the radar. Cash-in-hand jobs, avoiding making friends, let alone falling in love?"

"But you did, didn't you, make friends and fall in love?" Tom asked.

He nodded. "Melanie is… special to me."

"And Annabelle?"

"I couldn't leave her to that life with Alex. You might think I was involved with him, but I despise drugs. I've seen the damage they can do to people, to lives… When I found out what they were doing, what Stacy was doing, I was incensed. How could he? After everything we went through, he hadn't learned a thing!"

"And so, you killed him?" Tom asked.

Louis snorted with derision. "No… he was sent to kill me, after Alex found out what I'd been doing."

"Stealing his money?"

"Yeah, I took it, and Stacy was tasked to get it back. Only Stacy didn't know what I knew… that Alex was working with the police and Stacy was likely to end up doing serious time here in the UK. I told him, that's all. What happened next is down to Alex and his goons, and absolutely nothing to do with me. You saw for yourself how Marcus reacted… he knew it was true as soon as I said it…"

"Who told you about their operation?"

"Annabelle, of course. I think she liked me for a time, was attracted to me, but I wasn't interested. Not like that. She's sweet and I care for her, but as a friend. She asked for my help, and I was happy to give it."

"The escape plan?"

"Yes, I used the potential of a new mule route from Panama and I had Stacy get me squared away with checking it out. I used that to plan an escape, only for Alex to cotton on to my taking the money, little by little, and he set Stacy on me. After he confronted me, I told him what I knew about Alex. It was all I could do to save my life. Then… I went into hiding. I figured it would be for a few days, rearrange things with Annabelle and then get her out. But then… things got complicated."

"Stacy's body turned up?"

Louis nodded. "And everyone started to get jittery. I had to adapt… think again."

"Did Melanie know where you were?"

"No, no," Louis said, shaking his head. "She knows nothing about any of this. Melanie noticed odd payments being made… new accounts for businesses and names she didn't recognise. She mentioned it to me and… I have a thing with numbers. It was a puzzle that I got sucked into. That's how I found out what was really going on."

"James Newell?" Tom asked.

"Washing money," Louis said. "Initially he was doing it through legitimate companies but without the owner's knowledge. The numbers must have got so large they couldn't keep it hidden and that's where the Hunstanton location comes in. Small businesses, lots of them. Companies with turnovers of less than a million; consultancy firms, import, export businesses. None of them exist, except on paper. Newell was even fabricating business between these firms, purchases, contracts… loans. The people didn't exist, let alone the businesses." He shrugged. "No one is going to look out here for an operation of that size. Couple that with Alex's links to the police," he said, eyeing them suspiciously, "and he had a blank slate to work as he pleased."

"Why did you choose tonight to make your move?" Tom asked. "I mean, you did make that decision, didn't you?"

"I did, yes. Once I knew Alex had Melanie and definitely when he took one of your officers hostage, I figured you'd have to act. I gambled on Alex having crossed a line that he couldn't back away from. You'd have to act."

"That's a massive gamble," Tom said.

"I had no choice. I couldn't stay hidden."

"And why did Alex make such a rash move, do you think?"

"Because his investors know... that he's been fleecing them for the last couple of years, and they're not the sort of people you can hide from. He needs to pay them back or he's a dead man."

"And how did they find out what he was up to?"

Louis smiled. It was a knowing expression. "I guess they had someone paying attention."

Tom wondered if that person was Louis, and he'd decided to level the playing field with an anonymous tip off, much like sending Annabelle to see Tom. That set Tom to thinking about her. He took out his mobile and rang her number both Louis and Tamara wondering who he was calling.

The number you have dialled is no longer available.

Tom's eyes flickered to Louis, who smiled. He will have heard the automated message in the stillness of the hospital room. Tom shook his head.

"I'm not going to find her, am I?" Tom asked.

The smile left Louis's face and he glanced at the clock on the wall, shaking his head. "No, not without a great deal of investment in time and resources. I shouldn't think it will be worth it, do you?"

Tom held his gaze and then, he too, glanced at the clock on the wall. Annabelle had an eight-hour head start. She could be out of the country by now. Louis's actions were not only an opportunity to bring Alex Gillie down but also to act as a distraction to allow Annabelle to make her escape. Tom exchanged a look with Tamara. "No, probably not. You've funded her trip, I presume?"

"Not me, her husband… indirectly."

Tom put his mobile away. "You know, we're going to need that money back, Louis."

"The money?"

"Everything you syphoned off from Alex Gillie's laundering operation. That's what you had stashed up in the loft at the annexe, wasn't it? The records… hidden where no one would think to look for them?"

"Oh… yeah, that's right. I had to come back for that… As for the money, I don't think that's going to be possible."

"Louis," Tom said, sternly, "that money is part of a criminal enterprise. By withholding it you'll be making yourself an accessory."

Louis held up a hand in supplication. "No, you don't understand. I can't give it to you, even if I wanted to. Unless you can extract the money from the orphanage in Sighisoara, Romania… or seize the solar panels from the Gisozi School, north of Kigali, to name but a couple? And…" he winced again "… I don't see you doing that."

Tom laughed. "You gave it away?"

"No, I took something born of evil and I did some good with it. I changed lives for the better… and that's why I can't give it back to you. Besides the pittance I kept for myself, to live on you understand, I spread the rest around to those who need it. I sleep well at night… or I did, until very recently." His expression shifted, looking nervous. "These past few months, to be honest with you, have been a little trying. So… what happens now? To me, specifically."

Tamara moved to stand at the foot of the bed, meeting Louis' anxious eyes.

"That's hard to say. You know, no one is looking for you."

"What?"

Tom nodded as Louis looked furtively between them.

"There are no international arrest warrants,

nothing on Interpol... you're not wanted," Tom said flatly. "There aren't even any records relating to your trial or sentencing, as far as we've been able to ascertain."

Louis's forehead creased. "But... that's not possible. I'm not making this up—"

"No," Tamara said. "You're not but the authorities aren't looking to extradite you to Thailand. In any case, the British government won't extradite anyone to a country who practise the death penalty except in extreme circumstances." She shook her head. "I doubt your case meets those criteria. You didn't need to hide for so long."

Louis stared hard at her, possibly assessing the validity of her suggestion. He shook his head. "No... they must be looking for me. I was sentenced to fifteen years and a guard died during our escape. They would never allow me to get away with it, it would send a terrible message to anyone else who might try to smuggle... I mean, they would want me shot—"

"Which is why you would not have been extradited, Louis," Tom said. "And it may go some way to explaining why they've removed your convictions from the record. Stacy's too, by the look of it. His arrest was communicated to the British Consulate, but nothing further. His trial seems to have been erased too. The Thais don't want it to become common knowledge you escaped either."

Louis was shocked, his jaw unclenched, and he looked ready to cry tears of joy.

"There is still the matter of Alex Gillie… and his enterprise to consider. We'll need to understand your involvement, but…" Tamara said, choosing her words carefully, "if you help us to the best of your knowledge… then I imagine the courts will take that into account."

Louis swallowed hard. Tom moved to the door. "There are some people here who have been waiting to see you, Louis. They've been waiting a long time." He opened it, stepped out and beckoned the family forward. They approached tentatively, a nurse accompanying them.

"Not too long, and keep the excitement down please," she said.

The family filed into the room, Tom and Tamara stepping out to allow them the moment in private. Tom nodded to PC Marshall. "Give them ten minutes but keep an eye on them."

"Will do, sir."

Both Tom and Tamara were surprised to find Cassie in the family waiting area. She slowly got up from her seat. Her injuries were superficial, albeit cosmetic, but no less painful and she moved gingerly.

"What are you doing here?" Tamara asked. "I thought you were discharged hours ago?"

"I was... but Lauren... she doesn't want me at home," Cassie said, regret in her tone.

"Oh, Cassie. I'm so sorry."

Cassie shrugged. "She's never been keen on the job... and tonight, it all came a bit too close to home."

"But none of this was your fault—"

"It was though," Cassie countered. "I brought Lauren into it by using her connection with Melanie... and I put her in danger. It is my fault."

"Do you have anywhere to stay?" Tom asked.

Cassie shrugged.

"Yes, you do," Tamara said. "You'll stay with me."

"Oh... I..."

"You are, and that's that," Tamara said. "Come on, we'll have a lot to figure out in the morning. This is enough for one night." Tom looked back through the crack in the door, seeing Louis embraced carefully by his mother. The family had lost so much time together and he was pleased he would be going home to see his own. Life often has a way of sending you along paths you never considered, and he was grateful for the choices he'd made in life. Very grateful indeed.

FREE BOOK GIVEAWAY

Visit the author's website at **www.jmdalgliesh.com** and sign up to the VIP Club and be the first to receive news and previews of forthcoming works.

Here you can download a FREE eBook novella exclusive to club members;

Life & Death - A Hidden Norfolk novella

Never miss a new release.

No spam, ever, guaranteed. You can unsubscribe at any time.

Enjoy this book? You could make a real difference.

Because reviews are critical to the success of an author's career, if you have enjoyed this novel, please do me a massive favour by entering one onto Amazon.

Type the following link into your internet search bar to go to the Amazon page and leave a review;

http://mybook.to/JMD-blood-runs-cold

If you prefer not to follow the link please visit the sales page where you purchased the title in order to leave a review.

Reviews increase visibility. Your help in leaving one would make a massive difference to this author and I would be very grateful.

BOOKS BY J M DALGLIESH

One Lost Soul

Bury Your Past

Kill Our Sins

Tell No Tales

Hear No Evil

The Dead Call

Kill Them Cold

A Dark Sin

To Die For

Fool Me Twice

The Raven Song

Angel of Death

Dead to Me

Blood Runs Cold

Life and Death ***FREE -** visit jmdalgliesh.com

Divided House

Blacklight

The Dogs in the Street

Blood Money

Fear the Past

The Sixth Precept

Dark Yorkshire Books 1-3

Dark Yorkshire Books 4-6

Audiobooks

In the Hidden Norfolk Series

One Lost Soul
Bury Your Past
Kill Our Sins
Tell No Tales
Hear No Evil
The Dead Call
Kill Them Cold
A Dark Sin
To Die For
Fool Me Twice
The Raven Song
Angel of Death
Dead To Me

In the Dark Yorkshire Series

Divided House
Blacklight
The Dogs in the Street
Blood Money
Fear the Past
The Sixth Precept

Dark Yorkshire Books 1-3
Dark Yorkshire Books 4-6

Printed in Great Britain
by Amazon

28273093R00229